PRAISE FOR *NOPALITO, TEXAS: STORIES*

"The setting—replete with eight-cylinder cars, home perms, butane stoves, Buddy Holly glasses—is midcentury modern. It's 1955 in Nopalito, Texas, yet given the dearth of options for a girl who hopes to never be *husbanded*, and for a flibbertigibbet boy whose hands fly like birds when he talks, it might be 1855. These stories illuminate the other side of silence where words don't exist for desires that run counter to established norms. David Meischen's homespun but gorgeous words coalesce in a lush yet subtle style. Even bit players burdened with secret truth contemplate the world with attention to detail so tender it turns ordinary objects into sites of revelation. In this backwater outpost where everyone knows everyone, no one knows anyone. Each story is devastatingly beautiful, and the book, more than a sum of its parts, is a consummate work of art."—Debra Monroe, author of *It Takes a Worried Woman*

"In *Nopalito, Texas: Stories*, David Meischen is attuned to the quiet crises upon which a person's life turns. In clear, poignant, and often poetic language, we see the residents of a small South Texas town—daughters, sons, mothers, fathers, neighbors, friends, outsiders—pushing against the limits of their lives. Stubbornness, devotion, confusion, pride, and anger see them through the internal upheavals and seismic shifts of loss and grief. And at the end, you'll sigh deep and long and wonder at having held so much life, so much humanity, in such a slender volume."—ire'ne lara silva, author of *flesh to bone*

"The linked stories of *Nopalito, Texas* feel artfully distilled yet also boundless. As the characters grow older, they intersect in ways both surprising and deeply satisfying. This stunning collection, full of lyrical prose and deep compassion, belongs in the Texan canon."—Stacey Swann, author of *Olympus, Texas: A Novel*

"In this tremendous collection, David Meischen renders entire lives with extraordinary depth, breadth, and care. Like Alice Munro and Andrea Barrett, Meischen conveys the significance of the present moment by laying bare what has come before. *Nopalito, Texas: Stories* is a book to savor, and this is a writer to cherish."—Bret Anthony Johnston, author of *Remember Me Like This: A Novel*

NOPALITO, TEXAS

LYNN AND LYNDA MILLER SOUTHWEST FICTION SERIES
Lynn C. Miller and Lynda Miller, Series Editors

This series showcases novels, novellas, and story collections that focus on the Southwestern experience. Often underrepresented in American literature, Southwestern voices provide unique and diverse perspectives to readers exploring the region's varied landscapes and communities. Works in the series range from traditional to experimental, with an emphasis on how the landscapes and cultures of this distinct region shape stories and situations and influence the ways in which they are told.

Also available in the Lynn and Lynda Miller Southwest Fiction Series:

Hungry Shoes: A Novel by Sue Boggio and Mare Pearl
The Half-White Album by Cynthia J. Sylvester
Girl Flees Circus: A Novel by C. W. Smith

NOPALITO, TEXAS

STORIES

DAVID MEISCHEN

UNIVERSITY OF NEW MEXICO PRESS | ALBUQUERQUE

© 2024 by David Meischen
All rights reserved. Published 2024
Printed in the United States of America

ISBN 978-0-8263-6600-9 (paper)
ISBN 978-0-8263-6601-6 (ePub)

Library of Congress Cataloging-in-Publication data is on file with
the Library of Congress.

Founded in 1889, the University of New Mexico sits on the traditional homelands of the Pueblo of Sandia. The original peoples of
New Mexico—Pueblo, Navajo, and Apache—since time immemo-
rial have deep connections to the land and have made significant
contributions to the broader community statewide. We honor the
land itself and those who remain stewards of this land throughout
the generations and also acknowledge our committed relationship
to Indigenous peoples. We gratefully recognize our history.

Cover illustration adapted from photograph by Joshua J. Cotten on
Unsplash.
Designed by Felicia Cedillos
Composed in Alegreya

These stories are for Patrice Baumann McKinney.

A South Texas farm shaped me; a West Texas farm shaped Patrice. Since the day we met, more years ago than she will allow me to specify, Patrice has encouraged me with energy, enthusiasm, kindness, friendship, and heart. Her presence in my life has meant everything to me as a writer.

If we had a keen vision and feeling of all ordinary human life,
it would be like hearing the grass grow and the squirrel's heart beat,
and we should die of that roar which lies on the other side of silence.

—GEORGE ELIOT, *MIDDLEMARCH*

Contents

Acknowledgments

The following stories in this collection were previously published, sometimes in slightly different form:

Bellingham Review: "Waking Grady" (published as "Crossing Over")
Copper Nickel: "The Yellow Dress"
The Evansville Review: "A Husband to Bury"
The Gettysburg Review: "The Empty Rooms"
Limestone: "Beneath a November Sky" and "Nothing Happened Here" (published as "Robber's Trick")
Salamander: "Cicada Song"
Storylandia: "Crossing at the Light"
Talking Writing: "Agua Dulce"
Valparaiso Fiction Review: "Eldorado"

Heartfelt gratitude to Debra Monroe, mentor and close friend, for invaluable insights into the *how* of fiction; to Tim O'Brien, fiction master extraordinaire, for a magical semester studying the short story; to Daniel Mueller and Pam Houston, for insights and encouragement at the Taos Summer Writers' Conference; to Sharon Oard Warner, for making the Taos conference happen; to Twister Marquiss, fellow fiction aficionado, for shared enthusiasm; to Tom Franklin, for pointing out the potential in one of these stories, which afterwards found its way into the pages of the *Gettysburg Review*; to Tad Bartlett, Emily Choate, J.Ed. Marston, Maurice Ruffin, and Terri Shrum (RIP), for a magical week at the Winthrop Rockefeller Institute in Arkansas—and for the years of friendship and encouragement that continue today; to the Cherrypickers—Kirk Wilson, Stacy Muszynski, and Gary Cooke (RIP)—for the hours we spent reading each other's stories at Austin's Cherrywood Coffeehouse; to *Talking Writing*, for honoring one of these stories with the Short Fiction Prize; and to the Texas Institute of Letters, for honoring two of these stories with the Best Short Story award. I am blessed by these gifts.

A Note from the Author

Nopalito is a fictional town, but I can tell you where it is on the map: at the intersection of Highway 281 and County Road 227E, in Jim Wells County, Texas—a hundred miles south of San Antonio and fifty miles inland of Corpus Christi Bay. The county seat is Alice, fifteen miles south of Nopalito. The terrain is the brush country of the coastal plain, stippled with cenizo and agarita, prickly pear and yucca, huisache and mesquite. Agua Dulce Creek crosses Highway 281 a couple miles north of Nopalito. Like all creeks in this part of Texas, it is a dry creek, running only when it rains, and rain is intermittent.

NOTHING HAPPENED HERE

EVELYN SMITH, 1955–1975

ON THE DRIVE TO the Matthews place, Opal smoked a cigarette. Evelyn sat by the passenger door and stared. Grady was in the car—he would've been four that summer before Evelyn started first grade—but her memory preserves no image of her little brother in the back seat. Just Opal Matthews in profile at the steering wheel, her short-cropped hair shining like blackbird feathers. Opal was sixteen. Her voice came up out of her throat husky as Tallulah Bankhead, her cigarette, lipstick-stained, unfurling mentholated smoke out the open window.

"Rain is coming." Thunderheads gathered where Opal pointed to the far horizon. She gunned the engine. Opal had sass.

That was the word Evelyn's mother used for any kind of gumption she didn't like. "Got any sass in you," she had said just minutes ago, "best get spent of it at the Matthews place." Pausing, her eyebrow brush stilled before an arched brow, she locked eyes with Evelyn in the mirror.

In Evelyn's memory her mother was the only one left at home. Her father must've gone off someplace with Ralph, nearing ten and acting like a bantam rooster. Thick as thieves, Ralph and Daddy—her mother's words again.

Where was she going, all brushed and perfumed?

"I'll pack the two of you off. Opal can run the wickedness out of you."

The Matthews family had lived in the house on the rise beyond the creek for a year or so. Their arrival was clear in Evelyn's memory—a father and three sons who worked cattle for the Doyle ranch and a daughter, the youngest, who took the school bus weekdays and ran the household every day. There was no mother in the picture; given all the whispering, Evelyn knew she wasn't dead.

It was a two-story clapboard house—on the first floor boots and clutter, on the second ashtrays and unmade beds. The disarray would have driven her mother crazy, but the Matthews house delighted Evelyn—its smell of smoke and saddle leather, the jumble of dishes in the kitchen, sticky whiskey glasses unwashed along the drainboard. Opal shooed them into the living room, then set about clearing the mess so she could make lunch.

They discovered gold on the coffee table—a magazine unlike anything Evelyn had seen, her brother rapt on the couch beside her. She couldn't read, but she didn't need words. Swamp water glistened from the magazine's shiny cover, a frame of jungle growth draped in leafy green. A woman, all curves, stood in the water with a snake wrapped around her. Evelyn fell under the spell of the snake, the sheer abundance of it, coiled around the woman's body from hips to shoulders, mouth gaping and fangs agleam. The woman's eyes were wide, her mouth open as if inhaling a scream, lips red as crayons, fingernails too, the fingers of one hand draped in the V between her breasts, the pale, swollen flesh of them beneath a tattered neckline. Behind her in the trees, a darkly handsome man, muscled and confident, brandished a bladed weapon. It would be years before Evelyn encountered the word *machete* or discovered a stash of men's adventure magazines squirreled away in Ralph's closet, but at six she knew that the man would rescue the woman before the snake could work its evil. She looked and looked at the woman, the snake, the man behind them. Beside her, Grady did not stir. But she could feel him there, his heart beating.

The pages beneath held other images of women threatened and men hovering, though nothing like the glossy color cover. The woman there, the snake—they held her captive as the pages turned. It was like swinging too high, the way she felt inside, the moment of floating when she could no longer feel the anchor of weight and chains—breath suspended, horizon a distant shimmer. A deep pulse of pleasure on the downward plunge.

Opal snatched the magazine.

Cursing the Matthews men, their taste in reading, she sent Evelyn and Grady upstairs. They were playing onesies on the floor at the head of the staircase when the smell of rain arrived and the light at the window turned gray. Evelyn loved this game—metal spikes skittering across hardwood and the little ball bouncing, bouncing, as the jacks she scooped up prickled in her palm. She hardly noticed when footsteps came thumping up the stairs.

It was Opal, breathless with running, the look of a new game, a new dare, in the flush of her cheeks. "Robbers are coming! You've got to hide!" She swept them into her bedroom and behind a small couch in the corner. It was a loveseat, though Evelyn didn't know about loveseats yet. Whispering of danger, Opal swore them to silence. "Not a peep out of you." Then she was gone, her footsteps rapid on the stairs. It was quiet until the rain came, wrapping the afternoon in patter and rumble.

Shhh. A whisper. *It's okay.* The words seemed to come from inside her—and Grady dissolving, a shadowy presence, his head in her lap while she listened to silence beneath the rain.

When she felt that she would burst with waiting, voices came from downstairs—Opal's, higher than usual, and a man's gruff bluntness— quarreling, it seemed to Evelyn, like the sound her parents made when they closed the bedroom door to have it out. She heard the flat, hard sound of a slap, and a voice cried out—Opal's, Evelyn was certain— then the same voice in a warble, like someone being shaken. Evelyn went tingly all over. But Opal could take care of herself; she would send the robber away.

The voices stopped. The rain slowed. And Evelyn had to know.

The game she played with herself on the stairs was like fooling Momma while she napped, making herself so light that oak floorboards did not betray her. She made it to the bottom of the stairs, the house so still except for an odd shuffling sound coming from the kitchen and someone—Opal, maybe—trying to catch her breath. Evelyn made her way to the doorway and peeked around. On the kitchen table, in a jumble of limbs, a man's bare butt moved back and forth in a motion Evelyn had not seen before. He was wearing boots with dried cow dung stuck between heel and sole. His jeans were down around his thighs. He had on a chambray work shirt, and the breathing she'd heard was coming out of him. He was hugging Opal to the table, her skirt fanned out beneath her and up over her chest, her bare knees at cockeyed angles on either side of the naked flesh that moved against her. Evelyn couldn't see the man's face; he'd tucked his head into Opal's hair on the other side. Beside his tawny curls, Opal's eyes were wide, one eye puffed and smudgy, mouth open, lips like a bruise.

Rain trembled at the windows, mesquite trees drooping while Evelyn stood there and spied, unable to move, unable not to look. She might have frozen, like that woman in the Bible God turned to salt for looking where she oughtn't. But then Opal turned her head and looked right at Evelyn. She fixed Evelyn in her gaze and, with a movement of her eyes, signaled for her to get upstairs. Evelyn backed away, the motion of retreat lodged in her muscle memory. Then she was behind the loveseat again, a finger at her lips to keep what she had seen inside herself.

Afterward, Opal sat at her dresser as if nothing had happened. At the window, the eaves dripped. Grady must've gone outside to splash where the rain had puddled. In the mirror, Opal's puffy eye was darkening. She brushed her hair into place and went to work on her makeup. The eye seemed not to bother her.

When she'd finished, she sat Evelyn at the mirror and made her up with lipstick and powder and rouge, with spit curls at either cheek. Evelyn was wearing a short-sleeved peasant blouse. Her mother had sewed several such garments, with elastic at neckline and sleeves. They were easy to sew. Evelyn could run with her brothers and look like the daughter her mother insisted she be. This afternoon, when Opal had finished with the makeup, she put her hands at either side of Evelyn's neckline and tugged the blouse down off her shoulders. Evelyn stared at herself in the mirror and wondered what a snake would feel like against her skin. She caught Opal's eye in the mirror.

"Ooh, don't you look like a hussy. What would your momma think?"

Evelyn examined herself in the mirror. *Hussy* was another of her mother's words.

"What about that nasty magazine I found you looking at?"

"You won't tell?"

"Maybe I'll show it to her."

Evelyn was too frightened to plead. She simply looked at Opal and hoped. Finally, Opal got down on one knee, as if genuflecting, and fixed Evelyn with her one good eye. When she spoke, her voice came out lower than ever, the words husky with threat.

"Nothing happened here this afternoon. A game is all." Opal paused. The eaves dripped. "I didn't catch you looking at that trash." Evelyn looked down, but Opal gripped her harder at the shoulder. She looked up again. "You didn't see a thing downstairs. You'll keep your mouth shut to your brother."

Evelyn swore to her part in the promise—thank God Grady'd gone outside to play—and Opal was back to herself again.

"I got my black eye in the barn this afternoon." Her voice was blunt as truth. "I was horse-kicked, little miss. Jumped back in the nick of time. I am lucky to be alive."

Late that summer, the Matthews family moved away, gone without a trace before Evelyn's first day of school. Vernon Doyle hired three boys at the high school to ride herd for him, and the old house stood empty.

The following spring, Evelyn's mother whipped her with a hairbrush. She'd hatched a plan for mother-daughter Easter dresses—a prissy pattern, all frills and ruffles. When she gushed about puffed sleeves and dotted Swiss, Evelyn stomped her foot and said *no*. For a moment, she was light as air, dizzy with elation the word released in her. Until she was yanked into her parents' bedroom and her mother got hold of the brush. The spanking was like fever. Evelyn felt heavy with the shame of it while on the wall beside her mother's dresser a witness looked on. The Virgin Mary hovered there, sheathed in cool blue, serene calm in the drape of her clothing, the welcoming gesture of her open palms, the composure of an almost smiling mouth. Her eyes, their quiet reassurance. Even the Virgin's foot, poised to crush the head of the serpent, betrayed no hint of panic, no doubt about the outcome. Beneath the seashell roar of disgrace ringing in Evelyn's ears, she heard a whisper—*Be still*—an offering from her silent herald.

This was to be the first of three whippings with the hairbrush—and years between them—but always there was the threat. As childhood and adolescence passed, Evelyn had little time for idle thinking. Her every move was tactical, calculated to keep her mother from flaring up, to keep her father and brothers from discovering the rift between mother and daughter. The robber's game with Opal Matthews was just another of her secrets. She didn't dare mention it to Grady. He said nothing to her.

Grady giggled at the supper table whenever tension threatened. He laughed away their mother's stormy moods. He played dolls with Evelyn, chattering nonstop while they burped and pampered her collection. His favorites were a wedding set—a bride and her groom, two bridesmaids—a gift to Evelyn from her father's only brother, who shrugged off what folks might think about a bachelor farmer hooking tablecloths for his sister, his sister-in-law, himself. It was Grady who wanted the wedding party, who didn't mind the subterfuge it took to get them. He suggested the gift set for Evelyn, then made sure it would happen by teasing Uncle Aaron, saying his fingers weren't graceful enough for such delicate work. Starched and perfect, the wedding figures stood behind glass in the dining-room hutch Evelyn's mother was so proud of. On occasion, Grady worked his charm on Momma. She would place the wedding dolls on the dining table and let them orchestrate an afternoon-long ceremony.

Grady was the happy one—always sprinting ahead to the next adventure, ever swinging high, pushing higher, leaping free at the top of the arc, his voice like scissortails in a noon sky. While Evelyn stood anchored, watching. Her little brother seemed immune to the dampers that kept her quiet, the impatience that kept Ralph on a short fuse.

In the spring of 1960, as fifth grade drew toward a close, Evelyn's father invited the Wahrmund family for a Saturday feed. Her mother wasn't happy—*mousey* was her word for Dorene Wahrmund—but when Ralph protested, her displeasure melted away. Ralph was fourteen, and from the moment his voice had dropped, he'd wanted to be off alone with his best friend Jimmy Don, eldest of the Wahrmund brothers. Jimmy Don was fifteen. Evelyn's mother claimed there was nothing wrong with him a good slap wouldn't cure. "You're not too good for the rest of us," she told Ralph. And that was that.

When the Wahrmunds arrived, Evelyn's father was at the barbecue pit, set up out back among a cluster of mesquites. He'd built a fire and tended it, spread coals along the bottom of the pit, split chickens and mopped them with a special sauce—butter, vinegar, lemon, garlic, pepper—as he arranged them above the smoky heat. Robert Wahrmund joined him while the women went inside.

Ralph and Jimmy Don grabbed a bat and started knocking flies. They were good at showing off—pitcher putting a perfect ball across the plate, batter connecting every time, the ball arcing up and up, all but disappearing in the bright blue, suspended for a moment there, as if with an invisible parachute.

Max, second of the Wahrmund brothers, elbowed his way in, though it was clear to Evelyn the older boys were never going to let Max be one of them. She stood along the edges, knowing that when Ralph and Jimmy Don tired of showing off, they'd let her have a turn at bat.

Michael, Evelyn's age, third and last of the Wahrmund brothers, trotted to the edge of the outer yard, assigned by Jimmy Don to retrieve the baseball wherever it might land. Michael would have opted out, Evelyn suspected, except that otherwise Jimmy Don would needle him until he did what was expected anyway.

Grady laughed them off. Nine now—and immune to the allure of team sports—he stood beside Evelyn, openly mocking the older boys.

They didn't have long on the sidelines before their mother sent word with Mrs. Wahrmund and Evelyn had to go inside. Grady went along. He loved being in the kitchen whenever women gathered there.

Evelyn had a knack with seasoning; she was put to work assembling potato salad. Mrs. Wahrmund peeled and chopped eggs for her. Simple shirt-waist dress and flats, thick straight shimmering black hair in a blunt cut—Dorene Wahrmund was nothing like Evelyn's mother, with her lemony blonde do, her color-drenched sundress and heels. Evelyn had the sense not to say so, but she much preferred their neighbor's simplicity, her plainness. Of the women she knew, though, the one Evelyn most envied was Mrs. Wahrumnd's mother, Norma Pfeiler, who owned the café and bakery on Main Street. A widow, Mrs. Pfeiler had her own house, her own life. Evelyn wanted to be just like her when she got old. She didn't say that to Momma either.

When everything in the kitchen was ready, Evelyn was sent to summon the others. She headed for the boys first; they could wrap up their game while her father and Mr. Wahrmund carried barbecue to the house. Max was at bat, Ralph winding up for a pitch, Jimmy Don and Michael positioned to catch or retrieve whatever their brother hit. Everything started to unravel when Max gave a shout and dropped the bat. He walked toward Ralph, pointing.

"Look!" he called out. "Look! He's gonna do it!"

In the field beyond, separated from them by a single strand of electric fence, her father's newly purchased Hereford bull mounted the heifer Evelyn had named Violet. When the bull's rump started jerking back and forth, Max erupted.

"Atta boy!" he shouted. "Stick it to her!"

Evelyn had slowed, but she hadn't stopped walking. She found herself at Max's side, watching, transfixed, as Violet hunched into herself, her eyes wide and rolling. The bull made a final spasm against her and dismounted.

"What were they *doing*?" she asked.

"You're a farm girl," said Jimmy Don, approaching where Evelyn stood with Max and Ralph. "Animals been doing the nasty all around you. You telling me you haven't seen it?"

"Momma keeps her indoors a lot," Ralph said. "Wants to make a lady out of her."

"You really want to know what they were up to?" Jimmy Don said. "Making babies."

"Yeah," Max put in. "How do you think you got here?"

Evelyn spent a lifetime pondering the way a mind works, making you see the one thing you would rather not. As Max got to the end of his question, she had a vision—bright as sheet lightning—of her mother bent over the supper table with her bottom exposed, naked from the waist down except for the heels she was wearing today, the skirt of her sundress flounced up over her back. And behind her—why not at least her father?—Mr. Wahrmund wearing not a stitch, his butt muscles jerking like the Hereford bull.

And then flashes of memory: a skirt flared beneath pale thighs, dirty boots on a kitchen table, ragged breathing, a bruised and swelling eye. It wasn't the answer she wanted, but she knew in her bones that what Jimmy Don had said was true. *This* was how babies came into the world, how she'd arrived in her family's embrace. She wondered if Opal Matthews had a child. A boy, she thought, four years old by now.

The next day was Sunday—church and a midday meal at Uncle Aaron's house. That afternoon, back home, while Grady slouched on her bed, daydreaming aloud, Evelyn broke in.

"I'm not ever getting married."

"But you have to," Grady said. "I'm designing your dress."

At school, Evelyn was rewarded for the habit of silence, of focused attention. And at home—though her mother stressed clothing, carriage, chatter, popularity—any evidence of discipline had currency. Evelyn was left alone while she worked at her assignments. Somewhere in junior high—she could never place the season or even the year—the band director took her aside and told her she played flute well enough that he was moving her into Nopalito's tiny high school band.

Because she'd learned so well the art of being invisible, the older girls put no rein on their gossip when she drifted near. She heard bits and pieces, never the shape, even, of a coherent story. One day as she stood watching, the girls leaned inward, as if in a huddle, and she heard a single inscrutable pronouncement—"I heard it was rape"—followed by a tangle of whispers. Evelyn went to a dictionary in the library and turned to the word. *Carnal knowledge of a woman*, the definition began. Like fragments from a gospel reading, strangely disconnected from sense, these words were of little use. The closing phrase teased at her, though—*without her consent*. The notion of force lodged in her mind, and when she went back to the dictionary for *carnal*, she was visited by an image of flesh, a hairy butt rutting against Opal Matthews's pale thighs. The black eye cinched it. *He forced her*, she thought.

When Evelyn was fourteen, she found herself one evening on a patch of gravel beneath the lights at Otto Keene's. Ralph was out of high school and three months gone, but the remnants of his crowd were still on hand, flirting, eating burgers, bootlegging liquor from car to car. Evelyn was watching from the edges of the fray when a voice roused her. She'd heard the legend of Clayton Moore, the town's notorious heartbreaker, a decade out of high school by now and rarely spied in town after the sun went down. She'd seen his photograph in old yearbooks—the sideburns, the grin. She'd not had the pleasure in person, but when Clayton pulled onto the gravel in his hopped-up old Ford, she recognized him instantly.

He formed the center of a group, the voices around him merging like rain. Suddenly, his voice rose up. She didn't hear words but tone and timbre. In the instant, she knew it was the voice she'd heard that afternoon, the voice downstairs with Opal Matthews. Then Clayton turned and looked in her direction. She felt the burn of his eyes on her. "Well, look who's here. I think it's Miss Bopeep." Evelyn turned and walked to the car she'd arrived in. She was surprised her knees didn't buckle. Hearing Clayton's voice, feeling his eyes on her, she'd felt herself swing wildly out of control—a surging sensation that wed pleasure and panic.

In May of 1967, a month short of her eighteenth birthday, Evelyn finished high school. At summer's end, she moved into her first college dorm in Corpus Christi, forty-some miles east of the farm that had circumscribed her life so far—but far enough to spark feelings of freedom, release.

On September 22, shortly before midnight, as she stood at her window looking out over a campus still soaked from Hurricane Beulah, a knock came at her door. She was called to the phone, and the bits of happiness she'd collected over the years were taken from her.

At home after the winds quieted, Grady had gone out to look at the floodwaters along Agua Dulce Creek. He was not to be seen again—no body found, no gravestone carved for her brother. In the days, the years, that followed, Evelyn's mother could not bear to hear Grady's name spoken. Her father, sad-eyed and sagging, took refuge in silence. Ralph had come home to help with the searching, but when hope waned there, he went back to west Texas and the roughneck life. He returned only under duress.

As best she could, Evelyn made a life for herself out of the pieces left her—scraps of kinship, secrets she and Grady had sheltered. She traced the meandering line of Agua Dulce Creek from the family farm to the Cayo del Mazón, then to Baffin Bay and the salty waters of the Gulf beyond. She invented another life for Grady, picturing him whole and breathing on the far side of the flood that had swept him away. Year after year on his birthday, she drove to a seafood house on Baffin Bay. She ordered fried shrimp because her brother had loved them. Weather permitting, she sat at an umbrellaed table on the deck, sometimes all afternoon, the bay lapping at the piers beneath her feet while her clothes, her hair, wilted in the damp salt air. Overhead, the gulls, calling, calling.

Grady receded—time did that—memory offering up fragments when Evelyn least expected. Over lunch in a downtown cafeteria, someone in the next booth rattled a cup inside its saucer, and she saw Grady at three, holding one of her tiny cups at a tea party the two of them had set up on the front porch. Once, in an airport terminal, after hours of delay, she searched out an empty corner and, sitting, leaned against the wall to rest. She dozed into a shadowy place. Grady was there, napping too, his head on her lap.

Some mornings she woke knowing she'd dreamed of Grady, a secret he had left in her care the summer before the hurricane. Her brother had fallen for a young man who lived just west of the Smith place. Domingo Escovedo had recently arrived from Mexico—a sweet, shy boy, Evelyn seemed to recall, much favored by her mother, who had set cookies by the plateful in front of her brother's new friend.

High water murmured in the dreams that fetched Grady back for Evelyn. And her brother's voice, an urgent whisper—that she must cross the flooded creek, must take a message to Domingo.

"I've seen the way he looks at me," Grady had said, as if eyes alone might satisfy the eagerness trembling in their fingertips.

As the years went by, Evelyn took much comfort from what her brother had told her. That he had known—what?—love? Wary of attachments, cautious about the promises that seemed inherent in touch, she wanted for Grady what she held distant from herself.

Shortly after completing her MBA, Evelyn spent several days on the family farm with her parents. The occasion was her birthday; she was turning twenty-six. Unable to lure her mother to Corpus Christi for a celebration, unable to say no to her father when he got on the phone and said please, she agreed to a short vacation in Nopalito.

"My car needs servicing first," she told him.

"Take care of it here," he said. "Can't find a better shop than Clayton's."

Evelyn agreed without hesitating. Since the unsettling encounter at Otto Keene's a dozen years before, she'd seen no more of Clayton Moore than a distant glance. At some point during those years, she'd stopped being afraid. Facing up to her mother, seeing her defeated by Grady's disappearance, she'd learned something like calm in the face of bluster. As for the man who worked magic with cars, Evelyn had negotiated a life that didn't put her at risk of crossing paths with his kind of swagger. She'd had the rare encounter with an insolent male, what woman hadn't? She handled such occasions with a stiffening, a look, a tone she seemed to have inherited from her mother. Besides, Momma had been right about something, a kernel of truth wrapped in the trappings of insult. Evelyn Smith was not the sort of woman to attract notice from Clayton Moore and his ilk.

The morning after her father's request, she arrived at Nopalito's lone auto shop. The entire transaction might have gone off without a hitch—except Clayton turned from the register and didn't recognize her. Pulling a triplicate from the dispenser there, he took up a pen and paused, clearly waiting for her to identify herself. Evelyn said nothing.

"And who might you be?" he said. Something about his guileless look put a bur under her saddle.

"Miss Bopeep," she said. "That's what you called me once."

Clayton wrinkled his face into a question.

"Evelyn Smith," she said. "Ed Smith's daughter. I bet you remember Opal Matthews."

"Opal who?"

"Jim Matthews's daughter. He ran cattle for the Doyles. 1955."

"Why would I—? How would you—? That was twenty years ago."

"Big summer thunderstorm? You were there."

"This girl, Opal, what did she look like?"

"You tell me."

"Excuse me, Miss Smith. I don't know any Opal Matthews. I have a business to run."

Clayton didn't look as if what she'd said had rankled him; he looked like a man intent on other things. Just then a mechanic—smudged face, oily rag in his hands—stepped through the door behind the counter. From the quiet behind him came the sound of a wrench dropped on the cement floor.

The two men spoke briefly, and Clayton turned back to her, all business. Evelyn told him what she wanted done with her car and walked to the café. When she returned, one of Clayton's mechanics had replaced him at the counter.

She stayed on through her birthday and went back to Corpus Christi a couple of days later, stopping for lunch at Otto Keene's on her way out of town. Max Wahrmund ran the kitchen there now. He'd started as a short-order cook and quickly took charge. He was hard on everyone—cooks, dishwashers, waitresses—but the food coming out of his kitchen was some of the best in the county. Evelyn wanted a plate of his fried chicken.

Max had endured his share of heartbreak; it had not improved his character. Oh, he worked hard, always had. When he wasn't riding herd on the crew at Otto Keene's, he helped his father on the home place. Max clearly wasn't happy about any of it—might as well have stood out front by the highway in a sandwich board proclaiming how much the world owed him.

The lunch crowd was at its peak. Evelyn took a lone seat at the end of the counter. A clearly flustered waitress handed her a menu—"Be with you in a minute, hon"—and disappeared into the kitchen. Seconds later, raised voices. A woman—Evelyn thought it was likely her waitress—sounding angry, defensive, intimidated. And then Max, self-important, demanding, a voice that bent others to its will. Hearing him, she thought of the voice that had rattled her so badly that night outside on the gravel here. And the voice downstairs at Opal Matthews twenty years ago. It could have been Max that day of the rain. Evelyn smiled at the notion. He would have been eight the day she and Grady spent with Opal.

She took her time over a plate of chicken, letting the waitress refill her glass of iced tea several times. Reaching for her purse, ready to pay the bill, she looked up and saw Clayton at the door. She saw him seeing her. *You again?* his look seemed to say. He grinned. Winked. No hint of sex there—a goofy, disarming wink. Evelyn laughed as he moved toward her.

"Suppose anyone here would remember that girl?" he said, taking the seat beside her. "What was her name now?"

"Opal Matthews."

"How old was she?"

"Sixteen."

"Jail bait. Never liked girls that age—they don't know a thing about it. Twenty-four, twenty-five before they have a lick of sense." He raised a hand, as if to forestall the objection he expected her to make. "Men are worse," he said. "Take me. I've passed the four-O mark—might smarten up yet."

The waitress set a large paper sack on the counter in front of Clayton and started toting up his check.

"What happened to her?" he asked Evelyn. "This Opal Matthews."

"The family moved away."

He took the check and reached for his wallet.

"You still in touch?"

"No."

"Don't know where she moved?"

"No."

"How old were you?"

"Six."

He counted several bills atop the check, picked up his bag of takeout orders, and stood.

"Want to tell me why you asked *me* about her?"

"I think I'd rather not."

"Hmmm," Clayton said. "Opal Matthews, mystery girl."

He dipped his chin as a parting gesture and walked out of the place.

THE EMPTY ROOMS

DORENE WAHRMUND, SEPTEMBER 6, 1955

THE ROOSTER'S RACKET WOKE Dorene. She lay listening to the quiet between calls, an unfamiliar weight this morning to the silence. The oak in the yard whispered and stilled. Gray at the window. When the rooster called again, she rose and dressed and made her way to the kitchen. Raising a window above the sink, she turned to the percolator. Morning cool and sparrow chatter spilled into the room. When the coffee was ready, she woke Robert and set about fixing breakfast. Her hands were at the biscuit dough when he came through the house, footsteps heavy on the floorboards as he called to their sons. She poured coffee—black for Robert, a splash of cream in hers—and handed her husband a mug as he passed through on his way to the milking.

Minutes later, hastily clad in work clothes, her sons shambled in. Jimmy Don asked for coffee. "You're not old enough," she said. Her eldest was ten but wanted to be grown. She let him have a sip from her cup. Max, eight, was a surly riser. He shrugged off her good morning, leaning half-asleep against the doorjamb until Jimmy Don punched him and said, "Last one there." The two of them shot out of the house on a race to the pigpens. Dorene went down on one knee for Michael, her youngest, who still greeted his mother each morning with a kiss.

"Know what day it is?" he asked.

"Your first day of school. But the chickens need tending. Better get out there."

While bacon sizzled—jets of butane, blue flamed, whispering beneath the skillet—Dorene broke eggs into a bowl and whisked them. The sparrows were still at it, their noises enhanced by squawks from the henhouse, the occasional bellow of a cow from the milking shed. From the ridge of the smokehouse roof out back, the rooster claimed the morning with a final cry. Grinning at the bluster, Dorene pulled biscuits from the oven and dropped the pan atop the unused burners. Her days were filled with sound, a single interval of quiet arriving each night when Robert nodded off—and not a peep from her sons, two rooms away and sound asleep.

Robert returned first from the morning chores, a brusque kiss for her as she poured them each a second cup. A minute alone together at the little kitchen table, a few sips, a word or two, before the boys rushed in to get ready for school, the bedroom they shared erupting in clamor and their father raising his voice from the table, saying, "Don't fight," saying, "Hurry, hurry, hurry."

Minutes later she took her place at the dining table—one end for her, the other for Robert, with Max and Michael side by side between them, Jimmy Don opposite his brothers. They all talked at once, with little evidence of listening, though her sons had learned to hear their father beneath the clamor and respond as necessary. Robert was done first, then up and out the door, off to wrestle a grader along rough and rutted roads. He had several weeks of work with the county, thank God for that.

The instant the back door closed behind him, Jimmy Don and Max were out of their seats and off to their room for the zippered notebooks that held their school supplies, then into the kitchen, jostling at the refrigerator for sack lunches she'd assembled the evening before, and back to the dining room, chomping at the bit.

They wanted a head start to the bus, didn't want their little brother walking with them, most decidedly did not want their mother along.

"I'm coming," she said.

She'd walked Jimmy Don to the bus for his first day, with Michael on her hip and Max skipping along behind. She'd done the same for Max. It might've been the last thing she did for her second son that elicited a sign of gratitude. She'd do the same for Michael, closest to her heart, though she would never say so aloud.

She loved each of her sons with a wild, piercing joy that, as they grew older, she struggled to contain lest her affections embarrass them. But Michael soaked it up. He showed no sign of stepping back, as Max had done, watching his older brother. Jimmy Don had been sending her signals since the evening of his eighth birthday, when she hugged him in front of company.

They walked to the gate, the four of them, under a sky puffed with cloud, the house quiet behind them, the animals fed and fattening. Jimmy Don and Max were civil, though tight-lipped. Michael made up for their silence. He'd been at it, this patter of his, since well before his second birthday, when he'd discovered that he could make words from the sounds coming out of his mouth. He woke talking and fell asleep midsentence.

When the bus pulled up, Dorene hugged Michael and let him go. When he got to a window, she waved and turned to walk back. Scissortails cavorted above—swooping, zigzagging—their long tail feathers V-ing against a sky so blue she almost had to look away. The birds called to one another. They cackled. To Dorene it sounded like laughter. She felt happy just hearing them.

As she reached the back steps, she heard something behind her and turned. It was in the live oak across the yard, a rustling deep within the leaves, a short, sharp squawk, and then silence. One of the barn cats must have got up there, got himself breakfast with feathers.

Dorene opened the back door and paused midstep into the kitchen. Her hand on the doorknob behind her, she cocked her head. She listened. The window at the sink was still open, but nothing crossed the sill. The birds in the hackberries, the trees themselves, had gone mute. The cows beyond, their noses dipping to Buffelgrass, had nothing to add, no calf among them bawling. The air itself had stilled, dust motes listless in a shaft of sunlight from the window. She had only ever heard silence layered with the sounds that living creatures make—silence with heft, voices behind it somewhere, coming or going—one of her sons needing a Band-Aid, Robert trekking in from the fields.

What she heard was time. Not the ticking of clocks—none ticked in Dorene Wahrmund's life. Robert couldn't sleep while a clock ticked, wouldn't have a timepiece that tapped against the eardrum. The clock on the kitchen wall was silent, its rotations smoothed by the currents that moved within. What Dorene heard—what she felt from a deep recess she hadn't known she harbored, what came to her at shortly past 7:30 on the morning of September 6, 1955—was the silent movement, the stealth, the cheat. Her inner ear opened to the way time stops, or seems to. And when it starts up again, the clocks have changed—the calendar, the year, the decade even. Time has put someone else in your place. The face in the window, the eyes—who is that woman? How is it she has failed, until now, to hear what surely she must? What will she do about the stillness that waits in the rooms of her house?

She stood there trapped, shut off from the moment before the door had opened. That life had vanished, quick as a flash of feather scissor-tailed against the morning sky. Distant as someone named Dorene Pfeiler, age eighteen, lakeside at the clubhouse, sitting swim-suited atop a squat stone pillar, smiling for the boy she will marry. He holds the camera, the shadow of his head and shoulders visible in the bottom-left corner of the snapshot, fading now, shadow and girl, among the pages of an album stored out of sight beneath the window seat in this very house. Robert, his finger at the shutter. And Dorene, grinning into a future she cannot begin to imagine.

When she found that her legs would do as she wanted, she walked from room to room. Everything was as it had been. Hastily made beds in the room her sons shared, her own bedroom neat as a pin—from the meticulous arrangement of her dresser and the impeccably made bed,

Robert's doing, to the clothes rack on the back of the door, three of his shirts hanging there, perfectly pressed. There was work too. Dishes cluttered the kitchen counter, laundry in a tumble from the bathroom hamper. Beside the ironing board, a pile of starched khaki—her radio at arm's length—and the iron plugged in, biding, where she had switched it off the night before. She reached to the radio; music and voices leapt into the room. It was worse than the quiet. She turned it off.

The rocking chair beckoned, but habit was strong in her. She turned on the iron and began, stopped when a burning smell reached her, and she saw she'd ruined one of Robert's shirts, the imprint of her iron charred into a sleeve. The will to attention seemed to have escaped her. She took the shirt to the kitchen wastebasket and went out to burn the trash, letting flames dispose of the evidence. It was a thing she might have done on any other day, keeping something from her husband that would have served no purpose but to fuel his ire.

Walking back to the house, she thought of the eggs Michael had collected, waiting in the tool room for her to clean and carton. Tomorrow, Thursday at the latest, she would have to deliver her eggs in town. *I'll take care of them later*, she thought, *or have one of the boys do it after school*.

Inside, she walked again from room to room. She could find herself nowhere. For stretches she sat—couch, rocker, dresser chair, bed. Several times she had an experience like coming out of a daydream, aware gradually that her eyes were trained on something—the pattern of lace in her curtains at a living-room window, or a potted ivy, its tendrils trailing in a patch of sunlight on the window seat. Later, it was her rolling pin, biscuit-sticky on the board she used for working dough. Studying this one item amid the jumble on the counter, she realized that she was chewing—a lunch of crackers and sardines on the plate in front of her, the sardine tin with its key-wound top on the table beside her napkin, a dab of the fishy oil glistening there.

She cleared her things from the table, cleared dishes from the counter, arranged sounds into words when her boys returned from school. She was distantly aware of saying what needed to be said to Michael about his first day of school. With help from her sons, she got a meal on the table and greeted Robert when he arrived, dust covered, from a day on the road grader. After supper, claiming a headache, she left the men to clean up and went to bed.

She was half-asleep when Robert reached for her. She put his hand away. He reached again. Again, she put his hand away. "Woman," he said. He wanted her little enough. She had schooled herself to let him have his way in other things as well, schooled her sons in the habits of deference to their father.

Not tonight. "I'm going to the bathroom," she said, and sat in there for a while, giving him time to fall asleep.

He reached for her again.

"Robert, no," she said, and sat up.

He grabbed at her. She slapped his hands away. At some point they got out of bed and fussed at one another some more.

"I won't take no for an answer," he said. "I don't have to." His face was too close, his breath hot and ripe against her.

"Get out of here," she said, her words blunt as fists between them.

Robert raised his voice. She did the same, the two of them sputtering in the dark.

Jimmy Don knocked at the door. "Momma? Daddy?"

Robert yanked the door open. "Get on back to bed," he said. "You got no business here."

Jimmy Don backed up. He kept his voice civil. But he did not leave. "You all right, Momma?" he asked.

"I'm fine, Son," she said. "Your father and I will settle this. Go on now, don't wake your brothers." And Jimmy Don was gone.

Dorene was so tired she wobbled. She got back in bed. Robert gruffed at her for a bit, then walked around to his side and lay down, his back to her—stiff, unyielding. It was best, she knew, to make amends before they slept. But tonight, before Dorene could reach a calming hand across the space between them, tonight the weight of sleep pulled her under.

She was awake at dawn, but she turned from the light and slept. It was day outside when Michael woke her.

"Daddy's gone," he said.

She put on a robe and sat at the breakfast table, her sons tongue-tied at their places, snatching looks at her between bites.

Later the other places at the table were empty, but she was still there, vaguely aware of a gnawing sensation in her gut. She poured milk over cornflakes and sat there while the morning passed. Now and then she ate a soggy spoonful.

She was sitting at her dresser, still in her robe, when the boys came in from school. One look at their faces and shame got through to her, a burn like lye.

She got them out of the room and closed the door behind them.

She took a bath, put on fresh clothes, and went to the kitchen. That seemed as far as her resources would reach. Jimmy Don asked what they should have for supper. He marshaled Max and Michael to help. She stood by, and food was on the table when Robert got home, his eyes spilling questions as they passed the serving dishes. During the meal, he studied his plate, his brow knit as at a hand of cards that doesn't add up.

When it was time for bed, Robert followed her into their room and closed the door. They changed into bedclothes and, switching out the light, stood beside each other at the double windows, a ritual they'd fallen into years back, loving the air at the screens, the soft shapes out there in the night.

"What is it?" Robert asked, his voice mixing concern with impatience. "What's got into you?"

"I don't know," Dorene said.

"Not getting out of bed. Sulking."

Is that what she looked like?

"What did you do today?"

The night seemed answer enough.

"That's what I thought," Robert said. "It won't do for tomorrow."

Somewhere out there, a cow nuzzled chain-link at the gatepost.

"There's work to be done," Robert said. "For the both of us." He turned to the bed.

Dorene made herself get up as usual when the rooster called. She put on a clean dress. She brushed her hair and pulled it back with one of the plain knit headbands she wore for housecleaning. She took stock of Robert and her sons. She would do what she could for them—sack lunches for the boys, breakfast and supper, clean clothes. For Robert, what tenderness she could muster when he needed her. Starched khaki, attentively pressed. Her end of the farmwork. First thing after breakfast, she got the eggs ready to sell.

Twice—on Friday of the first week, and again on Monday—Dorene walked her sons to the bus, Jimmy Don and Max notwithstanding. Michael wanted her company. She was fine on the way to the gate, fine waving to the departing bus. But then the walk back, the quiet house. Monday morning, when she closed the door behind her and faced the empty rooms, it was too much. A cry came out of her, deep as any grief she'd known—a spasm in her ribcage, her breath forced up and out, her throat, her voice box seizing. It was like the sound she had made, alone in the house three years ago, in the aftermath of her father's funeral. She'd felt him suddenly—a shadowy presence in the gray leaching in from an overcast sky—and then this hurt erupted out of her. It had knocked her to her knees.

This time, when the sound came, Dorene held herself erect. "You will not do this," she said. "No one has died."

On Tuesday she kissed Michael in the kitchen and waved as her sons went out the door. She walked to her bedroom and sat down at the dresser. She would drive to town. She would see her mother. If she could do that, she could do anything.

She brushed her hair, put on a touch of lipstick, a hint of powder. She looked at herself in the mirror. Her hair would not pass muster, hanging heavy and straight and plain. She was overdue for a permanent, and she hadn't set her hair in pin curls the night before as she usually did before a trip to town. She pulled one of her headbands into place and took a look. Her mother would not be pleased. A scarf, perhaps, then. But that was worse. She looked like a church widow, or so her mother would say. Actually, Momma *was* a church widow, but while she espoused a spare, pared-down look for herself and other husband-less women of a certain age, she would call her daughter dowdy, plain and simple.

Dorene looked back through her scarves and chose one with a bit of color. She twirled it from two of the corners so that the scarf furled around itself, then replaced her headband with it, tying the ends of the scarf at her nape, beneath her hair. It would have to do. If Gloria Vanderbilt could carry off a turban in public, surely she could manage a fashionably furled scarf.

Her mother's little bakery-diner had settled into the morning lull when Dorene arrived, five cartons of eggs in her hands for the baked goods that had made Nopalito a stopping place for travelers up and down the highway. The screen door clattered behind Dorene when she released it, and from one of the barstools, a child swiveled to face her. Evelyn Smith was Michael's age. She ought to have been in school, though her mother, seated beside her at the counter, clearly thought otherwise. Mathilda Smith, blonde, combed, made-up, was running her mouth at Dorene's mother. While they talked, the child stared at Dorene. Not a stare, really. The wide-eyed look of a startled fawn, a child who has seen something she'd rather not. Until her mother noticed.

"Stop gaping," she said, and spun the child back around to face the counter. "Finish your pie. We have patterns to shop for."

Released, Dorene's mother turned to her. She took one look and frowned.

"What's bothering *you?*" She didn't trouble to lower her voice.

"Nothing," Dorene said, and sat down with her mother in one of the booths.

"Is it Robert, has he . . . ?" When Dorene said no, her mother launched into a litany of questions. Was it the boys? The mortgage on the farm? And back to Robert. Her mother had no patience with moody men and the way their feelings so often came to the surface like fireworks. Robert was Robert, Dorene reminded her mother. He'd been moody, mercurial, since he got back from the war.

"What then?" her mother said. "Tell."

"I don't know, Momma." Dorene didn't have the words. "I've got the blues is all."

"The blues." Her mother all but snorted. "You don't have time for the blues."

Dorene was three weeks shy of thirty-one. No matter. With a look, a few well-chosen words, her mother could make her feel twelve again—fidgeting, timid, dismissed.

"You can start with a permanent."

"I don't need a permanent."

"I'm closed Mondays, you know that. I'll give you one then."

"No," Dorene said. "You will not. I'll be fine. I don't want a permanent."

Time passed. Somewhere during the stretch of days, Dorene was aware, with curious detachment, that she had missed her time of the month. She went through her routine as usual, pausing now and again. What if she had a girl this time? What would that be like—to have a daughter's company in a house full of men? In the time before, she had wanted a daughter with such eagerness, such ardent hope. Just seeing a baby girl had taken her breath away. It was not like that now. There were no tears when she woke one night to the onset of her period. She went to the bathroom and took care of herself, got back in bed and was instantly asleep.

Never had she slept so deeply. Never had she wanted sleep more.

The days got better, the empty house, by degrees, bearable. With fall approaching she called for a butane delivery. She was at the washing machine when the truck pulled into the yard. No need to interrupt herself. Johnny Kramer would knock when he was done. She heard the door of his truck slam, and seconds later a shout came from the yard where the butane tank sat. She hurried to the porch door and out into the yard, arriving at the scene to find Johnny pointing the butane hose at a coiled rattler. The snake was clearly done for, the butane freezing it in place.

Johnny Kramer all but stuttered at being caught with his nozzle aimed at a snake. He apologized repeatedly for the waste of fuel, promising to knock some off the bill when the tank was full. Dorene didn't care. She was relieved to know that he was safe and that the snake was dead—one less danger to her sons.

She had agreed with other women that Johnny Kramer was one of the better-looking men in Nopalito. She hadn't considered the matter any further. In the weeks since Michael's first day of school, though, Dorene had begun to notice a curious phenomenon—that as she paid less heed to what was said around her, she was studying others, examining them, seeing things about them they might prefer she not remark on. It was like that with Johnny, the way she watched him while he filled the butane tank.

He had hair the color of cured hay. It would have been lovely to reach out and touch, to flip the curl back off his forehead, run fingertips over the muscles in his forearms as he connected the hose coupling to the butane tank. What she hadn't counted on was that Johnny would observe her observing him. What she hadn't counted on was the look he gave her.

She might not have noticed, except that she became aware he had stopped talking. Shifting her gaze from his hands to his eyes, she saw him looking at her, saw deep, quenchless need there. He would have followed her into the house and shucked the clothes from her. He would have bedded her, not hiding his eyes the while.

She watched herself watching him, watched the loneliness shining up out of his eyes. A person could drown, she thought. Not *I could drown*. No. *A person could drown*. The words came to her so clearly she hoped she hadn't spoken them.

"No thank you," she said, her voice audible in the air between them.

"Pardon?"

"Lowering the bill." Dorene thought fast. "It's kind of you to offer, but no thank you."

They had disposed of that issue at the outset. Johnny Kramer clearly wasn't fooled. He knew what she'd said no to. Wilting back into himself, he scribbled an invoice for the butane and left.

At some point after the first cold front, a weepy period ensued. It was like a lingering cold. No sobs, no crying jags. Her eyelids were puffy, her nose ran, her tear ducts seeped. She slogged through her days, not caring what she did or how she looked. She stayed out of town, turned a deaf ear to her mother when she called and peppered her with questions. More than once she stayed home on Sunday. Robert wasn't Catholic, but he'd made promises when they married. He loaded up the boys and drove them to Mass.

Dorene was aware of feeling grateful to her husband. When she suffered a lapse, he stepped in. He did what needed to be done, but there was no hint of kindness in him, no gesture that might be traced to affection. Over supper one evening, when she reached for a handkerchief and dabbed at her cheeks, she caught Robert's eye. He looked as if he wanted to backhand someone. She tried to reach for him when he came to bed. She wanted somehow to comfort him, to find a bit of solace with her head on his chest. Robert sat upright at her touch and scrambled to a sitting position at the side of the bed, his back to her, his shoulders rigid with refusal.

"When is this going to stop?" he said.

What could she say to him? That when she was alone, silence did its work inside her, hard and sharp as a harvesting blade? That when he was there—and her sons—their noises came at her, that sorting the sense from words was something she couldn't remember to do? Robert would think she had lost her mind. For the first time in what had never been an easy marriage, Dorene made her way alone.

With her tears came tantrums. She didn't know what else they could be called, these fits that came on her. Mostly they happened when she was by herself in the house. One morning, feeding a load of clothes through the wringer, from washer to rinse tub, she didn't notice when a pant leg wound around the upper roller and started back through again, the other pant leg well on its way so that when the slack played out, the wringer stalled. Dorene yanked the release catch and disentangled the mess, but it was too late. The pants, an almost new pair of

Robert's khakis, were torn at the crotch. She gripped them at the tear and ripped the back seam open to the waistband, then threw the ruined khakis to the porch floor and stomped on them, an ugly, wet growl coming out of her.

Days later—it might have been weeks—the phone rang from its nook on the kitchen wall and wouldn't stop. Dorene snapped it from the cradle, but before she could frame words suitably rude, her mother spoke.

"Where are my eggs?"

Her eggs were in the tool room—some in cartons, some not. They weren't getting any fresher.

"I'll bring them tomorrow," Doreen said.

"You'll bring them tomorrow." Her mother had a knack for draining her voice of everything except contempt.

"*Yes.*" The word came out of Dorene as a shriek. "I'll bring them tomorrow."

"I'd planned on feeding my customers today."

The party line roared in Dorene's ear while she tried to get a grip on her tongue.

"Give me half an hour," she said. "I'll bring them now."

"Make yourself presentable. You might not care how you look—"

As Dorene slammed the phone down, her eyes lit on the cookie jar, sitting on the counter in a pool of sunlight. It had been a wedding gift from her mother, a ceramic jar in the shape of a freckled, hatted farm boy sitting at rest with his head on his knees. The top lifted off—hat, head, forearms—revealing a cache for the cookies her sons loved.

Dorene reached a hand to the jar and sent it sailing. The sleeping boy whacked against the refrigerator and crashed to the linoleum floor, head and hat intact atop broken legs and body. Oatmeal cookies lay scattered among the pieces. She was on her knees contemplating the mess when she felt a presence at the door. She looked up. Robert looked back at her. He was holding the eggs, all in cartons, that she was supposed to have taken to her mother. It was too much.

"Get out of here!" Dorene shouted.

Robert answered her with terrible calm. "That is the second time you've told me to get out of my own house. It had better be the last."

Dorene looked at her husband looking back at her. She looked until her nerve failed her. She picked up a jagged section of the jar. Beneath it was a dent in the linoleum they'd bought last year. She knew that Robert saw it too. There wasn't a scratch or nick on the place he hadn't registered.

Robert finished what there was to say between them, his voice husky now—with anger, with something like regret. "You don't start carrying your share of the load around here, there'll be something broke besides that jar."

He slept on the couch that night, a Friday. In the morning he wolfed his breakfast and left her at the table with their sons. Max looked as if he might spontaneously combust. Beside him, nearer Dorene, Michael made a study of his breakfast. Jimmy Don had his eyes on her. She didn't like what he seemed to be seeing.

"You're not so big you can't be slapped." The words—they were her mother's words—came out of Dorene before she knew she would say them.

Jimmy Don went pale, but he kept his eyes on her.

Max spoke. "He didn't do nothin'."

"Mind your tongue," said Dorene.

"Why should I?" Max let his temper off its leash. "Look at you. Don't even comb your hair. No wonder Daddy—"

Jimmy Don sat opposite his brother at table, but he could move with alarming agility when roused—one moment in his own chair, the next pulling Max up out of his.

"Take it back," Jimmy Don said, and twisted the arm he held behind Max. Max struggled but didn't say a word. Jimmy Don adjusted his grip, and Max went still. He apologized, then, his face purpled by rage and shame.

Jimmy Don let go, and Max rushed out of the house.

"You needn't have done that," Dorene said.

"Somebody," her eldest answered, "has got to take charge around here." Then he too was gone.

Dorene felt like Max—one minute so angry she wanted to break a roomful of things, the next sick with knowing that Robert had seen her worst. Alone in the house with Michael, she put him to mopping the kitchen floor. He'd wanted to help, and while he was small for the task, she trained her boys for housework whenever opportunity offered. Michael did the best he could, but his hands were simply too small, his coordination too rudimentary, to wring a mop properly.

"Give it here," Dorene said. "I'll do it myself." And that might have been the end of it. Except that, turning too quickly after Michael handed her the mop, she struck her shin on the rim of the bucket. "Goddamn it!" she shouted, flinging the mop into a corner. She threw herself to the floor and pounded her fists on the wet linoleum, warbling like a turkey in the throes of a stroke.

The look on Michael's face when she was done—a pale, blank mask, eyes glittering with shock. Dorene fled to her bedroom, slamming the door in a surge of loathing. She wanted to reach inside herself and stifle the rage that poisoned her. Dropping into the chair at her dresser, she pummeled the wood veneer that held her things and gave one last ugly cry. She was finished. She sat at her dresser and stared at the map tears made of her face. She sat quietly until the tears stopped. Her weepy period, her tantrums—she was done with them.

She got up out of her chair and went back to her chores. When Robert returned from his work outside, their sons in tow, she met them on the porch and asked the boys to give her a few minutes with their father.

"The mail," Jimmy Don said. "We'll walk to the mailbox." He ushered his brothers away.

Stepping to the sink, Robert unbuttoned the cuffs at his sleeves, rolled each one twice, and began to soap up. He had little use for apologies, even less for a promise, but right now Dorene didn't care. She had to offer her husband the words, puny as they might sound. "I'm sorry," she said. And she was. "You deserve better." Robert washed the dirtied soap suds from his hands and lathered up again.

"The way I've been acting," Dorene said, "it won't happen again."

Robert rinsed the soap from his hands a second time and spoke. "The damage is done." He shook the water from his hands.

Dorene opened the cabinet beside the sink, took out a fresh white towel, and offered it to him. "You're strong," she said. "We are. We can handle it."

Robert faced her for a minute, his dripping hands held up between them in an attitude almost of prayer.

"We'll see," he said, and, taking the towel from her, he dried his hands.

Dorene made good on her word, though sometimes her energy flagged, and she was not to recover the enthusiasm Robert and the boys had taken for granted. As the days turned into years, Max was perpetually impatient with her. Jimmy Don ran interference.

"I'm the man around here," he would say to his brothers when Robert was out of the house. A day came, too, when her eldest stepped between mother and father, deflecting Robert's ire from wife to son. Jimmy Don's fearlessness unnerved her, his insistence that she live up to a standard he had set. More than once, during an hour, a morning, that weighed too heavily, he pounded on her bedroom door and delivered a brief, blunt sermon, the gist of which was that life was hard, self-pity her least attractive feature, her presence as woman of the household needed elsewhere.

"Get your ass outta there, Momma, or do I have to open this door and escort you?"

When Dorene looked back on her difficult interval, and she often did, she could not identify a time marker between the days she had thought she could not bear and the succession that passed of its own accord.

One morning, humming at her Singer, she was aware of feeling something like contentment. It might have been April, before the heat came, or midway through October, with windows open to the first cool. It might have been six months after the day she stepped into her house and heard the stillness—or two years.

Moments came, too, when she was aware of Robert—sometimes drying dishes beside her at the sink, sometimes in their bed before sleep, when quiet words crisscrossed the space between them. More often it was morning at the kitchen table, with cups of coffee going empty between them and no words needed. Luminous moments, these were, when Dorene could see that Robert was *right there* beside her. She could touch him, he was that close. She did not reach out. She was afraid she wasn't strong enough, afraid to have that kind of hope.

Once, halfway through a permanent, she caught her mother's eyes on her in the mirror—an ache there, a question.

"I'm all right, Momma," she said. "I'm all right."

AGUA DULCE

CANDACE LAMBERT, MAY 11, 1960

CANDACE LOVED THE MUTED sheen of the old bridge beneath a full moon. It was like the gauzy lighting that fell on the faces of beautiful women while a projector whirred in the dark. Harlow, Garbo, Hayward, Monroe—they looked lit from within, breezes gentle in their hair, like the stir she felt at her nape, the night air cool on shoulders left bare by the sundress she'd hidden just for this. When Buddy's headlights appeared, she stepped to the edge of the bridge, the planks solid beneath her and the creek below dry as drifting sand, a waterless dark roiling from under the trees that lined the banks.

The lights on Buddy's car followed the property line of a neighboring farm, turning and then climbing up a rise toward the cattle guard— its moonlit grid—then another turn and down the road toward Candace and the creek, the lights ever closer and brighter. He drove quietly, a '58 Bel Air his parents had given him two years back on the evening of his graduation from high school. Candace had just arrived for the ceremony, in tow behind her parents, when Buddy got out of his shining new Chevy, combed and suited and dapper. She'd decided on the spot

33

that when her last night came and she needed to get this step behind her, Buddy Grant would be the one.

Other girls lost it with Riley Clark or someone like him, all swagger, bruising what he touched. Other girls might bleed the first time—but not Candace. She'd have Buddy. He would kiss her through the pain and after. Except for his name, it might've been perfect. Thank God for the luck of her own. She loved the sound of Candace, the look of the letters together, as she imagined them, with her photograph on magazine covers. Her mother's name was Winnie. Rhymed with ninny. How could she be anything but old—doilies everywhere—with a name like that? If only Buddy were a nickname or he had a middle name worth the bother. But no. Buddy Grant was the whole of it.

Candace felt no hurry tonight as he drove toward her, a deep-throated purr emanating from the Bel Air's big engine, the quiet where she stood amplified by the muffled crunch of tires on crushed rock. The Chevy eased to a stop—headlights going dark, engine stilled—and Buddy stepped out, moonlight casting his silhouette across the hood of the car, its polished surface glowing white against the bar ditch, the fence line, the pastureland beyond.

She hadn't expected the shaking—tremors running along the inside of her ribcage, pinging like the after current of an electric fence. And cold—a cold let loose in her, so cold her teeth rattled. There was something in her that wanted out.

Buddy ambled from the car to the bridge and stopped. He stood as if the road were his territory, the bridge hers, as if she must cross the line between. As best she could, she held the shaking and stepped off the bridge.

"Hey, babe," he said when she reached him, and that growl went all over her. They grabbed each other, his body hard against her, the close-shaved whiskers along his jawline rubbing rough against her cheek. She pulled his face down along her neck, onto her chest above the bodice of her sundress, and then it was too much. She tried to pull away.

Buddy took his hands from her and fumbled at his belt, his zipper. "No," she said, backing away, the Chevy bumper a cool band against the backs of her legs. She felt hands at her waist, lifting, and she was on the hood of the car. His hands were everywhere.

"No!" she said and pushed him away.

"But you wanted me—You wanted us—" His voice was husky, raw.

"Is this what you did with the others? Here?"

Buddy tucked his shirttails; he zipped and buttoned and buckled himself at the waist.

"I know you've had girls," Candace said.

"I'm twenty years old." His words gave an edge to the silence that followed.

Candace waited.

When Buddy spoke again, his voice was tinged with regret. "I shouldn't have told you."

I made you. She couldn't say that, though it was true. She hadn't wanted names, didn't care about gossip. What she'd wanted was to know that Buddy would know how to do what she wanted done. She would get tonight behind her, then get out. She'd chosen Buddy but not this. Not on the hood of his car.

"I thought you were different," she said.

"How?"

"Better."

"Than who?"

"All of them," she said. "Riley Clark."

At the sound of Riley's name, Buddy grinned, his teeth glistening like one of the mouth-breathing grease monkeys who leered at her when she walked by the Magnolia station, the Pegasus overhead flying places she would go without them. The moon would light her way.

"Look," she said, pointing. "Can you see her?"

"See who?"

"The woman in the moon."

"Looks like ink splotches to me."

"There's a woman," she told him. "Her hair is up—all feathery. She's sitting at her dresser. Holding a powder puff."

Buddy's grin flashed again. "You're kidding me, right?"

"Better behave yourself. She watches out for me."

Let him stand there looking amused. She had six years' worth of egg money stashed with a wad of earnings from babysitting. She had a schedule of buses between here and the West Coast. She had by heart the location of the YMCA in downtown Los Angeles. Come this time tomorrow, she'd be crossing West Texas, leaving Nopalito far behind. She knew where she was going.

The night darkened, the pale, powdery surface of the road dissolving into thickening gloom. When the moon came back, she moved to Buddy, leaned up on tiptoe and kissed his ear.

"Come," she whispered. "Let's walk down the creek."

Buddy pulled off his loafers, walked to the car, and tossed them through an open window. He reached behind the front seat and grabbed a picnic blanket. Candace walked to the bridge and stepped out of her fancy summer flats. She set them on the protruding end of a plank—a pair of jeweled slippers that might be ruined by the drifting silt below, moonlight glimmering in the cut glass pieces and on the silver prongs that held them. Together, then, they descended into the Agua Dulce, the creek bed loose and cool and fine, like grained silk, with patches of paleness where the branching canopy thinned.

"I know a place," she said, and led him to a wide, shallow bend where the moon poured in, the silt drifting like sand on the beaches in her magazines. Avila, Hermosa, Isla Vista. Capistrano, Corona del Mar. She would live by the ocean on a beach called Crown of the Sea.

When she had pictured what they would do, Candace hadn't thought about dirt. But there it was, sifting through the picnic blanket's thin fabric. She kissed him anyway. She let him put his hands on her, but then, just when it was feeling right—when she knew what was coming—Buddy pulled away and sat up. He dug around in a pocket on his jeans and produced a little square foil packet. She knew what he had. It was clear enough by the moon.

Three years ago—she'd just turned thirteen—Candace had encountered a used one in her locker, oozing onto a book cover. She didn't know what it was, hadn't seen one before, but the odor impressed her. Hearing a snicker, she turned to find Riley Clark studying her, his band of tagalongs in a slouch behind him. With a cupped hand, Riley shifted the equipment at his crotch. He wasn't smart enough to have groped himself as a hint about the smell spilling out of her locker. But she'd heard enough talk—school bus whisperings, drugstore gossip—to suspect that something squirted out of boys when they used their peckers for pleasure. Right there, facing Riley, she knew.

"What you got there?" he asked.

Candace turned to her locker and took the item in question between thumb and forefinger. Turning back, she let it dangle. "Looks like a sausage casing. You can have it." She draped the wilted mess across the shoulder of Riley's letter jacket. Afterward, she washed her hands and told herself that whatever it was she'd touched, she wouldn't have one near her again.

"Put that nasty thing away," she told Buddy.

"But, but," was all he could say.

She had her way, though. Always did. "Just pull out before you're done," she said. "I don't want a baby in me."

She whispered she was ready, but Buddy said no, not really. He used his hands and a few awkward directives to indicate that before he could proceed she would have to spread her legs. There was a tickle in his voice, as if he might sit up again, giggling this time, and forget all about why she'd asked him here.

She'd thought of what they would do as making love. In those words. Buddy would make love to her, and then later, when she was gone away from here, she would know how it was done. The act itself she had pictured in soft lighting—graceful, veiled in shadow. In the instant when she comprehended Buddy's request, though, she knew sex would be anything but.

There was pain when she complied—when their bodies came together as she had thought she wanted—though she hadn't thought the hurt would take her breath away. Buddy kept whispering things. What he was doing. What it felt like. What he wanted to do next. She didn't mind him doing any of it. If he would just shut up and do it, just shut up and put his lips on her, his tongue. There. There. Yes. Then it was over, and he was still inside her. He shouldn't be, but he was.

He was apologizing, words tumbling around her in that little-boy tone he took when he knew she was mad and he didn't want her to be. The anger she felt was distant, though, as if it weren't even part of her. She felt heavy in her bones, a thickening in her as if her blood had slowed, a kind of sadness that had visited her before, when she turned away from a moment that hadn't gone as planned. Or on days when she lost sight of who she was going to be, how she was going to get there. Moments like now, when sleep entered her.

Buddy woke her. She cracked one eye to a sliver of early light, then squeezed it shut and turned away. She didn't want to see what he looked like rumpled with sleep, with dirt in his hair. She didn't want to see him seeing her.

"I been trying to wake you." He sounded flustered. "Tried to keep you from sleeping. Wanted to get you home."

The early-morning cool was lovely. If she could get him to leave her alone, she'd sleep some more.

"What about your momma and daddy?" Buddy asked.

"They get up at five. They'll know I'm gone."

"There'll be hell to pay."

"Always is."

From somewhere in the trees a mockingbird erupted, its call harsh and scolding.

"You got to think now," Buddy said. "How're you gonna patch it up with them?"

"What do you care?"

"You're my girl now."

Surely not. She couldn't let that happen. Couldn't let herself be trapped. With grinning, well-meaning, fumbling Buddy. With her hopeless, faded parents.

The mockingbird started up again, a series of wild variations swirling in the treetops.

Buddy stood. "You don't show up in time for the bus, all kinds of talk will get started."

"I'll stay home. I'll say I was sick."

"What about your folks? What are they gonna think, seeing you like this?"

"I'll handle them," Candace said.

"We ought to get going." Buddy bent and kissed her cheek.

"Go then," she said. "I'll be along."

"You're gonna mess this up." Buddy sounded peeved. "Guess I'll see what I can do."

Candace curled to sleep again. Just a few minutes, that's all she needed.

In the moment of dozing, between waking and dreaming, something stirred in her, a tiny something, so small she almost didn't notice—like a comma shifting in the middle of a closed book. The briefest flutter, almost imperceptible. Then nothing.

Sparrow chatter roused her, a patch of sun on her face through the trees. She remembered that Buddy was gone and sat up, heavy with sleep. There was silt inside her bra, beneath the waistband of her dress, everywhere. She ached inside, but almost pleasantly, a muted tenderness.

Except for the birds, it was quiet at this bend. Schoolchildren had come here once for picnics—forty, fifty years ago. Her father, her mother, too—if they could be believed, if ever they had been children— had spent days here with their classmates. Poppa tossed horseshoes on the outer bank with the boys. On the inner bank, a flat treeless space rounded by the Agua Dulce's lazy curve, Momma skipped rope with her girlfriends. At lunch they spread tablecloths on the creek bed, opened tins of sardines, pulled wild onions where they grew each spring along the banks. They had molasses cookies for dessert. Naps, even, or so her parents said, before trekking back to their one-room schoolhouse and the mules that carried them home. To furrows they'd never get out of. Old as grandparents they'd been when she arrived—their only child.

Rising, Candace shook out the picnic blanket and began to fold it. But she would not see Buddy again, and there was no need to try explaining the blanket to her parents. She tossed the flimsy thing aside and walked toward the bridge, sparrows quieting as if to mark her way with silence. The creek curved and curved again, the banks on either side a tangle of underbrush, with oaks and hackberries and pecans blotting out the sky.

Minutes later, as she rounded the last curve hiding the bridge from her path along the creek bottom, Candace heard a rumble from beyond the rise and knew the school bus was coming for her. Mr. Jamieson would pull over when he got to the mailbox. Old fool would crank the door open and sit there gaping—as if she might materialize out of sunlight and road dust. He'd wonder aloud at her absence and then drive on while her parents fretted behind Momma's ancient, ugly curtains, that dumb-struck look on their faces, not knowing where she was.

She'd locked her door from the inside and climbed out the window. She wondered if they had tired yet of knocking, of calling her name. What would they say when they saw her—shoulders bared to the world, the flesh of her breasts visible along the line of her bodice?

The bridge appeared in a band of sunlight beyond the trees, then came a flash of yellow-orange as the bus clattered across. Candace heard shouts from within, and by the time she came out from under the oaks and up the bank to the road, Mr. Jamieson had stopped the bus. A gaggle of seventh- and eighth-grade boys hung out the windows, a thin film of dust behind them, drifting over the ragged edges of the bridge and into the shadows that pooled below. When the air cleared, the bridge was empty except for her jeweled flats, their facets catching sunlight and scattering it back.

She heard gears grind, and the bus started backing toward her, a chorus of shouts erupting from the boys in the windows.

"Hey, Candy, where yuh goin'?

"Bet it's a beach party."

A lone girl stuck her head out a window. "Look at the dress, stupid. Candace Lambert's goin' someplace ritzy."

"Hope there's martinis," shouted one of the boys.

"Thinks she's better than us," the girl announced, her voice sharp as broken glass. "Thinks she's Kim Novak."

"Hey, Candy Kim," one of the younger boys called out, "will you dance with me?"

A boy her own age, from a window in the last row, let loose a nasty chuckle. "Looks like she'll do more than dance."

Candace put a hand to her hair and made smoothing motions. She wished for her compact mirror, her brush and comb. They were on her dresser at home—inside a patent-leather clutch that looked lovely with her sundress. She'd decided against it, though. She hadn't been able to picture herself holding a purse when Buddy got out of his car at the bridge, hadn't been able to think how she might gracefully dispose of it when their moment arrived.

A fist rapping on window glass drew her attention. Beside the boy who'd insulted her, face framed in a back-facing window, Riley Clark winked at her, and then, wetting thick lips with the tip of his tongue, he kissed the air at her.

The bus stopped backing, and the door cranked open. "All aboard!" shouted the boys.

Candace waved them on.

Mr. Jamieson appeared on the road beside the door.

"Young lady," he said, "do you need an engraved invitation?"

Candace stepped back until she felt the planks of the bridge beneath her feet. She stooped, reaching to where her shoes sparkled, set them in front of her, and stepped into them. She folded her arms and waited for it to be over.

Mr. Jamieson was no match for her. He shook his head and got back on the bus. The door closed, and the calling boys retracted their heads. The engine revved and the bus moved off, its plume of dust drifting, expanding, until Candace was enclosed in a cloud of powdery light.

The house she lived in needed paint. The walls were the same color as the hard-packed dirt of the yard, flowerbeds dead and empty in the aftermath of the recent drought, the cenizo hedge out front indistinguishable from the color of dust. Seen from afar as Candace came over the rise, walking homeward after her encounter with the bus, the house with the yard and hedge that framed it looked like a backdrop for a movie, something about poor folk and hard times. Just one thing was out of place this morning—Buddy's Chevy at the side of the house, Buddy's beautiful Bel Air, white as a wedding dress filmed under brightest light, a band of red shiny as lipstick flashing from fender to fender. Candace kept walking. There was nowhere else to go.

Turning in at the gate, she could see her parents on the front porch in the swing they sat in Sunday mornings between breakfast and church. Before them—speaking, gesticulating—stood Buddy Grant, his voice a sound she intuited before she was close enough to hear it, his tone something she could interpret from the rise and fall of the words. This was Buddy in sincere mode, calling forth a calm over disturbed waters.

As she neared the house, her mother turned and, seeing Candace, pointed. Buddy looked in her direction—the conciliatory gesture of his hands frozen for a moment—then turned back to her parents and went on with what he was saying as if he'd known them all his life. As for her parents, their faces gave evidence they were listening, that whatever petition Buddy Grant was casting before them, his words were falling on receptive ground.

As she approached the cenizo hedge, Buddy ran out of words. The sudden quiet unnerved Candace. She stopped. Buddy turned from her parents and, crossing, came midway down the porch steps. He paused there, his hand on the wrought-iron railing. Sunlight fell harshly in the space between them, the shadow of a scissortail crossing the yard at an oblique angle.

Buddy stood there as if appointed to save her. Behind him, attentive, sat her parents, silent in their unmoving swing. Inside the house, behind her locked bedroom door—hidden—lay a packed suitcase, a

Trailways bus schedule, a roll of bills to feed her where she fled. Between here and there, an alliance she would have to breach—Buddy, his face happy, confident as he waited; her father, his brow stern but approving as he looked at Buddy; and her mother, eyes shining with hope as she faced Candace. A tableau, the three of them, welcoming her into the fold.

As the sole of a single jeweled flat made contact with the bottom step of the porch and Candace pressed down to rise up, whatever force inside that had fueled her movement forward, her resolve to get away— the strength she'd thought was hers—was gone. Wilting, she climbed the steps and crossed the porch without a word to the three who plotted to keep her. She opened the front door and stopped. Her bed beckoned, but her room was locked; she hadn't thought to bring the key.

Her mother's couch blocked her way. The springs groaned beneath her when she sat. The coarse brocade upholstery smelled old. Like wool put away with mothballs. Like stale pipe smoke, unused chewing tobacco. Like air in a funeral parlor when someone has died.

THE YELLOW DRESS

THE WAHRMUNDS, MARCH 8, 1958–APRIL 29, 1961

I

Dorene purchased the fabric on a rare shopping trip to Corpus Christi. Six weeks ago she'd circled the date on her calendar: Saturday, March 8, 1958. Other purchases taken care of, she was browsing among bolts of cotton, fingering first one print and then another, when Michael tapped her at the elbow and said, "This one." He'd asked to come along as a birthday treat. The youngest of her sons, he'd been nine for all of four days. Dorene had almost forgotten he was with her. Ordinarily, when Michael had his mother to himself, he chattered nonstop. He hadn't said a word, though, since they'd entered the store. Colors, textures, varieties of print—cotton, linen, satin, velveteen—they seemed to put him in a trance. The bolt of fabric he wanted for her was a lovely mercerized cotton, a solid among aisles of prints, a shimmering lemony yellow.

Dorene hadn't worn anything so bright in years. She said as much.

Michael pulled the bolt of fabric and led her to a mirror.

"Look," he said, draping the loose end of the swath on her shoulder and unfurling the bolt down across her torso.

Dorene had a naturally dark complexion. On occasion, where she wasn't known, she'd been addressed in Spanish—once on her honeymoon. She'd said, "No habla español," and then laughed Robert out of the ire the mistake had sparked in him. This color, though, so thick it made her think of egg yolk, this yellow glowed against her skin.

When Michael said buy it, she didn't say no. Minutes later, browsing pattern books, he tapped her again and pointed.

The dress in the color sketch was what Dorene would call a dancing dress—a full swirling skirt set off by bands of rickrack, a scoop-neck top much like a tailored peasant blouse, with elastic at neckline and sleeves. More rickrack too, circling the scoopneck, the sleeves.

Why not? she thought. It's time.

Over supper that evening, after Robert came in from the fields, she held back and let Michael tell about the material, the pattern he'd picked out for her. Jimmy Don, her eldest, smirked. Max, ever the instigator, made a fist and socked Michael on the arm.

"You are such a pantywaist," he said.

"Not another word," Robert answered him. "Not at this table." But the look on his face carried the same judgment.

"Apologize," Dorene said to Max.

"That's okay." Michael waved off the insult. "I don't care what he says." Excusing himself, he fetched the shopping bag from Dorene's dresser chair and, with a magician's gesture, pulled the fabric from it.

"Something bright for a change," Jimmy Don said, clapping in her direction.

"Look at what she's gonna make with it!" Michael handed the pattern to Jimmy Don.

Her eldest gave an appreciative whistle and spoke to Robert. "You'll have to step out with Momma."

"Give me that." Robert lay hold of the pattern. His face soured. "Look like a floozy wearing this thing."

In a single motion, smooth as quicksilver, Jimmy Don stood up.

"You can't talk to Momma like that," he said. "Nobody can."

"This is my house," said Robert, standing as he spoke, menace edging his voice. "I'll say whatever I goddamn please."

Dorene stood and said her husband's name. "Robert."

"Woman."

She didn't waver under his threat. She hadn't wanted this, but it was here and she wasn't afraid.

"Jimmy Don," she said.

Her son turned to her. With her eyes, she indicated his chair. Then she sat down.

Jimmy Don sat down.

Robert stood for a moment longer. "Next time you go shopping," he said, "leave your boy there home with the men." Then he too sat down.

Dorene admired in Jimmy Don the calm that came over him when he sensed someone near to him was threatened. He betrayed no fear, didn't even seem angry. Only intractable. He would not back down. Robert called it disrespect—often and loudly—but his bluster was like air escaping under pressure. Harmless. Anyone could see that he admired his firstborn. Jimmy Don was the son who wouldn't be intimidated.

The confrontation at an end, Dorene put the fabric and the pattern back in the shopping bag. Michael didn't object when she put them out of sight beneath the window seat. He took it to heart, though—she could see that. It wasn't the dress that had triggered the scene at the supper table. Michael surely knew, as Robert privately confessed, that what bothered his father was the role their youngest had played.

"Max got it right," Robert told her. "The boy's going girly. You encourage it."

Michael had weathered his father's looks—he'd taken flak from his brothers—with hardly a ripple. But the scene over the yellow dress put a bit in his teeth. He avoided games and outings with his brothers, kept a rein on his enthusiasms at the supper table. On the rare occasion when he broke free of caution, he was likely to stiffen mid-gesture, as if hearing his father's voice.

Three years passed, and then one afternoon, with an April breeze drifting into the house, Dorene raised the window seat and saw a corner of yellow fabric down among her sewing things.

She was at the table looking over the pattern, the material laid out before her, when Jimmy Don passed through. As before, he whistled.

"Do it," he said. "Daddy'll get over it."

Jimmy Don was sixteen going on thirty. He'd been fully grown at thirteen, with a man's voice that men listened to. He'd discovered himself in the mirror, regularly looked there while he smoothed the wavy black hair he'd inherited from her. The eyes, the cheekbones—he was too good looking for his own good, trailing the scent of a heavy, oily cologne wherever he went. Around his brothers, his friends, he was still the cocky prankster. But he could shed his boyish self with ease.

His *do it* was curt, hard-edged, but it was enough. Dorene arranged the sections of her pattern, pinned them into place, and got to work with her scissors. Over supper, when Robert asked about her day, she told him she'd started the dress.

Max gave her a look. Michael smiled but held his tongue.

"Get ready for a night on the town," Jimmy Don said. "Where you taking her, Daddy?"

He didn't let up until they'd settled on the last Saturday in April—a dance at the Cotton Patch. "Like old times," Jimmy Don said, his voice all mockery now, a reference to the stories she'd told her sons when they were small. They knew their father had once been more outgoing, that—especially before Robert shipped out to the South Pacific—their parents had spent many a Saturday night dancing in the open air.

Gulf breezes made the Cotton Patch the most popular dance spot in the county—a slab of cement a mile or so outside Nopalito, unroofed, with a tall picket fence in place of walls. Picnic tables and benches framed the dance floor, with tin-roofed sheds for bandstand and bar. It was a pathetic sight by daylight, with huisache and prickly pear bristling up out of hardpan, no cotton fields in sight. But when sundown came and cars drove up and people walked in and sat down and started talking and the music started up, there was nothing like it. Dorene had been happier there, without even thinking about it, than any other place her life had offered.

Afternoons, then, when she could find the time, she worked on her dress, a puzzle forming as she hummed at her Singer, a change in Jimmy Don she couldn't explain. Without notice, the humor had disappeared from his wisecrack commentary. His words were knife-sharp, his sarcasm, his judgments of others tempered by withering heat. He was especially harsh with Michael. Cupcake, he called him. Marmalade. Mr. Bubbly.

One afternoon she walked in on them—Michael trapped between the kitchen counter and the stove, Jimmy Don waving his arms wildly, a cruel parody.

"You don't like it?" he was saying. "Learn to use 'em. Put 'em up." He hunched into a boxer's stance and made sparring motions, this time aping what his little brother might look like if he tried boxing. But Michael had a surprise in store. He made a fist and socked Jimmy Don in the gut.

During the bent-over gasping for breath that followed, Dorene stepped in.

"That's enough," she said, and when Jimmy Don threatened to throttle his little brother, she stood between them. Her power with him held. He wouldn't touch her. He wouldn't insult her by getting around her or shoving her out of the way.

"I'm used to him" is what Michael said when Jimmy Don was gone. "He's got a mean edge lately."

"Wonder what's wrong."

"You know Jimmy Don. He wouldn't tell you if you asked."

II
—

Jimmy Don's trouble was Patsy Geistweidt—something she'd told him ten days back. A blunt, bare sentence that had changed everything. Patsy had a dazzling temper. The fire in her, that's what he'd noticed first—it's what drew him in. And he'd discovered that having sex with her after one of her flare-ups—or even during—could be spectacular.

Patsy was twenty-one. What there was between them had started up last fall on the evening of her birthday, when he approached her, celebrating with friends at a dance.

"Have you even started shaving?" she said, brushing his cheek with the back of her hand.

"I've got hair where it counts."

"Well," she said, "I guess you can dance with me then."

Before the night was done, they had fucked in a cornfield. For the rest of the fall, they carried on secretly. He didn't mind staying out of sight with her. He'd been with women before Patsy, but he hadn't gone out with any of them, hadn't given them a second thought outside of arranging to bed them. Patsy changed all that. What they did when they got off alone—he liked it too much. He liked her too much. After sneaking around with her for a couple of months, he suggested public outings, but even after he turned sixteen—that was back in January— she'd been embarrassed about his age. Patsy claimed she hadn't even told her cousin Carter, and they were all but joined at the hip.

Then one night in March she got in Jimmy Don's car and said, "Let's do something respectable." They spent the evening with Carter and Arlene, newly married. Carter would have liked Jimmy Don if he had vampire teeth and a cape. The Geistweidt cousins had been dancing partners—incurable show-offs—since Carter was six and Patsy five. They finished each other's sentences, passed a drumstick back and forth from an order of fried chicken. Whatever one did, the other approved. If you wanted Patsy in your life, you got Carter. They were a package deal. Patsy's first big blowup at Jimmy Don had come when he'd made a wisecrack about all the time she spent dancing with someone she couldn't enjoy after.

For a month, then, in the eyes of the town, Patsy and Jimmy Don were a couple. On Friday, April 14, they had supper at Carter and Arlene's. Whiskey sours afterward. A game of spades. Patsy had little to say during the evening; she wanted to go straight home when they were done at cards—said she was tired, didn't want to rumple her skirt. She lapsed into silence on the drive. Jimmy Don switched on the radio and whistled along. At her house he killed the engine and cut the lights. A quiet minute with Patsy was the most he could expect. Her parents would be waiting inside; she didn't want them to fret.

When he turned to Patsy, she turned away, her nose to the passenger window.

"I'm pregnant," she said.

For moments at a stretch, looking at the back of her head, he wondered how far the stillness reached, what had happened even to the sound of breathing.

"Well?" she said, as if to the window.

"You can't be."

"I think I'd know."

"It can't be mine."

Now she turned to face him. "You might want to think before you say another word."

"We use condoms," he said. "Every time." She'd cured him of calling them rubbers.

"One of them leaked."

"How would that happen?"

"You get pretty excited. Must've torn one."

"Look," he said. "It can't be mine."

Patsy slapped him hard, the flat of her hand connecting to bone, to the hinge in his jaw. The pain was like electricity, shooting into his nose and eyes.

He had never hit a woman. He didn't intend to now. He grabbed her hands and held them.

Patsy sucked air into her lungs and shouted. "I have a baby in me! It's yours, goddammit! You did this to me!"

A light came on at her parents' bedroom window. A minute later, the porch light too.

Patsy got out of the car and leaned into the open door. "Congratulations," she said. "You're a father." She slammed the door and was gone.

Jimmy Don was good at juggling the difficult things. He'd been playing referee at home since before he was ten, stepping between his parents when his father threatened to get out of hand. For several years already he'd been earning money by taking on work where he could find it, all the while juggling school and the help expected of him in the fields. A week after turning sixteen he'd bought himself a car—announced the purchase by dropping the keys in the middle of the supper table, told his father he'd made the down payment with his own money, that the monthly installments would come out of his earnings. He was used to things going his way.

He'd been just thirteen when he had his first woman—a rancher's wife where he was helping with the cattle. She was pretty enough, looked to be thirty, thirty-five. Invited him in one afternoon when the rancher had gone off somewhere and Jimmy Don was waiting for his father to pick him up. He'd been told he could pass for sixteen; he said seventeen when the rancher's wife asked. He learned a lot from her, learned the signs to look for in other women, kept his mouth shut about them, made up stories about made-up girls to cover with his friends.

And then Patsy.

After the night she slapped him, he didn't see her for a week. She wouldn't come to the phone. After school one afternoon he tried the drugstore on Main Street where she worked. Patsy disappeared into the back room and waited him out. By sunset on Friday he was edgy with worry and anger. "Fuck it," he said and drove to her house. Her parents were nice people—and no match for Patsy, who would've made it clear he wasn't welcome. A minute of their muddle was all he could stand. "I'm sorry," he said. "I've got to see Patsy." He left them standing at the door and took the stairs up to her room. An old iron bedstead with a pink chenille spread. A dresser, the mirror edged with bric-a-brac. Patsy turned from the window. She would have seen him driving up, would have heard his voice downstairs.

In the week gone by, he hadn't thought once about what he might say. He'd only wanted to see Patsy. What he said, when the words came, was not pretty.

"I don't want this."

Patsy looked tired. She looked worried. Scared. But her words matched his for bluntness.

"You did your part to get it."

Jimmy Don's answer was what he willed to be true. "You can't have a baby in you."

"So I should get rid of it? Is that what you want?"

"I don't want this."

"*What*, then? Want to drive somewhere and have your way with me? Wouldn't have to use protection—that damage is done."

Outside, the tamped rumble of a car at the stop sign. A breath—and the engine revved, the driver taking on speed as laughter spilled into the dark. Patsy closed the window—a thump where frame met sill—and the voices were gone.

"I need some time," he said.

"What do you suppose that'll get you?"

Patsy drifted from the window to her dresser. She touched a dried corsage fading among the things on the mirror's frame. For a moment, Jimmy Don was certain he smelled carnations.

"If you do that," he said—a crazy hope, that she would get rid of it. "What you said—if you do that—what about after?"

By the look on her face, Patsy hadn't thought about after.

"What about us?" It was the wrong question. He knew that before it was out of his mouth.

"Us?" Patsy said, the word like an intake of breath, like a tonic she swallowed to strengthen the words that came next. "Go home, Jimmy Don. Find someone else to ruin."

Another week went by. He tried to reach Patsy at work. She hung up. Tried to reach her at home. She wouldn't come to the phone. Parked his car outside her house for hours on end. Nothing. At two in the afternoon on Saturday, her parents called, worried sick. Patsy had gone out the night before and hadn't come back. All morning they'd been calling her friends. They'd tried to reach Carter. No luck there. Jimmy Don was clearly a last resort; Patsy must've poisoned her folks against him.

He drove straight to the Geistweidts and questioned them for clues. They were no help at all except to kindle the beginnings of dread. He drove to Carter's house. Neither of the cousins was there. Arlene was evasive, said she didn't know where her husband was or when he'd be back. She wasn't happy that Jimmy Don said he'd wait. When the phone rang, she jumped like a rabbit, closing the door on her way to answer it. He couldn't distinguish words, but Jimmy Don knew worry when he heard it. And he was persuasive. Within the hour, he had a street address in San Antonio, a room number.

A hundred miles later, he pulled up to a shabby motor court on the city's south side.

Carter answered his knock, a dim room behind him. A dresser top, its finish a pattern of pale circles where beer bottles and drink glasses had stood perspiring. A dingy window to the courtyard. A narrow bed, a rumpled, washed-out coverlet. Patsy's head on the pillow.

Jimmy Don crossed the room and went down on one knee at her side. She was so pale. He knew the answer to his question before he asked it.

"What have you done?"

Carter's voice behind him. "This was your call."

Jimmy Don crouched low at Patsy's side and waited for her to look at him. "Tell me you didn't," he said.

"You wanted it." Her voice was as weak as she looked, and there was a note in it he didn't want to hear. Loathing or its near kin.

Carter's voice behind him. "You aren't wanted here."

Jimmy Don turned, springing, and pinned Carter against the wall. Carter didn't try to get loose. He looked at Jimmy Don.

"We got rid of you," he said, and it was like when Patsy had slapped him—the stinging in his nose and eyes, the nearness of tears.

Jimmy Don let go. He turned to Patsy. "I'll stay," he said. "Carter can go."

"No," said Patsy.

He babbled a bit then, a series of promises delivered kneeling at her pillow. He'd be with her when she felt better. He'd make it up to her. They'd be together again.

To each one, Patsy mouthed a silent no.

"I love you," he said, nothing to lose now, knowing it was useless.

"Now you're gonna say it." Carter's voice again, sad now, no longer angry.

And Patsy. "It's too late for that."

"Go home," Carter said. "This is what you wanted."

III

Jimmy Don sat in his car at the motor court until the neon arrow beside the highway started blinking. By the time he turned his key in the ignition, Robert and Dorene had stepped onto the floor at the Cotton Patch for their first dance in ages.

She was wearing the yellow dress, and whatever Robert might have felt three years ago, when Michael presented the fabric and pattern at the supper table, it seemed forgotten now. In the car, as they pulled into the parking area, she'd adjusted the neckline so that it clung just off the shoulder.

"You're gonna raise some eyebrows" was all he said.

Inside, Michael trailed them to a table. "Save a number for me," he told her and drifted to the edges of the dance floor, hanging out there with others his age. Max was gone for the weekend, working cattle in place of Jimmy Don, who'd made the last-minute arrangement and then gone running off God knows where. He'd been impossible lately.

Robert brought two beers from the concession stand, so cold, what with the ice they'd been plucked from, the first swallows almost hurt going down. They danced a waltz, afterward dawdling as they made their way back, open-air voices from the tables and benches rising and falling and all jumbled together so that you couldn't hear any one person, all of them talking at the same time and nobody really listening to anybody else, just being part of something more than the words they tossed into the fray.

Several times Michael came and danced with Dorene. He'd inherited her love of dancing. He was smooth, effortless in his movements. At twelve he was still short—a thin boy, light on his feet. He smiled and smiled dancing with her. She knew he gave himself credit for the dress, for the good times she would have wearing it.

The last dance of the evening was a waltz. Robert took her hand; he spun them in circles and circles as they rounded the floor. It might have been the beer—she'd had several—or the dizzying motions of the waltz. Or happiness—perhaps she'd forgotten how that felt. But circling, circling with Robert—*one* two three, *one* two three—Dorene felt as if she were dancing out of herself, and Robert with her, dancing out of whatever it was that had snared them, waltzing to the last song, no one wanting it to end, the band letting it play on and on. A blur of colors, faces, voices outside the circles they spun, her yellow dress swirling and swirling.

Midnight found Jimmy Don sitting in his car on a narrow rutted dirt lane that ran between fields to Agua Dulce Creek, a swath of curves, dry most of the year, that wound between his father's farm and Nopalito. In the months before, he had come here with Patsy. They'd spread an old blanket beneath the oaks along the watershed. After the drive from San Antonio, instead of going home, he'd driven county roads until he found his way here. The windows were down, the night air cool, the memory of being here with Patsy so strong he could put fingertips to his tongue and taste her there.

He arrived at the gate to the farm just as the lights in the house blinked out, his parents and Michael home from the dance and gone to bed. Not wanting to wake them or face his mother's worry, the questions his mother might ask, he switched off the headlights and pulled to the side of the lane just inside the gate. He leaned back in the seat. He wasn't surprised that he didn't doze.

Their dancing clothes discarded, their good nights said, his parents surrendered the house to a quiet so deep Michael knew they'd fallen asleep. He had the bedroom to himself—Jimmy Don gone from the bed they shared, Max's narrow single bed empty against the far windows. Michael lay wide awake atop the sheets. He felt that he was waiting—for what, he didn't know. While he lay there, he thought about the dance and his mother in the yellow dress. It was right there, he could see it through the open door to the bathroom where she'd made herself ready for bed. She'd put the dress on a hanger, left it hanging from a knob to the storage space above the bathroom closet. It was a pale shimmer in the moonlight spilling into the house.

They were asleep; the house was his. He tiptoed through the stillness to the dress. Even by the faint glow filtering into the dark, it was lovely, the fabric light as touch against the back of his hand as he lifted the skirt at the hem. Stretching up on tiptoe, he unhooked the hanger from its knob and held the dress against himself, feeling the weave against bare thighs, bare knees, bare shins.

He carried it into the bedroom, closing the door to the bathroom quietly behind, and stood before his grandmother's old dresser, the big mirror rising from it, his jockey shorts white against pale skin, the dress like amber in the mirror's muted light. Taking the dress from the hanger, he raised it over his head, slipped his wrists into the armholes, and let the cool cotton drop down over him. He straightened the skirt and tugged the neckline into place just off the shoulder. He was Michael and not Michael looking back at himself in the yellow dress. Reaching, he pulled the switch chain on the lamp that sat on the dresser, yellow light spilling through the shade against yellow fabric, against rickrack blue and red and purple, against the pale, pale skin of Michael and not Michael.

Jimmy Don walked the lane beneath an almost-full moon, the house quiet and dark before him. He was crossing the yard toward the back door, hackberry leaves shushing above him, when a light came on in the windows to his bedroom. He ducked behind the hackberry trunk and peered around.

Michael stood there looking in the mirror—steady, as if becalmed by what looked back—himself in the dress their mother had sewed for the dance tonight.

A day ago, seeing what he saw, Jimmy Don would have walked into the house and trounced his little brother. He didn't have it in him now. He whispered to himself, his brother's name, whispered, "Michael, Michael," not sure in the moment if he heard disapproval or wonder in his own voice.

He would have turned and walked back to his car, would have slept there. But a sound from elsewhere in the house drew his attention—a dark form at his parents' bedroom window, his mother pausing there and then fading toward her bedroom door, a habit she'd not put behind her, checking on her sleeping sons. More than once, coming in late, Jimmy Don had found her sitting bedside at his place, waiting, wanting to know that he was safely home. And now no way to warn Michael.

In the time it would have taken her to walk through the house, the door from the bathroom opened into the bedroom where Michael stood, their mother a dark shape where the door had been.

Michael turned and froze as surely as if some evil creature had cast a spell on him. Their mother stepped across the room, and when she touched him, a calming hand—Jimmy Don knew this about her—when she touched Michael, he struck out at her, writhing, a brief silent struggle that stopped when Michael cried out, a short, sharp, wordless shout. For a moment, nothing. Then their father's voice calling from the dark of the bedroom their mother had left. She raised her head, like a deer testing the air. Then she turned and was gone. Moments later, her voice from the dark where their father had called, her tone reassuring. Finally, her shape at the window, and behind her, quiet.

Through the other window, in the light of the lamp on their grandmother's dresser, Michael tore at their mother's yellow dress, yanking it over his head and flinging the dress away from him. He crossed to the bathroom and closed the door there, walked back to the dresser and pulled the chain on the lamp. As dark flowed out and moonlight flowed in, Jimmy Don's eyes adjusted. Michael stood facing the mirror.

He reached for the band of white that clothed him and, pushing down from the waist, stepped out of his jockey shorts and dropped them. He stood again facing the mirror, all of him pale, no patch of dark yet where his penis drooped.

The youngest son, the eldest, their mother—awake too late. Michael, fixed in place, as if he will not move, will not lie down to sleep. At the bedroom window opposite, Dorene, standing watch over the night. Beneath the hackberry tree, a witness, his face streaming tears. Behind him, from a tree out by the wash line, an owl calls. Michael turns toward the sound. Jimmy Don swivels behind the tree, his back to the trunk, his shadow absorbed by the dark there.

A HUSBAND TO BURY

CANDACE LAMBERT GRANT, DECEMBER 8, 1960–APRIL 6, 1961

CANDACE WAS GOOD AT picturing a life to die for, though her luck had run in the opposite direction—a husband she hadn't wanted, a child growing in her through a string of empty days, and the occasional storm when she fancied something, a milkshake for instance, and Buddy tried to reason with her. It was too late, he'd said, and too far, a dozen-mile drive to the Burger Dell. Then, as luck would have it, the winking neon arrow went dark as he pulled off the highway and set the brake, a lone carful of teenagers burning rubber in the rush to be elsewhere.

"Get me a milkshake," she said, though clearly the place was closing. "Go. Use your famous charm. Smile. Do whatever it takes."

Buddy got out and closed the door behind him. The silence was delicious—crisp December night outside the car, perfect stillness inside, and the baby not kicking. For moments at a stretch, she was the person she'd dreamed, sitting starlit beneath palms on a costal boulevard with an exotic name—Ventura, Santa Monica—alone and far away. A car approached the intersection behind her, the highway angling in from the southwest, headlights cutting across the parking lot to the window where Buddy stood wheedling. He turned for a moment, captured in a brightness like klieg lights, the beams sweeping past him, arcing across the blacktop as the car traced the angle at the intersection and headed north toward Nopalito.

And then, the oddest thing: following the path the headlights had marked across the parking lot, a cattle truck was moving slowly across her field of vision, moving toward Buddy at the Burger Dell window. It seemed to come from someone's dream, like the ghost truck of a double exposure, lights out, engine still, moving toward Buddy, his back to the danger, laughter ringing out of him. The driver was dead of a heart attack, though no one knew that yet, the truck that propelled him quiet as the night, its movement so smooth she could hear the shuffling hooves, oddly muffled by the raised car windows, as Buddy turned from the Burger Dell window and flashed a smile of success. She heard herself cry out. And sat listening to the quiet that came after the crash, the knocking hooves, the plaintive cries of cows, until the fire truck came, the ambulance. She stayed in the car while they disentangled the bodies and put them out of sight on covered stretchers—her husband, the girl at the window who'd been flirting with him, a short-order cook who'd died behind her. "I'm cold," Candace told the sheriff's deputy, refusing to budge. He sat with her, sat behind the wheel, waiting with her until Buddy's parents arrived.

Shock, the deputy said—Buddy's mother adding that a baby was coming—how pale Candace was, how calm. How she didn't cry. What they didn't know was how far removed she was, how many doors had been closed and locked behind her before a truck loaded with cattle mangled her husband of four months.

The event unfurled like a script intended for someone else. Sirens and flashing lights, bawling cattle, their smell spilling out of the slatted truck into December's late-night chill. The deputy's kindness, too, his questions, surely not meant for her. And the feeling of rote, of distance, in her answers. Buddy Grant, age twenty-one. Candace Grant, his wife, age seventeen, pregnant, seven months along.

Mr. Grant let out a howl when they told him his son was dead. Candace recognized a word—*No!*—in the anguish spilling out of him. It didn't sound like human speech; it sounded as if he'd been kicked in the side. *Yes,* she thought. *That's it.* She'd witnessed such an injury—a neighbor stove in when he paused behind a mule, his liver ruptured, so much pain distilled into a single syllable.

Mildred Grant maneuvered her husband into the back seat of the car he'd driven there, put Candace in the front, locked Buddy's car, and told the deputy she'd send for it in the morning. She drove them back to Nopalito.

The Grant residence was a low-slung expanse of creamy brick, like something out of a magazine you might find in a doctor's office on Ocean Drive. Mildred let them in. She and Mr. Grant were the only people Candace knew who carried household keys with them, who locked their doors before bed or before driving away. Mr. Grant walked into the kitchen and put a fist through the sheetrock.

I can't be here, Candace thought.

Mildred left the room and returned with a prescription bottle. She tapped several tablets into her palm, fingered them, and put one back. She filled a glass of water at the sink.

"No," Mr. Grant said when she handed him the pills—a husk of the objection he had raised at the scene of Buddy's death. Still, he took the pills and washed them down. Mildred led him to bed.

"No," Candace said when her mother-in-law returned. No to calling her parents in the dead of night. No to the Grants' guest bedroom. She didn't want her parents, and she couldn't risk witnessing what Mr. Grant might do on waking. No bed but her own would do.

"I'll be fine," she said when Mildred offered to stay the night with her. "Mr. Grant needs you."

"With what I gave him"—Mildred raised the bottle of pills between them—"my husband will sleep until noon. I'm not leaving you alone."

A person who didn't know her might have suspected a lack of feeling. Candace knew better. Mildred Grant was like that saying about cards held close to the chest. Her face, her eyes, she'd mastered. They gave no sign. But there was fire inside her, as Candace had learned. She'd paid a price for thinking otherwise.

Over the months of her marriage to Buddy, she'd studied her mother-in-law, parsing out clues. The moment Mildred Grant stepped out of the car at the Burger Dell, Candace could see that something had shifted. She'd been watching to see what it was. As Mildred excused herself to pack an overnight case, it came to her. Finally, this woman looked her age. No, that wasn't right. She looked like other women her age. She looked as if in the time since she'd taken the deputy's call, a weight she'd evaded had settled in her.

Mildred returned and drove them to the apartment Candace had shared with Buddy. She would take the couch. "Try to sleep," she told Candace. "You'll need it." And she closed the door between them.

Buddy wasn't there. He wouldn't be, Candace knew that. But the smell of him was everywhere—the skin bracer he splashed so liberally at the bathroom sink, hair oil scenting the pillowcase beside hers when she slipped into bed, his sleepy man smell down under the sheets.

Candace slept. She woke, coming up from so deep it felt like drowning.

When she opened her bedroom door, Mildred Grant was up and seated on the couch, her sheet and blanket neatly folded on the end table, face freshly touched up, hair smoothed, not a strand out of place—a perfect silvery sheen—artfully swept back into a modest French twist. She looked like the banker's wife she was: gray wool suit, sleek black pumps, rich black leather handbag.

If Grace Kelly were in her mid-forties—and not married away from the movies—Candace could imagine her in the role of Mildred Grant. Both had that serene look of certain beautiful women. This morning, though, her mother-in-law's calm was a mask that didn't lie. Even in the soft light bleeding in through the blinds, Mildred Grant looked haggard, her eyes emptied of hope, of possibility.

"We should call your parents," she said.

And without thinking, Candace knew what her mother must bring.

"I want my scrapbook," she said. "Tell them I want my scrapbook."

"You're not going to make trouble again."

"No," Candace said. "I need a black suit. I want Momma to sew it. For the funeral."

Mildred Grant merely looked at her.

"It's in my scrapbook," Candace said. "The suit I want. A picture."

And it was. A glossy magazine page, a black-and-white photo, at its center a beautiful woman, a black-gloved hand to her face, eyes downcast behind the black netting of a perfect hat, at either arm a handsome, suited, solicitous man, behind her a bleak March sky. Elizabeth Taylor come to bury a husband.

Candace had cut the page from one of her movie magazines. She had studied it—the famous actress, her companions, their impeccable mourning. Since the death memorialized in the photo, another March had passed, then another, and then Buddy, a baby in her she hadn't wanted, the months ticking by.

"But that's a fitted suit," her mother said. The scrapbook lay open on the apartment bed. Her mother's gaze shifted briefly from the photograph to Candace, her middle draped like curtains.

"I'm pregnant," Candace said, her mother flinching at the word. "Make a suit that goes wide in the jacket. But tailored. Not all these ugly gathers."

"But that *woman*," her mother said, indicating the photograph. "What will your father say?"

He was on the couch in the next room, the door open between them. Everything they'd said would have carried.

"I don't *care* what he says!" Candace crescendoed into a shriek, the old impatience kindled in her, a bright hot anger that always surprised her, sudden to announce itself and just as suddenly gone.

Mildred Grant stepped in. "I'll cut a pattern," she said. "For a dress—comfortable over your middle. I'll cut it to look like a suit, with a jacket hem at the waist. Buttons. Tailoring."

"Winnie," she added, "can you ask Hugh to drive you? Get butcher paper from the icehouse?"

She took measurements, and when the butcher paper arrived, she went to work sketching out a pattern, then cut out the pieces and marked them for sewing.

"I've got just the fabric," she said. A decade ago she'd set up shop on Main Street, a women's clothing and fabric store—told folks that raising Buddy, being the banker's wife, she'd go stir-crazy with nothing more to do.

"I don't have a hat that'll work," she said.

Dispatching Candace's parents to pick up the fabric so that her mother could start sewing, Mildred palmed her car keys and departed for Corpus Christi. "Don't worry about the netting," she said on her way out the door. "If need be, I can purchase that separately and stitch it on for you."

She was always Mildred, this woman, always Mildred Grant when mentioned outside her own hearing. Nine or ten years ago, on the street downtown, Candace's mother, fifteen years older and apparently feeling her seniority, had addressed the younger woman as Millie.

Mildred Grant hadn't said a word, but it was clear that this lapse was not to be repeated.

"What's *your* name, Momma?" Candace asked as soon as she was alone with her mother.

"You know my name, child."

She'd only ever heard her mother called Winnie.

"I mean your real name."

"Winifred."

"Oh," Candace had said, disappointment blooming in her. Winifred. It was worse even than Winnie.

On a fall afternoon the year Candace was ten, she found herself alone in the house with her father. Her mother had gone to the neighbor's to work on a quilt three farm wives had taken on together. Candace loved being alone, her attention drifting from the play of light at her window to birdsong beyond, a swing chain squeaking in the breeze, and back to the sound of water running in the bathtub, where her father had excused himself after coming in from the fields. Murmuring to herself, wordless imaginings, she left a book she'd been browsing on her bed and wandered the house.

She passed by the bathroom door and found that she had left the story she'd been telling herself. The door had always been closed during a bath. Since her first day of school, even her own baths had been private. She had no interest in her mother at her bath. She was old, but she'd been a girl once. Still was, Candace supposed. But she wondered about her father, an idle curiosity that drew her back this afternoon to the closed bathroom door, something on the other side, something about Poppa that she must see.

Unafraid, with perfect calm, she put her hand to the doorknob and turned it—slowly, carefully, a secret between her and the house. She pushed and the door swung open. It was as if the door were attached to a puppet string that raised her father out of his bath, his hand reaching for a towel. She didn't have words for the parts of Poppa hanging naked before her, didn't have words for what she'd seen of herself when she undressed for bathing. She could only stand there and look: her father with his hand at the towel, her father arrested, looking back at her.

It was no longer than the double click of a ticking clock, but it was enough.

Poppa yanked the towel around himself and shouted, "Get out of here!"

She took a step back, and he slammed the door.

Afterward, he came into her room and paced. He didn't lay a hand on her, didn't need to. What he said was enough. Good girls don't open closed doors. Good girls keep their eyes where they ought. He talked about the woman in the Bible who looked where she was told not to. This was a warning, he said. Not again. Candace might be turned into a block of lick salt for the cows.

"If your momma knew." That was the last thing he said. And shook his head. For the rest of her life, when a man shook his head at her, it was her father she saw, his hand on her bedroom door. "If your momma knew." Then he was gone.

Nothing more was said, but what her father did with his eyes around her was never the same. At table he looked at the space beside her when she spoke, he looked at her mother, he looked at the light fixture. Sometimes, when Candace found his eyes on her, he looked confused—like a hermit from one of her fairy tales who opens his door to an orphaned girl and knows in the instant that, whatever her story, she, this wide-eyed child, is a mystery he will never unravel.

Her mother was a fool, but even she noticed that something was amiss.

"What is it?" she asked that first evening over supper. "What has happened?"

Poppa said nothing. Candace did the same.

In the days after, her mother settled on Candace as the source of trouble. Now and again, unannounced, she would stand in the doorway of the bedroom she'd entered so freely before.

"What have you done, child?" she would ask. "What have you done?"

The dress sewn for Buddy's funeral was a disappointment, though it was perfectly made. As Mildred Grant had promised, it looked like a tailored suit. Well, Candace thought, tailored for a penguin. The hat was perfect, though, and so were the black gloves Mildred had brought back from Corpus to go with it. The night before the funeral, alone in her apartment, Candace put on the dress, the gloves, the hat. She stepped into her new black pumps and stood before the full-length mirror Buddy had installed on the bedroom door before they moved in. She practiced gestures that would pair the gloves and the hat. A hand to the hat, as if to secure it as she walked. A hand to her face, her eyes cast down.

She walked to her dresser and, reaching into the right-back corner of the top drawer, pulled out a handkerchief from the trousseau her mother had assembled so quickly. A dazzle of white from the bluing it had been rinsed in, the silky cotton was edged in delicate hand-tatted lace. Unfolding it, pinching the pristine cloth at its exact center, she shook it so that the edges draped like flouncing on a skirt. Protruding fanlike from the fingers of her black-gloved hand, it was the perfect complement to her outfit. She tilted her face as she imagined she would tomorrow and, holding the handkerchief with the center tufted up, leaving the veil on the hat in place, dabbed through it at the corner of an eye, pleased with the dress, the veil, the gesture, the eyes she saw looking back at herself from the mirror.

When the minister launched into the eulogy, Candace felt herself floating away. She heard Buddy's name, with dates on either side like brackets. The rest of it was church words, blurry words, nonsense. She had never been able to take in this kind of language, had always heard it from a distance, dreaming herself elsewhere. Beside her on the right sat her mother, losing her battle with the decorum of mourning. The pew squeaked with her twists and turns, her hen-like peeking to see where folks were sitting and what the wives were wearing. Beyond her sat Candace's father, still as stone. Mildred Grant sat next to Candace on the left, looking the worse for lack of tears. Beyond her was Mr. Grant, so heavily sedated Candace wondered what, if anything, he'd remember of his son's funeral. He'd cried beforehand when they closed the casket. He was seeping tears now, the word *No* at his lips quietly and repeatedly.

Opening the clasp on her purse, Candace reached inside and palmed the compact biding there. She wanted to lift it out and snap it open. A glance would have done the trick.

Mildred Grant slipped a hand into the crook of her arm and touched her just above the piping that edged her glove. Her fingers were cold as the grave. Candace knew this about her mother-in-law, that she was cold-natured, that even on warm days her hands conveyed a chill. A warning, Candace had thought, though she envied Mildred Grant the cool calm with which she'd orchestrated her own life, her husband's, her son's, the way she didn't ruffle when things didn't go her way. Faced with Candace, she'd simply enlarged her plan to include a daughter-in-law she wouldn't have chosen, a grandchild arriving well ahead of schedule. Candace had made elaborate plans too. She'd watched them unravel from the window of a marriage she hadn't wanted, a succession of airless days in the little apartment that made her husband so happy while a child she couldn't imagine battened inside her—someone else's life veering out of control while she looked on.

Nothing reached her.

Until that moment in the middle of Buddy's eulogy when Mildred Grant touched her, the cold in her like a voice that must be answered. And from a deep place Candace hadn't known was there, a wakening cold, like the chill of midnight, like the weighted hum of truck tires moving over pavement, like the grip she should have felt watching Buddy at the Burger Dell window, Buddy swiveling the wrong way, swiveling away from the truck behind him on the blacktop, tossing a split-second smile when his eyes swept by her, swiveling still, and then his smile gone, the truck upon him.

On both sides, her name was spoken.

"Candace?"

Had she cried out?

"I can't breathe," she whispered to Mildred, standing. "Let me out."

She rushed the length of the church, in her wake a rustling as the faithful turned in her direction. She could feel their eyes on her, their judgment. Moving faster, she pushed through heavy swinging doors into the vestibule and walked full tilt into Stan Meyer.

He was a tall man. With her head down, Candace almost knocked the breath out of him.

"Buddy's dead," she said, sweeping past him through another heavy door and out and down the steps, where she stopped and took in deep, deep breaths, trying not to cry out when her lungs released the healing air.

When she found that she could slow her breathing, she turned back. Stan Meyer stood waiting at the bottom step.

"Buddy's dead," she said again. It was the best she could do by way of explaining herself.

"I'm so sorry," Stan said. He seemed to struggle with himself, between the impulse to hug her and a voice suggesting otherwise. He took her hand. "Beg pardon for being late," he said. "I only just got home." Stan Meyer made his living as a roughneck. Between stints on a drilling platform in the Gulf, he returned to Nopalito and helped out on his father's farm.

"Go on in," she said. "It's not over. The preacher's going on about Buddy."

"What about you?"

"I can't be in there. I can't breathe." The panic at her again, she turned, thinking he shouldn't see this. On the street beyond, a car braked for a cat, which leaped away at the last second and came bounding across the lawn in her direction. Removing a glove, Candace went down on one knee and put out her hand. The cat nudged her there and purred as she smoothed the fur between his ears.

"My husband loved me," she said.

"Of course he did." Stan knelt beside her and reached; the cat licked the back of his hand.

She said what hadn't been said to anyone: "I didn't say it back."

"Buddy knew how you felt," Stan said. "I'm sure he knew."

The cat gave Stan's hand a sudden nip and pranced off. Stan rose and helped Candace up.

"I said mean things," she told him. For a moment she was almost with Buddy in the little apartment kitchen. "I don't want this," she said. "I don't want a baby."

"Hush now," said Stan. "You don't mean that."

From inside the church, a hymn started, the organ first, then voices joining in.

Stan spoke again. "Stay out here long enough, Mildred Grant will send a posse after you."

Stan's brother Jackson, two years younger, had been Buddy's best friend. The three—Jackson, Buddy, Stan—had run with the same crowd when they were all in high school together. They would have paid a penalty for crossing Mildred Grant.

A strange laughing sound came out of Candace. It was like being punched in the gut and having the gasp escape as strangled music. The sound came again, and then she was calm.

"Maybe not," she said. "I think my mother-in-law has had the starch knocked out of her."

"How about you, Candy? How're you holding up?"

"No one calls me that. Not anymore."

"Sorry. Still picture you in grade school."

"I'm a woman now," she said, putting a hand to her midsection as proof.

Stan Meyer blushed.

"Walk with me," Candace said. She took his arm. "I should get back in there."

She let him escort her to the front of the church. She let go of his arm there, moving along the pew to her seat between her mother and Mildred Grant while Stan walked back to a pew with empty seats. On the walk up the aisle, she'd been aware again of rustling as watchful eyes followed their progress. Taking her seat as Mrs. Buddy Grant, widow, she knew that with a man beside her she'd attracted extra notice. Afterward, when memory summoned Buddy's funeral, it was this moment that came back to her, walking the aisle with Stan Meyer at her arm and all eyes on them.

She'd been a happy child, perfectly satisfied with her parents, blissfully unaware that in the world outside their isolated community, her family might seem out of step with the times. If there were any sign of what was to come, it was in her parents' awkwardness as mother and father. It was clear even to Candace they couldn't quite believe she existed, so many years they'd accepted being childless before she came along. She was a dreamy child; her parents lived in the here and now. They lived from chore to chore and expected her to do the same. They fretted that she didn't. When it was time for her to start school, they worried aloud that she might not be ready.

It didn't matter. The older children, the teacher too, seemed drawn to Candace. From the first day, they looked after her, not more than a dozen of them assembling each morning in the same one-room schoolhouse their parents had attended, one teacher and eight grades in a shabby, unpainted building that leaked when it rained.

On a breezy morning not long after her first day of school, she dawdled as the other students left for recess. Miss Freudenberg reached into her desk drawer and, pulling out a hand mirror and brush, worked at taming her windblown hair. Candace watched, fascinated. Each morning her mother carefully braided her own hair. On Sundays and special occasions, she wrapped the braids around her head and pinned them into place. She did this in front of her dresser mirror. She didn't use a hand mirror or carry a compact. She didn't pause in front of mirrors; she discouraged Candace when she found her at a mirror.

"Come here, child," Miss Freudenberg said. Sitting Candace on her lap, she ran the brush through her hair and then handed her the mirror. "Look at you," she said, her face beside Candace in the mirror. "Pretty as a picture."

Miss Freudenberg was not a pretty woman. She wore simple white blouses, unadorned black skirts, and plain black Minnie Mouse pumps. Her face, too, was plain, and that might have got her by, but her voice made folks think she was ugly. Her sentences came out in blurts, the words ragged and hoarse. At recess, when she was not around, sometimes the older boys would mimic her by braying. Stan Meyer policed the school, though, both indoors and out. A seventh grader, the tallest and strongest boy at the little school, he wouldn't allow even a hint of unkindness to Miss Freudenberg herself.

The boys were wrong about their teacher. Candace heard a lamb in her when she spoke, a lamb that has cried itself hoarse. If only someone would calm Miss Freudenberg, her voice might stop crying. Candace wanted to put a soothing hand on her; she wanted to let her know she was safe. Sitting on Miss Freudenberg's lap, the mirror before her, that's what she did. She reached and stroked her teacher's hair. "Sweet child," Miss Freudenberg said, her voice hoarse still but softened.

A year later, on the morning of the first cold front, Miss Freudenberg arrived at the school an hour late. Stan Meyer had them all in their seats, not daring to roam or whine, when the door burst open and their teacher rushed to the front of the room, clearly disheveled by more than the brisk north wind—weed stains on the back of her coat, tears in her blouse where buttons had been torn from the placket, her hair a tangled mess. She stood behind her desk, grasping at things there, rearranging her grade book, an ink bottle, a box of chalk. It was a mile walk from the farmhouse where she boarded. What could have happened along the way?

Stan Meyer rose and walked to Miss Freudenberg's desk. "Are you all right?" he asked, his voice soft enough that Candace intuited the question from his tone.

"I fell," the teacher said. "I think I cut myself."

Using a hand to brush back her hair on the side, she revealed a jagged cut running beside her ear from hairline to jaw. The collective gasp made it sound as if the room itself were trying to catch its breath.

"Someone hurt you," Stan said, both concern and anger tempering his words. "Who?"

"I *fell*!" she said, looking past him toward Candace and the others. "Please. Tell them I fell."

"You need to see a doctor."

"No!"

Candace heard the lamb in her teacher again—terrified, trembling, desperate to run.

Stan Meyer crossed to a cabinet along the side of the room and took out the first-aid kit kept there for playground mishaps.

When he approached her, their teacher started back, knocking over the chair behind her.

"No!" she said again, shrinking from Stan until she'd backed herself into the wall behind her desk.

Stan turned from her and got them all out of the building. There was no phone. He sent one of the older boys to the nearest farm. "Call Dr. Manning," he said. "Tell him what she looks like. He'll know what to do."

He sent the rest of them home, insisting they walk in groups and stay on the roads, stay out of the brush. Candace wouldn't leave. Folding her arms, she refused to take the hand of any neighbor who offered to walk her.

Dr. Manning arrived with his wife, a registered nurse, who assisted him in the office and ran his practice. "Go home," she told Stan. "Take Candy Lambert home."

He didn't. He stood beside Candace looking at the closed door of the schoolhouse after Dr. and Mrs. Manning had gone inside.

There was a single cry—short and sharp—then silence. After a few minutes, Miss Freudenberg appeared on the schoolhouse stoop, Dr. and Mrs. Manning on either side of her. She let herself be led to the car and put inside before they drove away.

When Stan Meyer offered his hand, Candace took it and let him walk her home.

The school didn't open its doors again. Like the few children who had still attended there, Candace rode the bus to Nopalito instead. Teased without letup for her country ways, her clothes, her ancient, backward parents, she took refuge in the daydreams she'd always been drawn to.

Now and then she caught sight of Stan Meyer, six years older, among the coterie of boys who staked out the back of the bus. Stan waved when he noticed her looking. She smiled back and began to look else-where, careful of her attentions, protective of something her teacher had touched in her. Kindness, perhaps. She kept it to herself, even when Buddy came along. Until he died and she heard his father cry out.

When her little girl was born, Candace was expected to nurse the child. She wouldn't do it. She hadn't thought about names, had let her mother and Mildred Grant put their heads together, though now she wished she'd made herself care. Sylvia Laverne sounded like someone who might have carried her lunch to school in a molasses bucket.

"She favors you," her mother said, and Mildred Grant concurred. Candace handed the child back and let them coo over her. She thought her daughter looked like a wrinkled, red-faced, hairless little old man.

After the hospital she let herself be put in the guest bedroom at the Grants', let Mildred take care of infant Sylvia while the weeks stretched on, her mother in the house daily, fluttering at her to be up and about, making such a fuss about having a grandchild a person would have thought *she* had given birth. When Candace tried to pull herself up out of bed or shift from her chair or walk about the house, heaviness sat in her, lassitude in her muscles she couldn't dream herself out of. If she sat perfectly still, she could empty herself until she was just her eyes and the cold light of February—and then March—at the window.

A month into her stay at the Grants', she found herself alone with the baby for an afternoon. She'd sent her mother home, and Mildred Grant had taken some time to put her shop in order. Candace was fine until Sylvia started crying. She tried to calm her with a bottle. She tried the pacifier and then a fingertip dipped in honey, with the same results. She tried walking Sylvia, rocking her, singing a lullaby. The crying only got worse, a series of sharp, one-note shrieks, surging like an electric fence. She lay the child in her bassinet and, closing doors behind her, locked herself in the bathroom and sat on the commode, hands pressed to her ears. After a few minutes, she rose and splashed water in her face.

The crying had stopped.

When she got back to the guest bedroom, the door was open. Mr. Grant stood beside the bassinet, singing a husky, wordless melody, Sylvia Laverne cradled on his shoulder, sound asleep.

In the weeks since Buddy's funeral, his father had scarcely moved out of a circuit from bed to table to chair and back. Little Sylvia's crying jag got through to him. In the days after, he seemed ever alert to the sound of her fussing. He would appear in the midst of the noise and rescue the child, no matter who held her. He had a deft touch. Sylvia Laverne would quiet to his voice and gaze at him, rapt, while she gripped the pinky he offered. Over lunch one day he announced his intention to check in at the bank. Within days he had given his afternoons over to the old routine, the house deadly quiet when both he and Mildred were gone.

Candace's parents only made matters worse—her father's awkwardness when he came into the house after driving her mother there, the shame of his only child's hasty wedding visible in every step. Of course, her mother talked to fill the silence. One morning, when she hadn't seen her granddaughter in several days, her mouth got away from her. She babbled without pause, spilling nonsense over the child until Candace thought surely she would hear herself and stop. Unruffled, Mr. Grant took Sylvia Laverne from Candace's mother and put the child in the arms of her other grandfather. Candace's father blanched. He kept the child; he rocked her back and forth, moving as if his arms were constructed of hinged wood. Candace's mother looked on as if none of it made sense to her, not a word out of anyone until Mildred Grant walked into the room.

She spoke to Candace's mother. "These visits are too short for you."

"I don't want to impose."

"Nonsense," Mildred said. "We have an extra room here. Have Hugh pack a bag for you. Stay."

"No!" The word came in unison from Candace and her father.

Sylvia Laverne gave every appearance of starting to fuss, but Mr. Grant took her. She quieted. Candace was afraid her mother would cry, so clear was her wish to say yes to Mildred, so painful the insult delivered by husband and daughter.

"Well," Mildred said. She looked as if she might deliver a homily on the benefits of manners. But Candace's mother spoke first.

"I don't want to impose," she said again. "I'll stay until Hugh is done with his errands."

Candace excused herself when her father was gone. She almost slammed the door behind her when she got to her room. She had never felt so mean. Her mother was a decent person; she harmed no one with her talking. But Candace couldn't wish this woman here with her, couldn't wish herself on the farm with those who claimed her as their offspring. Who were they, anyway, Hugh and Winnie Lambert? How had she arrived in the narrow embrace of their lives? They might as well have found her in the garden among the cabbages.

There was a time when she'd have come back to herself when she was by herself. Not that day. Her father returned and drove her mother home. The Grants left for the afternoon. Sylvia Laverne slept without waking. And Candace could hardly bear the stillness, her certainty, against all odds, that beyond the walls that shut her in, the town too was emptying, that she would grow old sitting in a house that wasn't hers, tending a child she hadn't wanted.

On a Monday morning, with Mildred gone to her dress shop, Candace sought out Mr. Grant. While he sat beside her, rocking Sylvia, she had a fleeting vision of herself in the guest bathroom at bedtime, a glass of water in one hand, a fistful of her host's tranquilizers in the other.

"No," she said, so sudden the temptation, so powerful her fear of what the little pills might do to her.

"No, what?" asked Mr. Grant, but quickly—Candace was practiced at this—she evaded his question.

That afternoon, instead of dozing while her daughter napped, Candace fell sound asleep. Her dream was dark like slumber. She was walking through the dark, but she was safe. There was no threat of tripping to hobble her step, no one lurking to catch at her throat. From out of the dark, she heard the voice of a mother sheep calling out reassurance. She bleated a reply. A hand slipped into hers and held firm, a voice at her ear she seemed to remember. "Sweet child. Pretty as a picture."

The dream was with her when she woke, the calm gone quick as vapor over a stock pond's surface, in its place a dread that chilled. It was the calm itself that so unnerved her, the dream's lovely certainty. And the quiet she woke into, the child asleep in her crib, Mildred napping down the hall.

Candace rushed out of the house and stood in the yard, her face to the sunlight, its warmth a prickly brightness against closed eyelids. Hearing noises, she opened her eyes and walked toward the sound of hammers. Three blocks down from the Grants', a new house was going up. She would find life there—movement, voices. Amid the pounding, she would think what to do.

As she approached, a pickup truck pulled onto the lot, and Clayton Moore got out. Despite the unease he inspired in men with budding daughters or attractive wives, Clayton had thrived. There wasn't an engine made he couldn't tune, a worn-out vehicle he couldn't get running again. Good head for business too. Not even thirty, with a service station, a shop of his own, a new house going up in Nopalito's respectable neighborhood. His charm was lost on Candace, no matter the collective opinion. Clayton was a bit on the shaggy side, a measure cockier than seemed warranted, even now, engaged in conversation with the crew boss but plainly aware of her presence. On any other day the town's Casanova wouldn't have earned a second thought, but this morning Candace found herself staring. What was it about Clayton Moore, this man who smirked and did what he wanted, stepping over the limits that governed others, immune to consequences?

Nearby, a couple of crew members started measuring two-by-fours, then switched on the electric saw, so shrill Candace had to cover her ears. But she loved the scent of fresh-cut lumber and, when the saw quieted, the pounding hammers, their lopsided rhythm—a house going up, framed walls and roof, rooms waiting for sheetrock and paint and furniture, waiting for footsteps.

Inside one of the rooms, a carpenter pounded a nail into place, then slipped the hammer into his tool belt and stood there, working his shoulder muscles with a free hand. When his gaze crossed hers, he gave a goofy grin. Grabbing at verticals in the wall there, he leaned toward Candace, as if through the bars of a cell, and winked. She felt her smile rise up and freeze.

That's it, she thought, her gaze moving to Clayton, still talking, still giving orders—a man who knew how to get what he wanted, putting up walls three blocks from the banker's house. Like that man in the story who got bricked in forever, except Clayton was building the walls himself. If she'd been standing close enough she would have slapped him awake. She would have shouted, *Run!*

Later that afternoon, after Mildred woke from her nap and before Mr. Grant returned from the bank, Candace slipped into the master bathroom and pocketed one of his tranquilizers. Back in her bedroom she slipped it into an aspirin tin she kept in her purse. She had no intention of taking the tranquilizer. Ever. Still, should it come to that, the little pill was there.

On Friday evening of the same week, Candace sat down to an early supper with the Grants. With a breeze visible in the trees off the patio, Mr. Grant got up and opened the sliding glass door. Hammering sifted in through the screen, the crew working late on Clayton Moore's house.

"They'll be finished soon," Mr. Grant said. And then to Candace, "You might want to hire them when they're done."

She had no idea what he was talking about. Mildred Grant confused her further still.

"You have a home here," she said. "With us."

"Not a minute to herself," Mr. Grant said. "No space to call her own." He winked at Candace. "My wife has the house of her dreams. Clayton Moore's getting his. Why not you?"

"Why would I?" Candace asked. "How?"

Mildred Grant raised a hand toward her husband as if to say, *Enough*.

"No," he said. He turned from her and answered Candace.

"The insurance money. It's yours, you know."

She had wanted a wedding, a honeymoon too. She'd wanted Buddy to get the Grants to fund them. Instead, they'd bought a hefty life-insurance policy, surely Mildred's way of flouting her wishes, though now the money was hers. She'd seen her name on the papers.

Her first impulse had been to run shouting into the street, waving the check, to get her hands on the cash and get out. But she'd been heavy with the child she was carrying, and Buddy was hardly cold in his grave, and then Sylvia Laverne arrived and this listlessness came over her. Until just four days ago, when she'd watched Clayton Moore's walls going up.

"No," she said. "I don't want a house." That word again. *No*. If only she had invoked it before. If only she could say no when it counted. And follow through. As a test, excusing herself, she went to her room, took the purloined tranquilizer from her aspirin tin, and flushed it down the commode.

By noon of the following day, she had a replacement tranquilizer in the aspirin tin. She felt like a yoyo, a fool. Within days, four of Mr. Grant's little pills had found their way into her cache. On a calm day, without need or pressure, she swallowed one and washed it down with water. She watched herself. While she was under the influence, she was fine; she could see why certain women might be drawn to this kind of respite. And though surely Mildred Grant would never take one, that seemed a shame. One of her husband's pills might take the edge off.

Afterward, though, Candace worried about the lull that came with the tranquilizer in her blood. She was reminded of the distance she'd felt for years before Buddy's death, always watching herself, always wondering who is this girl, how will she get away?

She hadn't let herself believe she was pregnant, had railed at Dr. Manning when he insisted otherwise. "I won't have a baby," she had told him. "You can't make me. I'll get rid of it." When he threatened to tell her parents, she laughed.

He took another tack. "What about the child's father?"

"I'm not saying who that is."

"Word gets around."

"Go ahead. Call him," Candace said. "I don't have to do what he says."

Doctor Manning picked up his phone and dialed. "Let's see if Mildred Grant can talk sense into you."

Buddy's mother issued steely ultimatums. Candace answered them with a steely silence all her own. She ignored the fuss her mother made, stared down her father's silent confusion. She let Buddy think she'd marry him. She was sure she wouldn't, right up to the day Mildred Grant boarded the Trailways bus where Candace sat with her ticket out, the banker's wife ordering her off, a heat Candace hadn't suspected coloring the woman's face, her voice. When Candace said no, she was dragged off the bus, spitting curses the while, every vile thing her tongue remembered. She stopped when Mildred Grant slapped her.

What happened after that happened to someone else, someone named Mrs. Buddy Grant, the signature she practiced endlessly before their quick civil ceremony, thinking, *Who is Mrs. Buddy Grant?*

Albrecht Meyer died unexpectedly on the first of April. He'd fathered seven sons, hardy himself as any two of them combined until they found him slumped over his wife's garden plow, startled into a heart attack, apparently, by a rattlesnake, the fang marks plainly visible on either side of the wedding band he'd worn for thirty-eight years. Breck was seventy. He left behind his wife, Alouise, age fifty-three, and their sons, ranging from twenty-one to thirty-seven.

Candace spent the morning of April second, a Sunday, baking her mother's burnt-sugar cake. She put on a simple black dress and drove out to the Meyer place.

Jackson Meyer, Buddy's old friend and last of the Meyer boys, answered the door and invited her in. Jackson had stayed on to help his father run the home place. Two of his brothers had leased farmland in the area; a third ran a feedstore in the county seat. The other brothers were en route. Angus, the eldest, had gone to college on the GI bill. An engineer in Houston, he was expected by suppertime. Gib, the middle son, ran a small drilling outfit in west Texas. He was driving in from Odessa. It would be two more days before Stan, second youngest, could get there from the Gulf.

Jackson sliced the cake and handed Candace a plate with a thick wedge on it. "Of the two, my daddy had the sweet tooth," he said. "But let's take Momma a bite." He led her through the house to the front porch, where his mother sat rocking, the rhythmic groaning of hardwood on hardwood like the slowed counting of a clock that has no hurry in it.

"My boys and I are much obliged," said Mrs. Meyer, tipping forward in her chair to take the plate Candace offered. She lifted a single forkful to her mouth. "Delicious," she said. "Breck just loved your momma's cake." She set the plate on the floorboards and went back to rocking, her eyes moving to the distance.

Alouise Meyer looked every bit the age of the man who'd died plowing her garden. Her fingers were all knuckle and bone, bent like claws where she gripped the arms of her rocker, the hands darkly stained with liver spots. Her hair—mostly gray, no rinse to silver it—she kept in a knot just above midpoint at the back of her collar. She wore no makeup this afternoon, nothing to mask what the years of sun and worry had done to her face. Seven living sons she'd borne, a stillborn daughter, and now, since yesterday, her husband gone. On the porch facing her in the warm spring light, Candace felt drawn to Mrs. Meyer's eyes, her unfaltering gaze, a depth there that seemed to have no bottom. Looking, Candace felt suddenly untethered, as if gravity were turning her loose from the floor beneath.

Mrs. Meyer came up out of the rocker and took her hand.

"It's Buddy Grant she's missing," she said to Jackson. "Poor thing. Too young for such a loss."

Jackson turned and disappeared into the house. He was gone almost before Candace saw the panic he surely hadn't wanted seen—Buddy's friend, not wanting to cry, not wanting to be seen shedding tears.

Alone with Mrs. Meyer, she couldn't think how to correct the widow's mistake. She let it stand, let herself be put in Mr. Meyer's rocking chair, let Alouise hold her hand for a few minutes, though not another word crossed between them until Candace rose to take her leave.

Inside, she stepped into the bathroom and took one of Mr. Grant's tranquilizers.

She found Jackson in the kitchen.

"Daddy's the one she talked to," he said. "Gonna be mighty quiet around here." He gave a wry smile. "Might have to find myself a wife." The way his eyes lingered when he said wife made it look as if he thought Candace might do. Jackson Meyer was nice enough—and easy on the eyes. But it gave her chills to think of Buddy's best friend that way. Besides, he was stuck here. Long ago, she'd crossed farm boys off her list.

For Breck Meyer's visitation service, held midweek at the funeral home, Candace wore a dress she'd sewed herself. She didn't have her mother's patience at the machine, but she hadn't felt like quarreling. The pattern showed a bright party dress—full skirt with belted waist, fitted sleeveless top with a modest, wide, square neckline in front and a lovely plunging neckline in back that would have set her mother to fretting. Immediately, Candace had pictured the dress in black satin.

First thing on the morning after driving her cake out to the Meyer place, she laid out the pattern and went to work at her Singer, humming as the dress came together. Tuesday noon, when it was done and she tried it on, she couldn't stop smiling at herself in the mirror. Wednesday evening, as she entered the funeral home, she was pleased when Stan Meyer caught sight of her. She watched the change in him looking at her as she approached and took his hand.

"I'm so sorry," she said, raising her free hand and touching his cheek.

As she turned, Mildred Grant came in through the front door, Mr. Grant behind her, his eyes glassy from grief and tranquilizers. So far Candace had used only two of his pills, and one of those didn't count. She'd only wanted to see what it would do. The other she felt silly about—her brief scare Monday afternoon on the porch with Alouise Meyer. She made a mental note not to have another tranquilizer.

After the service Mildred took Mr. Grant by the hand and moved toward Breck Meyer's widow and her sons, lined up to receive anyone who wanted to shake hands with them and say a word or two. Candace edged past Mr. Grant and nudged Mildred.

"Don't put him through this," she said. "I'll sit with him."

She offered Mr. Grant her arm and walked him to a bench along the wall of the foyer. Her parents followed Mildred to the receiving line, her mother holding Sylvia Laverne.

"You shouldn't be here," Candace said to her father-in-law.

"I shouldn't be anywhere."

She took his hand in both of hers. He let her, but the hand lay limp, unresponsive, in her grip. She could think of only one thing to say.

"My daughter needs you."

"Your daughter needs her father."

And then, surprising herself, a confession of sorts, an odd conviction she'd not spoken aloud: "I made him drive me."

She saw a question forming in Mr. Grant's eyes.

"Buddy," she said. "That night. I wanted a milkshake. A dozen miles I made him drive me for a milkshake."

"It doesn't matter. What was said or who was with him. He's not coming back."

She looked up to see Stan Meyer approaching. He'd left the receiving line.

Mr. Grant repeated his thought. "He's not ever coming back."

"No. He's gone," Stan said, doubtless thinking it was his father they were talking about.

As on the porch with Alouise, Candace kept quiet. She saw no point in correcting Stan's mistake.

By the next morning, Mr. Grant was so bad Mildred wouldn't leave him, plainly afraid that whatever strength her husband had left he might use to his own detriment. "I've called your parents," she told Candace. "About Albrecht's funeral. They'll come for you."

"I can drive myself," Candace said.

"This will be hard for you. You'll want kin beside you."

Candace objected, but Mildred would have none of it.

"A young widow alone," she said. "At such a public—such a difficult—event. It isn't seemly."

Candace relented; she could read between the lines. Mildred had seen her with Stan Meyer before the visitation service. She had seen her hand at Stan's cheek.

The funeral had been scheduled for late afternoon with the burial at sunset, Breck Meyer's favorite time of day. Candace wore a slim, fitted black suit, one of two her mother had sewed for her after Sylvia Laverne's birth. As on the day of Buddy's funeral, she carried a white handkerchief edged with her mother's lace.

By the time the casket had been lowered, it was all but dark. Her mother was fretting to be gone, her father palming his car keys, but Candace held back, taking her place behind the last of the mourners queuing up where Alouise Meyer sat with her sons. As before, it was hard to face the widow, the loss carved out of her, but Candace had learned to use breath and voice to feign a calm she didn't feel. She needn't have worried. When her turn came, when Alouise Meyer looked up and saw her there, the widow rose and took her hand.

"I want to thank you again," she said. "My sons have savored your cake." She turned to Candace's parents. "Your daughter has been so kind," she said, and as the neighbors exchanged pleasantries, it was as if all had forgotten where they were and why. Seven Meyer sons and four daughters-in-law rose and joined the circle, grandchildren approaching at the edges. Candace murmured a greeting to Stan as he arrived beside her.

There was to be food and visiting on the Meyer place, though when Mrs. Meyer turned to Candace's parents and said please come, she was met with a flurry of excuses.

"I'm afraid we've overstayed our welcome," Candace's mother said. "Your house is full to the brim with kin."

"Well, then," Alouise said, "we must have Candace."

"Please, ma'am," Stan chipped in, "let Momma have her wish." And to Candace: "Please say you'll come. You can ride with me." And back to her parents: "I'll see your daughter home after."

Candace suspected Stan's car had carried others of the Meyer family to the funeral and burial, but as they left the graveyard, all of them got into other vehicles.

A mild front had moved through, and with the sun down, the evening cooled quickly. She rolled up her window and asked Stan to do the same. It was a quiet drive, the night starless, deepening, the pavement skimming smoothly beneath the car.

When they reached the turn to the Meyer farm, Stan got out to open the gate, then got back in and drove through. Getting out again to close the gate, he left his door open, cold air spilling inside, and suddenly hooves were coming toward her in the dark. Cows would do that, she knew, whether out of curiosity or the expectation of being fed or simply the foolishness of cows. But alone in Stan's car, the night so dense she could see nothing outside the beams cast by the headlights, Candace chilled to the approaching hooves.

She had to get away. Before it was too late, she had to be gone.

Without thinking, she scrambled across the seat, squeezing past the steering wheel and up into the night air. She rushed toward Stan, silhouetted by the faint red glow of the car's taillights, hooves scattering as cows shied from her, a stranger.

Her foot struck a rock in the road, and she went down on one knee. The pain made her cry out.

"What the—?" Stan said.

She scrambled up. "I've got to go," she said. "I can't be here."

"Whoa." Stan lay a calming hand on her. "Been in town so long you forgot about cows?" As if to illustrate the lack of danger, he took a step and, clapping, gave a shout. Hooves scattered farther into the night.

She couldn't explain, couldn't even say to herself what it was that so unsettled her.

Stan pulled her to him, held her there while she tried to breathe.

"Okay now?"

"Yes," she said, willing a resolve she didn't feel. "I'm fine."

He put her back in the car and they drove on. The hooves were gone now, surely, though still she heard them, like the beating in her chest. She reached into her purse, her fingers searching. The aspirin tin wasn't there. She withdrew the hand and clasped it with her other hand. The night felt thicker here, the caliche topping of the narrow road glowing eerily ahead, and as the car approached a bend, the headlights pouring into a stand of huisache in the pastureland beyond, the road curved distantly into a dark where she couldn't see.

ELDORADO

EVELYN SMITH, MARCH 18, 1964

ON THE AFTERNOON OF Aggie Doyle's birthday, Evelyn got off the bus and went straight to her room. She stepped out of her school clothes and slipped on the sundress her mother had sewed for the birthday outing—a simple, coral-colored affair with lemony piping to set off a modest, straight-line bodice and wide straps. Even with no one to see her, Evelyn felt naked as she sat down to her dresser mirror, her shoulders and collarbone exposed to the afternoon cool.

She hadn't wanted a sundress, had held her ground, but when her mother threatened the hairbrush, she danced out of her clothes on the spot, a breathless chant coming out of her. "Oh Momma, please. Please, no. I'll get your tape measure. Here it is. See." And she babbled on, anything to create a distraction. It was humiliating, but she didn't want the greater shame that came after a whipping with the hairbrush— hiding the bruises, keeping her part of a wordless pact. That this was between her and Momma. That her father, her brothers, must not know.

Grady's job this afternoon was to keep their mother occupied.

Evelyn heard voices from the kitchen and crossed her fingers. She put on the barest minimum of makeup, then took a brush and touched up her hair. She took special care with her nails, using a translucent polish with enough color to soften her mother's displeasure. Evelyn's fingers were smooth and slender—graceful, even—her nails perfectly shaped ovals. Aggie chewed her nails to the quick, and Fran had bony fingers. As the polish dried, her brother peeked in and gave a thumbs-up. Their mother had said yes. Grady wanted to swim and laze around at the Doyles'. Evelyn wanted him along as a buffer.

At half past five Fran pulled up beside the hackberry tree outside Evelyn's window and honked. She was driving her father's station wagon. Momma knocked at Evelyn's door and entered without waiting for an answer. She was a pretty woman. Everyone said so, but for days now she'd kept her hair—unwashed, unbrushed—in a knot at the nape of her neck, its blonde light dimmed.

"Don't keep your cousin waiting," she said, her mouth pulled out of whack. "She'd ditch you like a rusty wagon if you weren't blood kin. Look at you. Pretty dress like that wasted. Stand up straight." She gave Evelyn's shoulders a parting yank.

Fran sat behind the wheel in a white spaghetti-strap sundress sprigged with tiny flowers. She didn't look happy. Grady took the back seat wearing nothing but a swimsuit and a smile. Evelyn took the front passenger seat, and Fran maneuvered the dusty Chevy out of the yard. From his tractor in the field beyond, cultivator sweeps raising dust, Evelyn's father waved.

As they turned into the county road, Grady launched into a stream of chatter. He was irresistible. Within minutes Fran was nattering back at him. It was warm, more like May than March, with the smell of freshly turned soil tickling at the edges of Evelyn's consciousness. She drifted along, hearing her brother and cousin—the dip and sway of their voices, but not the words.

A mile or so farther down the road, on a curve beyond the creek, Fran gunned the engine and the rear of the old Chevy lurched to the right. She yanked the wheel left, then right, Grady whooping like a tilt-a-whirl rider while the station wagon fishtailed on crushed rock. Evelyn grabbed at the armrest on her door and felt the drag of the car sluing behind them, a lovely, crazy, terrifying weightlessness rising up inside her. The engine surged again, and when Fran stomped the brake pedal, the tail of the car made a dizzying half circle and stopped. Evelyn cranked wildly at the side ventilator window as dust engulfed them. She turned to her cousin, bent over at the steering wheel, hugging herself. And laughing as if she would never stop.

She's hysterical, Evelyn thought.

Grady gave a great shout. "Goddamn, Fran," he said. "You made that look easy."

"Pure luck," Fran said, flopping against the back of the seat.

"Luck," Evelyn said. She felt hot and cold and dizzy all at once. "You might have got us killed."

The laugh faded from Fran's eyes.

"What is *wrong* with you?"

Evelyn turned to Grady. He shrugged and looked out the window.

She stepped out of the car. If only she were wearing a shirt and pants, a pair of decent shoes, she could step to the fence and slip between strands of barbed wire. She could walk into the pastureland beyond and not come back.

"Get in the car," Fran said.

Evelyn started down the road.

Behind her she heard the Chevy engine turn over, and then the big wagon was beside her, Fran insisting—*Get in the car, Get in the car*—her voice oddly like birdcalls against the tamped purr of internal combustion, the smooth crunching of tires on caliche.

And all the while—*Stop, let me out*—Grady in a chorus from the back seat. *I'll talk to her. Stop, let me out.*

On a Sunday in late February, Wadene Doyle had approached Evelyn and her mother after mass. Each time Evelyn heard Wadene's name, a smirk pulled at the corners of her mouth. A man was responsible, of course. Wade Keller—Two, he'd been called since he got grown and quit answering to Junior. Seems Wade had expected a firstborn son to bear his name. When fate intervened, he called his baby girl Wadene.

Three. That's what Evelyn's father called Wadene around his daughter and sons, any time their mother was out of hearing range.

"Three sheets to the wind." That was Ralph, Evelyn's older brother, who buttoned up in front of Wadene to keep her eyes off the chest hair he paraded so proudly otherwise. Twenty years married to Vernon Doyle, and the rancher's wife looked at recent high school graduates—Ralph seemed to be her favorite—as if she might undress them on the spot.

That morning after mass, Wadene was swathed in one of her winter suits, lush silvery-gray wool setting off the jet-black hair she pulled into a bun for church. The hat said money—the extravagant brim, the drape of net beneath it and Wadene's dark eyes behind the veil saying, *Look at me.* No liquor on her breath this morning, but beneath her perfume was the faint odor of mentholated smoke that trailed her everywhere.

"Good morning, Mathilda," Wadene said. "That's a lovely suit you're wearing." And the two women made small talk about clothes and the approach of spring. Evelyn's mother wore the blue satin she'd sewed in the dead of winter. Her outfit played up the curves beneath the satin, the top button on the jacket leaving the barest hint of breasts. She had covered a tiny pillbox hat in the suit's blue satin and perched it on top of her glorious hair. Lemon was her secret; she used it to play up the highlights. Her favorite perfume, a sweet, heavy musk, she kept in a crystal decanter on her dresser. This morning as usual, she had called Grady just before stepping into her suit. Thirteen and giddy and clearly his mother's favorite, Grady grasped the decanter in one hand, the fingertips of the other ready at the atomizer. On cue he squeezed, and their mother stepped into a cloud of mist.

"I suppose you're wondering where Aggie is this morning," Wadene said. "She missed her curfew last night. Would *not* get out of bed this morning." She trained her eyes on Evelyn. "You should double with my daughter. I bet you'd get her home on time." There was admiration in her voice, but mirth too, an edge of mockery. She turned back to Evelyn's mother.

"Aggie's birthday is coming," Wadene said. "A school night, but she's got Fran on her side. They expect me to surrender my keys."

Beyond them, in a slot at the curb, sat Wadene's car—a 1961 Eldorado convertible, three years old but shimmering like new, sleek and pearl-colored, its top up while the weather stayed cool.

"Evelyn must come too," Wadene said. "But it seems there's a problem with homework?"

"I assure you my daughter can take a night off." Momma turned to Evelyn. *Just wait*, her look said.

Around the last curve, the Doyle ranch house—a sprawling, stuccoed hacienda roofed with Spanish tiles—came into view at the top of the rise ahead. Fran revved the old station wagon up the drive and parked in a spot shaded by crepe myrtles. Evelyn got out. Below the rise, on a level patch of open grass, she could see the faint outline of the baseball diamond Wadene Doyle had laid out when she arrived here as a bride. Evelyn was not especially fond of baseball, but she loved anything that set her free outdoors. They'd grown up running base to base down there—Ralph and the friends he sometimes brought along, Aggie and Fran, Evelyn, Grady. And always, Wadene in their midst, coach and player rolled into one.

For years they'd celebrated Aggie's birthday here on the ranch—with baseball and swimming, hot dogs, roasted marshmallows. Evelyn would have shucked her sundress in a heartbeat, put on Bermuda shorts and a shirt, grabbed a bat and gone running for the diamond. Anything but the evening Aggie and Fran had planned.

But no. She followed Fran and Grady through the hacienda's dusky, open-air entry hall and into the palm-studded atrium. Wadene greeted them from a chaise longue by the pool, a drink beside her on a small white wrought-iron table, smoke curling from the ashtray beside it. She waved Grady into the pool and spoke to Evelyn.

"I half expected Ralph might drive you over."

Fran answered. "He's going back to Odessa Saturday."

"Well, but Grady's here."

"Grady's twelve."

"Thirteen," Evelyn said. But no one paid her any mind.

"Ralph was always here before," Wadene said. "I miss those days. Besides"—her voice, her eyes, hungered—"I could use some company."

"Ralph is busy," Fran said. "He's got other things to do."

"Besides flirt with you," Aggie added, arriving among them. She had on a backless sundress in a deep, shimmery turquoise, more green than blue, the heart-shaped bodice showing off the figure she was so proud of. Her skin was smooth and pale, her hair jet black like her mother's. She'd have been pretty, Evelyn thought, except for the eye shadow, gobbed on like Cleopatra's.

"Why weren't you in school today?" Fran asked.

"Out with a *man* last night," Aggie said, her grin spreading.

Ice clinked in Wadene's drink. Behind them, oblivious, Grady splashed in the pool. For a stretch of seconds, no voice rippled the calm. Then, squealing, Aggie and Fran jumped at each other. They grabbed hands and spun like girls on the playground.

"He's twenty-six," Aggie said when she could catch her breath. "Showed up out of the blue."

"What about Vernon?" Fran asked.

"He was not available," Wadene said, "to protect his daughter's virtue."

"*You* let her go?" asked Fran.

"We reached an agreement." Wadene unfurled a cloud of smoke. She offered nothing more by way of explanation, though her husband would've been the clincher. *Not available* meant not home. *Not available* meant chasing skirts somewhere. Wadene regularly balanced her husband's indiscretions by loosening her rein on Aggie.

"We had a burger at the drive-in," Aggie said. "He poured tequila in my root beer." She made a face. "Hadn't tasted the stuff. Wadene keeps the liquor cabinet locked."

Raising an empty glass, the rancher's wife produced a ring of keys and jangled them. "I think I'll have another." She disappeared into the house.

"Coming home," Aggie said, "I made him let me drive. He was *sloshed*."

Evelyn felt laughter coming. She couldn't help it—they were funny. Fran with her blonde do, her haughty attitude. Aggie with her hand on her hip and that ridiculous eye makeup. A Technicolor raccoon, Grady called her behind her back. They were just skinny girls with hips and breasts playing dress-up.

"What's so funny?" Fran asked.

"Her," Grady said, bobbing at the side of the pool. He was pointing at Aggie. "*Look* at her." He backstroked out of reach.

Fran stuck out her tongue at him. "Look somewhere else," she said, then—fixing Evelyn with a practiced glare—"You too."

Evelyn straightened and held her gaze steady at her cousin. She didn't blink. She had the unsettling sensation that her mother was present too, inside her, looking through her eyes, daring Fran to go any farther. This moment would come back to her in her mid-forties, one day when she caught herself in an airport restroom mirror and saw her mother looking back—Momma's facial bones, her mouth, her unflinching gaze.

"Who cares about her?" Aggie said. "Let her look all she wants." She went back to her adventure of the night before.

Evelyn watched them. Aggie and Fran, their breezy voices—they were lit from within, bright as sunlight beneath the murmuring palms. Grady, too, splashing in the pool. Whatever she'd felt laughing at her friends, staring Fran down, they hadn't noticed. They didn't *see* her, their attention given over to Aggie.

"He got all whispery," she said. "Wanted me to stop along the lane here, sit with him for a while."

Aggie had refused the request, though she did allow a hand on her thigh. Recounting this moment, she pulled up the skirt of her sundress as if the imprint of his fingers lingered there. Evelyn wished for a sweater. She wished for jeans.

The final half mile of Aggie's date had proceeded smoothly, but then a finger slipped beneath elastic on her panties. And tickled. "He didn't mean to," she said. "But that's what his finger did, it *tickled*." Aggie swerved and hit the brakes. "I stopped the car right there and set him straight."

"Interesting story," Wadene said, dropping into her chaise longue. "You're lucky a scare was all you got." On the table beside her, she placed her drink and a little box of the kind that held teabags on a grocery shelf. She flipped up the box lid and pulled out a shiny chain of foil packets.

Evelyn had not seen a box of condoms before. She hadn't seen them linked.

"Put those away," Aggie said. "I would never."

"Best keep your knees together then. I'm not ready to be a grand-mother."

"We're *Catholics*. We don't believe in birth control."

"Last time I looked in the catechism"—Wadene blew a cloud of men-thol at her daughter—"I didn't find a dispensation for finger-fucking."

"That is *not* what happened."

"Be glad he didn't tickle you with more than a pinkie."

Poolside, Grady lapsed into a snickering fit. Fran shooed him away.

"I can't wait to get out of here," Aggie said. "I'm not ever coming back."

"Won't be so easy with a baby on your hip. Or two. Ask Candy Lambert what that's like."

"Candy's going to be an actress," Fran said. "A movie star."

"She's getting out of here." Aggie dismissed her environs with a wave. "When her little ones are old enough."

"Me too," said Wadene. "Soon as I finish this drink. Fame awaits me."

"It's my birthday."

"Go on, then. Celebrate. Find some grease monkey with sideburns to knock you up."

"Eavesdropper."

"You're letting them go?" Evelyn asked. "After what you heard?"

"What do you mean, *them?*" asked Fran.

"I'm not going," Evelyn said. And she didn't.

Candace Lambert was twenty years old—once widowed, twice married. While husband number two was away on an offshore oil rig, Candace regularly left their two-year-old boy with the absent husband's mother. Her dead husband's daughter—three now, a pale, wide-eyed miniature of the young mother—was dropped with the parents of the deceased. Evenings, Candace parked her car on the gravel at Otto Keene's, rolled all the windows down, ordered a burger and fries. She invited admiring high school girls to sit with her and regaled them with stories of the life that would be hers. Between bites, she sipped Jack Daniels from a gleaming flask.

Though Candace had a skeptical attitude about the confines of her current marriage, the first time around she had tried on the role of wife. She'd practiced *Mrs. Buddy Grant* as her signature so often and so well that sometimes she forgot and signed checks with her dead husband's name. Others might snicker over this lapse, but not Evelyn's mother. For reasons of her own, she thought Candace Lambert was tragic—like one of the doomed beauties in the soap operas that halted life in the Smith household every afternoon between two and three. Candace had looked lovely in black, Evelyn's mother declared, which she'd worn exclusively for the several months of her widowhood, right up to the day she walked the aisle, four months pregnant with a second child. She'd eloped with Buddy Grant. The second time around, she had the wedding she'd wanted, white dress and all. *Candlelight*, Momma said, defending Candace, her wedding, the lace dress she'd purchased with Buddy Grant's money. The dress wasn't, strictly speaking, white. It was *candlelight*.

The sun was setting when Aggie and Fran departed—a red glow filling the entryway as they walked out to the Eldorado. It looked as if they were entering an element of fire. Grady adjourned to the record collection in the Doyles' music room, leaving Evelyn poolside with Wadene.

"What are we gonna do with you?" Wadene asked. She was lying back in her chaise longue. Her eyes were closed. Evelyn thought maybe she wanted to be alone, to nap for a while before dinner.

"I've got a book," she said. "I'll go inside and read."

"I don't mean tonight." Wadene's eyes were still closed.

Evelyn didn't say anything. A breeze rustled momentarily among the palms.

"You showed some nerve back there. Standing up to them." Wadene sat up. "Might try a bit of that with your mother." She looked at Evelyn. Evelyn looked away.

"I see the way she looks at you. You always look down."

"She's my mother."

"Ralph doesn't put up with her guff."

"He makes her so mad."

"What about Grady?"

Momma loves Grady. She couldn't say that. "Grady makes her laugh" is what she said.

"And you?"

"She doesn't want a daughter like me."

"We should trade."

Evelyn pictured herself let loose here—and Aggie blinkered by her own mother, stringent, steel-willed Mathilda Smith. It was a good joke. Only years later did it occur to her that the strange woman sitting beside her that night might have meant what she said.

"If you were of age"—Wadene raised her empty drink— "I'd fill two of these and make a toast." She held the glass between them for a moment, sighting on Evelyn across the rim. "You're a smart girl, Evelyn Smith. You're not like them. Like me. Buck up."

Pockets of dark settled in the cooling spaces between them.

How? Evelyn was never sure if she said the word aloud.

"You think I know?" Wadene searched the heavens, as if the few stars that had blinked on might send an answer. She brandished her glass again. "You won't find the answer in this stuff. Or a license to marry."

Midnight approached with no sign of Aggie and Fran, no hint of Vernon's return, and Grady fading on the couch beside Evelyn. Shortly after the hallway clock struck twelve, the phone rang. Wadene shouted from upstairs that she would take it. They heard her voice briefly and then silence. Evelyn put her book down and said it was time to turn in. Grady would take his usual bed in the guest room. Evelyn knocked at Wadene's door and announced her intention to sleep in the bed opposite Grady—said she didn't want to be disturbed on a school night, didn't want to be waked when Aggie and Fran came in. Wadene gave her an odd look. She seemed on the verge of objecting but then said fine, she didn't really care.

Grady was asleep when his head hit the pillow. Evelyn had just begun to drift off when she heard Vernon Doyle's voice downstairs, the angry rise of it, broken off when Wadene let loose at him. Grady slept soundly while they went at it, didn't wake at the sound of breaking glass. It was quiet after that. One minute Evelyn was listening, the next she was coming out of a deep sleep. There was liquor in the air and fumbling at the covers and then someone sitting, the weight of him on the mattress at her knees. Then, through the fabric of her nightgown, a hand on her breast. She reached out wildly in the dark, raked fingernails down the unshaven cheek her hand slapped up against. He was up cursing. The light came on, blinding bright. And Vernon Doyle stood there, a hand to the side of his face.

Grady sat up, drugged with sleep. Wadene stood in the door, a bat in one hand, the other holding a flimsy silk wrapper closed between her breasts. She pummeled the air with curses. When she paused to catch her breath, Vernon launched into a cover story. He was sorry, he said— should have slept in the bunkhouse. After all, that's what she had suggested when he got home.

Wadene brandished her bat. "Should've whacked you when you walked in the door."

Vernon shrugged in Grady's direction. "Had a few drinks tonight."

"You stink of mezcal," said his wife.

"Didn't trust my footing," the rancher added—another plank in his alibi. The bunkhouse sat below, at the bottom of a rocky, twisting trail. "Thought better of it," he said. "Decided to bunk with Grady." Vernon's eyes flicked at Evelyn and then back down again. "What's she doing in here?"

"Sleeping," Wadene said.

"Supposed to be in town." Vernon took a handkerchief from his pocket and dabbed at the marks on his cheek. "With Aggie and Fran. Least that's what I was told." He played the confused drunk flawlessly.

"Spend a little time here," Wadene said, "you'd know which beds are occupied."

Vernon backed up to Grady's side of the room, put Evelyn's brother in front of him like a shield. Grady stood there with his hands on his hips, wide awake now and clearly having the time of his life—a comic-book superhero in pajamas—while the rancher finished his tale.

"This young man takes the same bed. Always. Every time he's here. I was gonna take the other. Should've been empty."

They were still then, like figures in a tableau. Philandering husband, indignant wife. Grady looking on. And Evelyn, cold to the bone, her palms itching to get at the rancher's face again—anything to remove the feckless look she saw there.

"He's telling the truth," Grady said, and a second hush came over the room.

No, Evelyn thought, but Wadene spoke to Grady.

"You don't know my husband."

"It was an accident," Grady said.

"He put his hands on your sister."

"You heard him. He thought the bed was empty."

Evelyn watched herself watching while Vernon played the injured party and Wadene harangued him, her bat gripped as if she might still use it. With Grady between them, so caught up in the drama of the moment he seemed to have forgotten he had a sister.

Finally, Wadene relented.

Vernon decided to risk a treacherous descent in the dark. Backing out of the room, he looked as if the bunkhouse wasn't far enough from Evelyn's nails. Wadene followed him and tossed a few dispirited curses down the staircase as he retreated. Then her bedroom door closed.

Grady turned to Evelyn. "Are you all right?"

"His hand was on me. Here," Evelyn said. She wanted to say more. She wanted to say, *How could you?* She was angry. At Vernon, yes. And Wadene. But mostly at Grady. For crediting the rancher's story—true or not. For making light of his drunken blunder.

Grady paled suddenly, as though he'd seen what she was thinking.

"Oh, Lynnie, I'm sorry." He moved to comfort Evelyn.

She backed away. "I can smell him."

"I don't think he meant to."

"I don't care. He was drunk. He—"

Evelyn had never felt so far from Grady.

"You want the light out?" he asked.

She did not. She went into the guest bathroom, changed out of her nightgown, and put on the clothes she'd brought for school. She packed everything back in her bag so she'd be ready to catch the bus in the morning. She took up her book and, with Grady behind her, knocked again at Wadene's door.

"I can't sleep," she said. "We'll wait up for Aggie and Fran."

"They're staying in town."

"Where?"

"Candy Lambert's house."

"What?"

"Fran called earlier. Before the hullaballoo. They'll be back in time for breakfast." Wadene closed the door and left her standing there.

Evelyn walked downstairs with Grady, switched on lights in the den, and sat down. She opened the book on her lap. She didn't read. Grady fell asleep, but she didn't.

The summer she turned twelve, the sounds coming from her parents' bedroom left Evelyn at the wrong end of her mother's hairbrush. She'd known for a year about the act that leads to conception, though she would have much preferred something more civilized, like the image she had conjured—entirely on her own—in the absence of specifics about the joining of sperm and egg. She had pictured a man and a woman—not her parents—dressed in their Sunday best, seated in facing stiff-backed chairs and holding hands as a kind of magical transference took place. Eventually, she had arrived at the truth about bodies, helped in part by the noises that sometimes issued from her parents' bedroom in the dead of night—bedsprings, muffled voices, cries that mixed eagerness and pain. More than once, from the bedroom her brothers shared, she'd heard Ralph shushing Grady, who wanted to know what was going on. Until one night, when Grady giggled. For the space of a heartbeat, Evelyn was appalled, hearing knowledge in Grady's giggle. And then she felt laughter, like a trigger in her throat. She put her wrist in her mouth and bit until hurt tamed the tickle itching to be heard.

The following afternoon Evelyn found herself alone with her mother, folding a pile of laundry. What happened was so predictable, so preventable, that afterward she could not stop rehearsing the scene, could not cure an aching need to reimagine her lines and come out whole on the other side. Her mother was talking, Evelyn drifting, not really paying attention, when Grady's giggle came back to her—a flutter of sound trembling at the edges of her, an answering tremor from within.

"What's so funny?"

Evelyn tried to get a hold of herself, but she felt the same tickle as the night before.

"Well?"

"A joke." This was dangerous territory. She liked it.

"Tell," said her mother. "I could use a laugh."

"Just something I heard."

"Well?"

"Last night," Evelyn said, breaking free. "What you and Daddy were doing."

Her mother was strong. She was angry. And careful. When it was over, Evelyn carried the imprints of the hairbrush in a dapple of bruises beneath her shorts. In the weeks after, she took extra care that no one see. It was the third time her mother had used a hairbrush on her. Evelyn meant for it to be the last, and to that end she set about insulating herself from Momma. She practiced the appearances of deference. She taught herself to hear if not to listen. More often than not, she succeeded.

Evelyn and Grady were at the kitchen table having a glass of orange juice when Aggie and Fran walked in, haggard, their hair wild about their faces. Aggie had an ugly egg-shaped bump thickening above her left eye and a milder bruise, barely showing at all, on her right cheek. Blood welled from a fresh nick on the bridge of her nose. She grabbed a cup towel and dabbed at her face.

"Don't ask," she said, dropping into a chair and putting her head in her arms on the table.

"What a night," Fran said. She picked up Grady's glass of juice, absently sipped from it, and put it back down.

A growling noise came from the direction of Aggie's stomach. "Sorry," she said, looking up. "I'm hungry."

"Me too," said Fran. "Starved."

"Pancakes," Grady said. "Please." Everyone who knew Evelyn loved her pancakes. Grady had confessed privately that hers were better than their mother's.

Evelyn assembled eggs, flour, sugar, bowls. Behind her, Aggie and Fran entered into a half-whispered exchange about their night in town, their stay-over at Candy Lambert's house. Grady urged them on. He thrived on gossip.

Their voices stilled at the sound of rain, heavy splatters on the roof, moving over and quickly gone.

"We're in worse trouble now," Aggie said. She looked at Fran.

"What about?" Evelyn asked.

"Never mind."

Evelyn broke eggs into the mixing bowl and switched on Wadene's

KitchenAid. As she flipped the switch again, she heard Aggie behind her at the table.

"She uses a diaphragm. You know? For birth control?"

Evelyn banged a Pyrex measuring cup on the countertop.

"What?" Fran asked.

Evelyn nodded to indicate Grady's presence at the table.

"Goody two-shoes," Aggie said. "Bet he knows more about it than you do."

"I don't want to hear another word about Candace Lambert," Evelyn said.

"She gave us fashion tips," Fran told Grady.

"Like what?"

"How to prop these up," Aggie said, cupping both hands beneath her breasts, lifting them up and together beneath her heart-shaped bodice to create the kind of cleavage Candy regularly displayed.

Grady erupted.

Aggie watched Evelyn. She didn't seem to like what she saw. "You needn't look at us like that," she said. "Someone's mother puts hers on display." She paused, as if waiting for that to sink in. Then, with her eyes on Evelyn, not seeing the look coming over Grady's face, Aggie made a tactical error. "I'm not talking about Wadene." She turned back to the table and registered the change in Grady.

"Take that back," he said, his voice curdling.

"No need to jump the fence," Aggie said. "I take it back."

But it's true, Fran mimed to Evelyn. Grady didn't seem to notice.

"Slut," he said to Aggie.

Fran grabbed him by the wrist. "You can't talk like that."

"Cocktease," Grady said to Fran.

"Grady?" Evelyn said. She could tell he was on the edge. She wasn't sure she wanted to call him back.

Grady turned to Aggie. "Dick licker."

Aggie slapped him. Grady's face went pale, the imprint of a hand coming up on his cheek—faint, then darkening, like a Polaroid photograph.

Evelyn picked up Wadene's flour scoop, dipped it into the canister, turned, and flung the flour at Aggie. She turned, dipped again, turned, and flour arced across the kitchen at Fran. The room was dead silent for a moment, a powdery cloud hovering above the kitchen table. Aggie and Fran wore masks in white that streaked up into their tangled hair. Beneath the flour, their faces were wiped of all expression. They stared. They seemed not to know what they were seeing.

Evelyn removed the apron she'd put on to mix the pancake batter, wadded it up, and dropped it on the table. "We're going home," she said. "One of you can drive us."

"What about school?" Grady asked.

"We're not going."

"What about our faces?" asked Fran. "Our hair?"

"We're leaving now," Evelyn said. She picked up her overnight bag and her book satchel from their place beside the kitchen door. Grady followed suit. They stepped out the kitchen door. Morning light poured into the atrium, palm trees stirring as the cool shifted.

Carrying kitchen towels, Aggie and Fran stepped out behind them. They dusted the flour from their faces and batted at their hair. When they were done, Aggie took the towels and dropped them into a chaise longue. By the look of her, she had begun to simmer. But the rancher's daughter didn't say a word.

Wadene's Eldorado stood just outside the entryway. The driver's side headlight was smashed, the bumper beneath it bent back, and the fender behind crumpled. The top was down. Rain splatters pocked the dusty finish, wet marks stippling the leather upholstery. They stood there as if memorizing what they saw. Then Fran palmed a ring of keys and led them to her father's station wagon.

Half a mile from the house, just beyond the cattle guard, sat Vernon's pickup truck. Fran slowed as they approached. Vernon was standing to the side, inspecting the damage his wife's car had done to the welded pipework there. Aggie rolled her window down as Fran eased the Chevy over the cattle guard and stopped. Vernon rested an arm along the bottom of Aggie's window, his cheek scabbed and swollen from the night before. He did not look happy.

"What happened to you?" Aggie asked.

"Might ask you the same," Vernon said. "Your face looks kind of like my cattle guard. I don't suppose you were driving? Face hit the steering wheel?"

"Right on both counts," Aggie said. "Satisfied?"

The rancher broke into a grim smile.

"Wadene do that to you?" Aggie asked. "Or one of your floozies?"

Vernon got red in the face. He kept his eyes on his daughter, hadn't once looked in Evelyn's direction. He seemed to be groping toward words, but Aggie didn't wait.

She turned away from him, turned to Fran, said, "Gun it," her voice blunt and ugly. Fran hit the gas, wheels spun beneath them, and the big car leaped ahead.

Evelyn turned to look back. She thought of Vernon's hand on her breast in the dark—the drift of liquor distilled with bad breath and sweat. In the years that followed, she had occasion to be grateful to the rancher. One moment with him in the dark of night and she'd been cured of men who drank.

"She's gonna be mad," Grady said as Fran drove away with Aggie, leaving them beneath the hackberry tree she'd parked beside the afternoon before.

"I don't want you in the middle," Evelyn said.

"I can sweet-talk her."

"No."

"Or play the clown. Let her chase me around the house."

Evelyn heard her brother's words, her own, against a backdrop of silence—the fields, the grazing land beyond, empty and still—their voices thin, wavering, like heat mirage.

"I can't take you with me everywhere," she said.

"You're mad at me."

"No."

"About last night. For believing Vernon."

It wasn't the rancher on her mind. It was the quiet that unnerved her, the unrevealing windows of the house she must enter, the chill of her mother's presence.

"I'm sorry, Lynnie."

"It doesn't matter. You can't fix this."

She extracted a promise from Grady—that he would stay well out of it until she called for him. He headed for a stand of trees behind the barn. She watched until he disappeared into a scrim of shadow beneath the leaves. The yard was even quieter now, the lane and the county road beyond bone white beneath the morning sun.

The hackberry stirred above her, leaves trembling in a momentary gust. Her mother would've heard the car, would've gone to a window and watched. Aggie and Fran, Vernon, Wadene—they were nothing now. Evelyn stood there summoning what courage she could. From behind her, in the trees by the wash line, a jaybird scolded. Above in the hackberry branches, a mockingbird answered.

She had loved church until sometime during her fifth year. She didn't know what Latin was, but the flow of sounds that came from the parish priest, the altar boys, entranced her. So too with her mother's voice, the blended voices of assembled churchgoers during a litany. She was ten before she realized that *prayfrus* was not a Latin word recited in response to the name of a saint but rather three distinct English words, *Pray for us*, soothingly blended by generations of repetition. Incense smelled like old men and their cigars, like old-fashioned spice cake. It swirled out of censers and rose through light that was like shade and sunshine all at once. The saints, the vestments, the colors—they enchanted her. Until one day when her mother's whispers failed to reach her.

"Sit still," she told Evelyn, her lips so close, the words like tissue paper. Evelyn tried, but there was so much to look at. She couldn't understand Ralph, on the other side of their mother, rigid as one of the statues. She stood, leaning, and tried to catch his eye. Gloved hands grasped her at the waist and sat her back down. Thumb and forefinger found the tender under-flesh on her upper arm and pinched. Evelyn gasped. She would have cried out, except that Momma took her by the chin and looked right down inside her. Words were not necessary.

When Evelyn entered the kitchen that morning after leaving the Doyles, her mother was at the sink washing dishes. She was humming. Evelyn wasn't fooled. She took a breath and plunged.

"I'm not going back there. Ever."

Her mother reached for a cup towel and dried her hands. "You will go where I say."

"Not the Doyles'. Not with Aggie and Fran."

"You will pick up the phone. Whatever you've done, you will apologize."

"No, Momma. I won't."

"We'll see about that." And her mother was gone.

Evelyn heard a dresser drawer being yanked open. She knew what her mother was getting from the drawer. In the drain tray on the counter, she saw the rolling pin, freshly washed. She picked it up. She didn't know what she was doing, but she stood there with it. Momma stopped in the kitchen doorway, hairbrush in hand.

"You wouldn't dare," she said. "Look at you. Shaking like a leaf."

Evelyn shivered. She couldn't stop. She raised the rolling pin and brought it down, her forearm ringing as the wooden cylinder slammed into the stovetop. In the quiet that rippled from the noise, she looked down. There was an ugly chip in the stove's enamel.

"How are you going to explain that to your father?"

"Maybe I'll tell him." Evelyn took a breath and steadied herself. "What you've done." She indicated the brush. "With that." Tears were close, but she held them back.

"He wouldn't believe you."

"Grady might."

"You haven't got the nerve."

Evelyn looked at her mother while her mother looked back. A fly buzzed at the window. In the far distance, almost inaudible, a tractor engine rumbled.

"Maybe I do," Evelyn said. "I am your daughter." The shaking inside her stopped.

Her mother stood there and looked at her. She looked for a long time. Then she spoke.

"Well, I never." She turned and walked away, her footsteps retreating through the house.

Never. Momma's final syllables hovered in a shaft of light that poured in from the kitchen window, dust motes dancing in the wake of her departure, the sound of her bedroom door closing. The loveliest combination of sounds Evelyn might live to hear. *Never.*

CROSSING AT THE LIGHT

ALBERT DECKER AND GRADY SMITH, JULY 14–15, 1965

ALBERT WOKE AT 6:30, aware in the instant that it was Claude's birthday. He made up the Murphy bed he'd slept in since 1934 and folded it back into the wall, bands of summer sun along the seams of the closed window blinds suspending the room in a glow that brightened perceptibly as he stood watching. He shared this modest apartment—and the package store below—with his mother, his days dispensed behind the counter, selling liquor to the locals, inhaling the dust they trailed behind them as they browsed these narrow aisles, five thousand miles from the one place he could imagine inhabiting. Still, each morning until Mrs. Decker woke—each morning was his.

After a quick breakfast of toast and jam, Albert fetched his cosmetics case from the cabinet beneath the bathroom sink and flipped the switch for the makeup lights he'd had installed around the mirror. He didn't like what he saw. He'd always enjoyed being slim, but the skin at his throat had begun to let go, a sag at his Adam's apple the brightness exaggerated. Before attending to his face, he unfastened the top shirt button and laid his collar open to the burn scar—like the negative of a shadow across his left collarbone—a private reminder of his mother's skillet, the frying grease splashed from it so many years ago that without the scar he might not credit memory.

He smoothed liquid foundation over the shadows beneath his eyes, still his best feature, set off by the wonderful lashes that Claude had so admired. He crimped them with his eyelash curler—no need for mascara—and then applied eyeliner, a thin, thin line of it. Finally, a dab of oily rouge massaged into the flesh of his cheeks until you wouldn't know it wasn't natural. Done, he leaned in, his breath fogging the mirror, and whispered his name: "Ahl-baíre." His voice took on a French accent, the only way he had pronounced his name since Claude first spoke it.

Fingernails were next. Albert took the cosmetics case and moved to the kitchen table. Yesterday morning he'd removed the polish he'd been using for years—almost clear, with just a hint of pearl. Last night he'd filed and buffed his nails, then massaged the cuticles, making of each nail a perfect oval. His hands were lovely still, the fingers long and slender, the skin smooth, with a smattering of faint, hardly noticeable liver spots.

He'd wanted something new for a while. A hint of color, perhaps, something to brighten the days. Three weeks ago—with Claude on his mind, the approaching birthday—he'd turned a page in one of his mail-order catalogs, and there it was, a translucent nail polish quickened by a blush of coral. Nothing flashy. Flashy wasn't his style.

Several months ago a stranger had come into the package store—wandered off the highway, apparently. Albert's life was Nopalito and its residents, the boundaries they had negotiated over the years. The women—some of them, anyway—treated him like one of themselves; others, like an errant child with whom they had come to a grudging truce. The men were prone to smirks, the occasional wisecrack. Or clumsy silences, not knowing what to say or where to look. The children gave him a wide berth. His temper was legendary.

The stranger was something else again, a stunning specimen of a man, his cheeks darkened by the blue-black of four o'clock shadow, a way of carrying himself that said he was at home inside the body God had given him. Albert took in the boots, the hat, the fit of the man's khakis.

"Good afternoon," he said. "And welcome. You must be lost." He was used to his voice, long since inured to the transformations it effected in men's faces. The upper register came naturally to him—a lightness in his words, a whispery lilt.

"You sell rye?" the man asked.

"We do."

"Feels cool in here. Your air conditioner running?"

By way of answer, the condenser turned on, a pitch beneath the fan whirring from the unit in the window.

"Well, then," the man said. "I'm not lost." For a leisurely half hour he wondered the aisles, pulling the occasional bottle from a shelf and seeming to study the label before he put it back. Between times his eyes were on Albert. At the end, with a pint on the counter between them, Albert let his patience off its tether.

"Surely you know that staring is rude."

"Seems to me you're asking for it. Made up like that."

"I want to look my best. Same as you." Sliding his fingertips along a shelf beneath the register, Albert flipped open the cigar box sitting there, and beneath an oiled cloth nestling in the box, touched his snub-nosed Smith & Wesson. The revolver's heft, its cold, smooth surfaces, heartened him.

"You've got nerve," the man said.

"In a place like this"—Albert glanced from the face before him to the front window, the dusty edges of the town beyond—"I'd drink up all the profits if I didn't."

The stranger laughed out loud. "You're an odd one."

"I suppose I am."

"Gerald Hamilton," the man said, extending his hand.

"Ahl-baíre." Albert took the man's hand in his. "Ahl-baíre Decker."

Gerald Hamilton screwed his eyebrows into a question.

"It's a long story," Albert said. "Perhaps another time."

The man paid and left, his presence lingering as the afternoon slipped away, the gruff timbre of his voice rippling at the edges of hearing. It was the kind of voice that came to Albert sometimes in dreams. Odd dreams these were, drained of motion, color, participants, reduced to the husk of a whisper in the dark, the prickle of whiskers at his earlobe. No words, at least none that he remembered waking.

The rare dream put him with Claude—the two of them at a sidewalk café near the Seine, a table between them and never alone, the cobblestone thick with strangers and their blurring words. Never did this clamor fade to the room on the Rue Saint-Jacques, as on the afternoon when Claude kissed Albert and led him to the bed, took off his clothes and touched him, touched him all over, nibbling at the skin of his throat and chest, his stomach and thighs—the first time he had come unabetted by dreams or his own right hand. And that smell at the back of his throat, that smell drenching the shadowed room.

His nails painted and dried, a second coat put on and dried, Albert took the stairs to the floor below. He was still not used to the open stairwell—no door at the top to unlock and lock behind him as he went down to look at his roses, no dark to descend, no locked door to negotiate when he reached the bottom. Both doors had been removed to make room for the chairlift he'd had installed early in the summer after Mrs. Decker had announced her imminent retirement from the package store. Her bones, she'd said, her declining strength. She'd let him run the business.

He was doing that already, as he'd taken pains to remind her. He tended the store and ordered more of what they needed, restocked the shelves and kept the ledgers in order. He'd taken over in the kitchen forty years ago, did all the necessary shopping. Mrs. Decker went out exactly once a week—and only with Albert beside her. Vanity forbade the use of her cane outside the apartment, so she linked her arm in his and slowly, maddeningly, they attended to her social requirements.

His days were given to the store; at breakfast and after closing time, his mother's company. Asleep, even—or waking in the night—he felt the weight of her presence a room beyond. The one time his mother took up the burden of herself was each afternoon after her nap, when she came downstairs to mind the store.

He'd had no intention of giving that up. He'd made phone calls, arranged for the chairlift to be installed. Mrs. Decker had the money, decades' worth of oil royalties collecting interest at the bank. When the crew arrived from Corpus Christi, he got out her checkbook and faced her down. While the lift was going in, he arranged to have the apartment repapered and engaged painters for the woodwork. They were almost done, their tools and buckets stashed in the back room that led from the package store to the yard. Albert crossed through the clutter and let himself out.

There wasn't much of a yard—a wide flower bed that ran from the door to the storefront, a driveway paved with crushed rock, and the carport they'd added when Mrs. Decker turned fifty and bought the car that sat beneath it, a 1938 Bentley coupe.

The flower bed was ablaze with Albert's roses—a dozen hardy vines, tea roses all, chosen for color and fragrance. Each morning of their bloom, he visited the roses.

He'd started them a decade ago, some months after the rough encounter he'd had in San Antonio, the terrible thing he might have done by way of recompense. The first had come from Grace Hoffman, a cutting she'd given him on a visit with his mother, who hadn't wanted to leave him alone on a Sunday afternoon for fear he might harm himself in her absence. Mrs. Hoffman and his mother had wandered ahead of him, stopping to admire first one planting and then another.

Drifting, emptied out, Albert tipped his head to a cluster of blossoms and closed his eyes. In the moments that slipped away before he opened them again, he breathed among roses at the Tuilleries, a scented breeze fluttering at his collar while somewhere ahead Claude and his mother practiced their charm on each other.

"Good morning!" A voice came from the street—Grady Smith, approaching Albert where he stood among his roses. The boy was like a colt, all bones and angles and unbalanced grace. He never stopped moving even when he was standing still, never stopped talking. He had lovely, curly, honey-blond hair—shorter than it ought to be, but his father was in charge of haircuts.

There wasn't anyone the Smith boy wouldn't talk to. Mrs. Decker's word for him was *fresh*, by which she meant that somebody should have put a bit in the boy's teeth by now.

"I'm on my way to work," Grady said. "Spent the night at Granny Grace's."

"Mrs. Hoffman isn't your grandmother."

"She's Janet's. Janet got me invited. Her momma is my daddy's sister—that's how we're cousins. Her daddy is Mrs. Hoffman's son—he's my uncle, but no, his mother isn't really my grandmother." The boy stopped and looked around, as if trying to get his bearings.

"It sounds confusing," Albert said.

"Seems like all the folks I know in this town are either blood kin to me or blood kin to somebody I'm blood kin to."

"I don't have family here—anywhere, really, outside these walls."

"When everybody's kin, everybody knows everybody's business."

Albert smiled. "Now *that* I understand."

"They mean well, though, the people who live here."

"I'm not so sure."

"Ralph—he's my brother—"

"I know who your brother is."

"Ralph says somebody ought to be driving that car." Grady pointed to the Bentley, which had been a riddle for the townspeople since the day it arrived at the package store.

"Everyone has ideas about the Bentley," Albert said. "What is your opinion?"

"My momma would wallop me for sass, but why don't *you* drive it?"

"I never learned to drive."

"It's a crime, Ralph says, for a car like that to sit there and rust."

"The Bentley doesn't have a speck of rust. Our mechanic takes it twice a month. He checks the tire pressure and keeps it tuned—whatever's necessary. He even takes it for a spin."

"Who's your mechanic?"

"Clayton Moore."

"You should hear what Momma says about him."

Albert was not surprised. Clayton Moore had made a second career of sniffing up skirts. Still, he was the best mechanic in the county, and Albert said as much to Grady, adding, "The man has motor oil in his blood."

"Sure is nice to look at," Grady said. Then, as if recognizing the tug his voice had betrayed, he blushed to the roots of his hair.

"Yes," said Albert. "I suppose he is."

"Hey, what do you feed your roses?" the boy asked. "They're about the prettiest I've seen."

"Eggshells and banana peel."

Grady put his nose to a whorl of petals. "Mmmmm," he said.

"They were chosen for their bouquet," Albert told him, saying *boo-káy* instead of *bó-kay*.

Grady scrunched his brow. "I thought a bouquet"—he followed Albert's example—"was a bunch of flowers, you know, picked and put in a vase."

"The French use it to describe the scent."

"Where did you get them? Your roses?"

"Cuttings. This one your Granny Grace gave me." Albert pointed to the cluster Grady had smelled. "The rest came from Miriam Koehn's rose garden. Rupert let me take the cuttings after Miriam passed."

"Know what I heard? I heard Mr. Koehn wooed Granny Grace when they were young. Don't you love that word? *Wooed?* Momma says he'd marry her this afternoon if she'd say yes this morning. Evelyn—she's my sister, I guess you know that too—Evelyn says it's ridiculous at their age, all that love stuff."

A bee buzzed past Albert's ear and dived into a rose.

"Can you picture it?" Grady asked. "Mr. Koehn kissing Granny Grace?"

"Kissing is private. It's not for us to judge."

"Would you kiss someone? Now? Ten years from now?"

"What a person feels inside," Albert said, "sometimes that doesn't change with age. The heart wants what it wants."

He'd been seventeen that summer with Claude, and thirty-two before a man touched him again—a young soldier in transit six months after Pearl Harbor, an exchange of glances in the San Antonio bus station, two minutes against a downtown alley wall at three in the morning. In the years that followed, when the hunger was on him and would not be hushed, Albert took the bus to San Antonio perhaps a dozen times. He felt no shame afterward on the bus ride south, but what happened with the men he met—it wasn't what he wanted. The driver always woke him when they pulled up to the stop in Nopalito. Stepping down from the bus, he had a rancid taste at the base of his tongue, and the least of it was that he'd taken a stranger's cock into his mouth.

But then he met the married man, a successful businessman, from the looks of him—expensively tailored suits, lush silk ties, gartered socks. He was an older man, had a wife, grown sons, and grandchildren already old enough to be in school. Albert spotted him in the lobby of the Gunter Hotel—restless, casting about, clearly looking. He put himself in the man's path, had lunch with him, followed along afterward to a lovely room upstairs. They had sex immediately, talked a while, and then had sex again. They talked the sun down, had room service for dinner, had sex a third time. As dark descended and the downtown lights blinked on, they talked some more. Albert never knew the married man's name. "Call me Bill" is what he said when asked. "I'll be back," he said as Albert dressed for leaving. "In a month. Please say you'll come." He put his arms around Albert from behind, put lips to his ear, whispered, "We'll have lunch," the promise of their bodies biding in the words.

Six times they had lunch at the Gunter. Six times they went to Bill's room afterward. In bed, the married man was gentle—no roughness ever, no penetration. He wouldn't kiss or be kissed on the mouth. He would curl up behind Albert, reach around and touch him—nipples, belly, hips, the tender spots below—take him in hand and whisper, stroking the while until he made him come, then turn and let Albert do the same. Bill trembled when they were in bed together, as if beneath his gentleness a desperate hunger ached untamed.

When they weren't making love, they talked, though no family names, no place names surfaced in the married man's stories. Albert observed no such caution. He talked about his mother, the package store, the residents of Nopalito. He showed Bill his scar and told him about his father. It wasn't that he lacked for conversation otherwise. His days were marked by words, but they were only sounds rehearsed to fill up space. And when his neighbors spoke to Albert, their eyes went here and there, vacantly. On the rare occasion when a gaze crossed his, he could see clearly that not one among the people with whom he spent his days wanted him to say a word about the life unfurling inside. Across a lunch table from Bill, though, or side by side on their long afternoons in bed, Albert felt that he was seen.

Finally, on the evening of the sixth visit, he found himself talking about Paris. He spoke of the cafés, the long walks, the delirium he'd felt eluding his mother and going out alone with Claude.

"So," Bill said when the story was over, "a boyhood crush. And you're still not over it."

"A crush."

"Puppy love," Bill said. "You were seventeen." His voice, his smile, had not changed. What came out of his mouth was cordial and affectionate as before.

"It was the one chance I had."

"Everyone has second chances."

"I haven't."

"But you were so young."

"Life gives what it gives. Life doesn't care how old you are."

On the street below, tires screeched and a horn honked. As the noises rippled into quiet, Albert wished he'd kept Claude to himself.

Bill got out of bed, slipped on his shirt, and walked to the window. He stood there for a while, his face lit up by the light beyond.

"Get out of that town," he said, still facing the window.

"And go where?"

"Here." Bill's wave took in the city beyond the window.

Albert laughed out loud. He had been to San Antonio.

"Look at all these people," Bill said, as if awed by the throng below. He turned back to Albert. "You could find someone."

"I have."

This time Bill laughed. He came back to bed and they made love again.

A seventh date was proposed and agreed to. A seventh time, Albert rode the bus north. A seventh time he arrived as planned. Bill wasn't in the lobby. Albert had lunch alone in the dining room, willing a calm he didn't feel, and then sat in the lobby until he felt conspicuous. He spent the afternoon on the street outside the hotel, walking to the corner, crossing at the light, walking back opposite the hotel to the Majestic Theater, where he stood beneath the marquee for a few minutes before retracing his steps to the hotel entrance. And then again. He'd made a pact with himself—that he must keep the hotel entrance in sight, that if he looked elsewhere for the space of a minute, Bill would choose that interval for his arrival and would be inside the hotel by the time Albert looked back. If he looked away, he said to himself, he would never see Bill again.

At ten that evening he walked to the bus station and boarded the last bus. He was surprised by his calm on the ride south. He assumed that Bill came to San Antonio on business, though he had no idea what the business might be or who Bill met with. Or where. He knew that anything could have happened to prevent Bill's meeting him today—a family emergency, a development at work that sent him elsewhere or kept him home. Hearing Bill talk, Albert would have placed him somewhere in West Texas, but he'd known better than to ask. It didn't matter. He couldn't cross over into the world Bill inhabited outside the room they had shared at the Gunter. It was likely that business would bring Bill back to San Antonio, but Albert had no way of knowing when, and he couldn't imagine Bill picking up the hotel phone, asking for a long-distance operator, placing a call to the package store.

He had taught himself to live without hope, had cautioned himself against the surge of expectation he'd felt each time Bill set another date with him. On the ride home, as the bus pulled into sleepy towns along the highway, the face in the window frightened Albert—pale and glassy eyed, like someone bleeding inside. Home again, stepping off the bus, he was a hundred some miles south of the Gunter—with no way back to where he'd been the morning before, approaching the hotel doors, knowing that just beyond, someone would be waiting.

By nine, Albert was done with his roses and back upstairs. He knocked on the bedroom door. While Mrs. Decker made herself presentable, he prepared her breakfast—one egg, over easy, with toast and coffee. He opened the blinds, and morning sun lit up the dining table. He poured coffee for himself and, when she arrived at the table, sat opposite her.

His mother had turned into a fragile little woman. Her bones had gone brittle, her spine curved, so that when she walked she carried her head out front like a bird. She was a living study in what age does to a body—the wreckage. Her hair was the exception, still thick and luxuriant, the color a variant of strawberry blonde she'd picked out of a magazine recently when she was in the mood for a change. It made her look like an aged tart, but it was what she wanted.

"Was that Grady Smith you were talking to?" she asked.

"How did you know I was talking to anyone?"

"That child is loud." She nodded toward the window that overlooked the driveway. "What was he doing here?"

"He talks to everybody, you know that."

"No need to encourage him. You'll never be rid of his nonsense."

"I seem to be rid of most everyone."

"You have a town full of adults. Grady Smith is not a wise choice."

"By which you mean?"

Mrs. Decker spoke as if to the slice of toast she had dipped in the yolk on her plate. "This isn't San Antonio."

"Don't," Albert said. And the table lapsed into silence.

Not speaking had served them well at times, as with the trips to San

Antonio she'd just alluded to. Mrs. Decker had tended the store on the days he was gone; she hadn't asked about the purpose of his absences. Once, during the half year of his trips to see Bill, she had commented on the frequency of his days in San Antonio, but she hadn't pursued the subject. Even after his final excursion to the city—though he had limped into the apartment and gone to bed for days, though surely she had been beside herself with worry—she hadn't asked him to explain.

Sometimes now a day passed without a dozen words between them. It was not the cure Albert would have prescribed. Still, this morning he watched his mother eat and didn't say a thing.

Her breakfast finished, she reached for a pack of cigarettes at center table and took out the first of her three cigarettes for the day, the only one she smoked indoors—an agreement reached between them years ago. The second cigarette came at shortly before two, just after her nap, the third at closing time. Because Albert hated breathing smoke, she had both of these in the driveway. But the first one each day, the best of the three, the one she wanted most, this one she smoked at the table after breakfast.

Lighting up, she took a deep drag, held the smoke for a moment, and then exhaled.

"I know what day it is," she said.

Albert did too.

She put her cigarette in its groove on her ashtray and reached across the table. Albert took his hands off the table and put them in his lap.

"Your hair looks nice," she said. "I did a good job this time, don't you think?"

"Yes," he said. "It's fine."

His hair had been black before he started going gray. It was black now, but without luster, just inky dye coating every strand. When he'd been young, people had reached for his hair, struck by its blue-black shine. "Comme des plumes d'oiseau," Claude had said, touching it.

"Write to him," she said.

"We've been over this."

"What will you do?"

"It's too late for letters."

His mother looked as if she would slap him if she could. Raising herself slowly from the table, she plucked her cigarette from the ashtray. "What about this mess, then?" She took a drag and blew a burst of smoke toward a section of wall beside her bedroom door, where the papering job was not quite finished, the plywood surface covered with meshed canvas backing.

"We could tear this place down and build a real house," Albert said. "We have the money."

"You don't have a dime."

"The ledger downstairs says otherwise."

"What you have you got from me. All of it. The roof over your head—"

"My hours are recorded."

Mrs. Decker reached for her cane and stepped away from the table. Reaching the mantelpiece above the stove the original builders had set into the wall and framed in like a fireplace, she turned and cast a steady gaze at him.

Albert was angry but sure of himself. His mother was a formidable opponent, but facing up to her over the chairlift had changed things between them. He wasn't sure she knew that yet.

"You'll get nothing from me," she said.

"You have five days to think so."

Mrs. Decker faltered. Clearly, he'd confused her. As if to buy herself time, she took from the mantelpiece a delicate porcelain bluebird he'd given her at Christmas and seemed to study it.

"This is Wednesday." Albert poured calm into his voice; he knew that would further unsettle her. "Before the week is out, I will tally my hours. I will figure an hourly rate. I can even adjust for inflation. Monday morning I will have a bill for you. You will write me a check."

By way of response, Mrs. Decker threw the porcelain bluebird at him.

Albert caught it. *Reflexes*, he said to himself. *Luck.*

His mother crossed to the unfinished section of wall, rustled at the edges of the meshed backing, and pulled a section of it loose. "Finish it yourself," she said.

Carefully, he set the figurine on the floor, put his foot on it, put his weight down, crushing it, and ground his heel. Crossing the room, then, he calmly took the stairs down, grabbed the remaining roll of wallpaper from the clutter the workers had left, and walked to the burn bin out back, an enclosure he'd constructed of hardware cloth held up at the corners by electric fence posts. Setting the roll of paper atop the cardboard liquor boxes discarded there, he lit the pile and watched it burn.

When he got back upstairs, his mother was at the table lighting a cigarette. Two freshly stamped-out butts lay in the ashtray.

Albert walked to the whatnot that stood where his bed folded into the wall. Pocketing his wallet and keys, he turned back to her. A thin stream of smoke rose, curling from the cigarette at her fingertips.

"I'm going to the icehouse," he said. "Is there anything you want?"

"I miss bacon," she said, tapping ashes into the tray. "Get me a few slices of bacon."

For so long, his life had revolved around his mother, an unspoken memory of how they came to be alone together, leaving his father behind. That was in early winter just after Albert turned ten. They had moved to a new farm in Hempstead County, Arkansas, not far from Hope. Josiah Decker was an itinerant farmer with a fondness for liquor and cards. Albert knew little else about the man who had sired him— nothing about how his parents had met, how a man swayed by whim, by volatility, had lured Ermalee Brown away from her elderly father and his respectable north Texas roots.

It was cold the day things got out of hand. They had butchered the day before, and wisps of smoke curled from the smokehouse against a slate-gray sky. Albert was in the kitchen with his mother preparing supper when the door opened and his father stepped in from the porch.

One of his moods had taken Albert, a moonstruck giddiness that lifted him trembling like a kite.

"Daddy," he said, breathless, dancing in place, "we made shoo-fly pie. Momma let me help."

"What have I told you?" his father said. "Get a hold of your voice. Don't jump around like that."

"You mean like this?" Albert did a wild imitation of himself, his hands unleashed, airborne. He meant no disrespect. It's just that he was happy. And as his mother often remarked, he had a short memory for disapproval. Something else, too. He'd begun to learn at school that it was fun to flaunt himself.

For a moment his father merely looked at him. When he moved, he moved so fast Albert didn't see it. He heard, then felt his head and back slam into the kitchen wall. It was not the first time he'd been knocked around for misbehaving, but always before he'd been alone when his father struck—and never a mark on him afterward that his mother might see.

There were distant, hollow moments when Albert could not hear. But he could see. His mother pleading with his father, her hands on his forearm. His mother shoved violently, colliding into the stove. His mother in a frenzy at the stove and turning with the skillet, the handle in both hands, underhanded, struggling with his father, the grip of his hands at her forearms.

Albert meant to help them. He didn't know how—only that the skillet must be returned to the stove, that if it could be righted the three of them might take up where they had left off. As he reached his parents, grappling at the stove, the balance shifted—a jerk in the hands at the skillet, a splash of grease. Albert heard himself cry out, and then it was over, the skillet of frying cutlets back on the stove and his mother rushing him into the bathroom, his father at the door in a frenzy of blame. If Albert had listened. If his mother had stayed out of it.

In the days that followed, keeping his father, his mother, at bay, Albert tended the burn. When it was healed, he hid the scar from everyone except himself—and years later in Paris, Claude.

His father was apologetic and then quiet and then brooding. Albert tried to stay out of his way, but one afternoon beneath the milking shed, Josiah Decker pushed him against a wall, squatted to his level, held him there, and looked him in the eye—no words, no sign of mercy.

Hours later, as Albert's mother approached her seat at the supper table, his father reached up and grabbed a fistful of her hair. He didn't even look at her, just tightened his grip, pulled, held. And released. Albert's mother didn't cry out. When she was let go, she cleared her face of all expression and sat down. But Albert had seen her face before, had seen the rage that flamed up, the steely will with which she tamped it down.

Over breakfast several days later, Josiah Decker came down with the flu. Albert listened from his place at the kitchen table, his mother's voice soothing, attentive, as she put his father to bed. Returning without so much as a word, she crossed the kitchen and disappeared into the pantry, searching for something, from the sound of it. Moments later, she set a small, much-worn suitcase on the table and, beside it, a tea canister he hadn't seen before. Raising a finger to her lips, she handed the canister to Albert and picked up the suitcase. On the porch she took Albert's winter coat from its hook and handed it to him, removed his father's winter coat and buttoned it about herself. She walked out to the car shed his father had built alongside the barn and swung the suitcase into the back seat of the aged Model T.

"Get in," she said, directing her attention to the crank.

When they got to the road, his mother turned right, instead of left toward town.

"Where we going?" Albert asked.

"Away from here."

"In Daddy's car?"

"This was my father's car," she said. "I took it. I guess I'm taking it again."

"Open that," she said, indicating the canister in Albert's lap. Inside was a roll of bills and beneath them, the weight of coins.

"I've been saving," she said. "Count it. That's all we've got."

They passed through Texarkana and drove on, a day and night of dusty roads and far-flung, hardscrabble towns. When they arrived in

San Antonio, his mother stopped. She seemed satisfied with the distance they'd put between themselves and his father, and with the money in her canister, they could make a start.

Two years later a letter made its way to Albert's mother. Her father had died, leaving a considerable estate to his only child. "He was old," she said. "There was oil beneath the land." As if that would suffice by way of explanation—like what she'd said when Albert asked if someone mightn't wonder what had happened to his father. "I'm a widow. That's all they need to know."

For most of a day, then, his mother sat at her dresser with the letter from her father's attorney. She let Albert brush her hair, smiled absently as he stood beside her and experimented with her makeup on his own face in the mirror, a ritual that had come of their time together, of the close quarters they shared—a shabby bedroom, stingily furnished, the wallpaper in tatters. His mother had not complained, but Albert knew she hated this room and the rooms beyond, brimming with boarders and no space to call her own.

"We'll get a fresh start," she said when morning came. She drove them out of San Antonio into the brush country that stretched south toward the Valley. The car broke down as they approached Nopalito. The place was tiny. The locals took his mother, her story, at face value.

"We'll stay for a while," she said. And so they had.

Grady Smith was behind the counter at the icehouse.

"Where is Ramón this morning?" Albert asked.

"The ice truck is here. I can't handle the big blocks of ice."

Candace Meyer pulled into the drive out front. She got out of her car and came in through the garage-style door that opened to the street. Hair swept back, spaghetti straps, lipstick, impeccable shoes—Candace looked dressed for a photo shoot, a clear signal she was having the rare good day.

"Good morning, Al," she said.

Albert winced.

"Oops. Good morning, Albert." She didn't say that right either, though he didn't mind. It was a pleasure just to look at Candace on a day like today.

She handed her list to Grady and followed him while he pulled items from the shelves. Albert didn't need a list. He knew where to find what he wanted, steering clear of Grady and Candace, though he rather liked the sound of their voices—up and down the aisles, and then Grady at the cash register, ringing up her purchases.

Afterward, Grady approached him. "Anything I can do for you?"

"Mrs. Decker is in need of bacon."

Grady's face broke open with merriment.

"I thought you had manners," Albert said. "What are you grinning at?"

"My momma would go up in smoke if I called her Mrs. Smith. Sorry, though. Let's get you some bacon."

Albert followed the boy to the refrigerated display case at the rear of the store. Grady slid open the panel at the back and pointed.

"That's the last of a slab," he said, and it was—about four inches left of the cured pork belly. "But look at the marbling. Lots of meat in this bacon, hardly any fat."

"It's fine," Albert said. "I'll have six slices, please."

"I'm always grinning when I shouldn't," Grady said. "Drives my daddy crazy. Ralph too." Turning to the sink in the corner behind him, he dampened a towel and started wiping down the slicer that sat beside the display case. "No harm meant," he said, as if explaining himself to the slicer. "By grinning, I mean. Sometimes I'm really bad. Somebody will say something to my momma, not even talking to me, and I burst out laughing. Momma doesn't like it, but I swear—I can't help myself. People are so funny, don't you think?"

Grady adjusted the slicer and flipped a switch. The slicer blade whirled, humming. Instead of swinging the pronged safety plate into place behind the bacon to secure it during the slicing, the boy locked his thumb around the handle and wedged the bacon into place by applying pressure with his fingertips.

Albert opened his mouth to say something, but Grady was moving so fast—back and forth with the bacon while thick slices dropped onto the butcher paper below the blade.

Under his breath Grady counted slices. On the fifth he cried out, spinning in a circle behind the slicer. Stopping, he held up his right hand. The middle finger, its tip sliced neatly off, oozed blood like a hose set to drip. Grady looked at Albert, looked back at his finger—the two of them frozen, entranced, until the welling red at Grady's fingertip broke streaming down over his hand.

Without knowing he had moved, Albert found himself behind the display case. He pulled a swath of paper towels from the dispenser on the wall and tried to get at the blood dripping from Grady's clenched fist.

"It hurts," Grady said. "It hurts." And then a sound from between his teeth. *Sssss. Sssss.*

"We must get this seen to," Albert said. "Come. I'll walk you."

"What about the store?"

"If anyone arrives while you're gone, Ramón can be summoned."

"What if he's mad?" Grady said. "I need this job." The boy was shivering.

"Can't worry about that now. Let's get you to the doctor."

As it turned out, there wasn't much a doctor could offer. Grady didn't have a cut that could be stitched; the tip of his finger was gone. It wasn't a deep slice. The finger would ooze, but it was done bleeding.

"It hurts," Grady said. "Hurts bad."

"A fingertip has lots of nerve endings," Doctor Manning said. "They're not happy about the damage you've done with that slicer."

Albert asked what could be done for the pain.

"Novocaine would deaden it," said the doctor. "Give the boy a couple hours relief." He turned to Grady. "You want a shot of novocaine?"

"I hate shots. I'll tough it out."

"I'll splint it then. Otherwise, every time you touch something . . ."

Doctor Manning rummaged in one of his cabinets and produced a U-curved piece of metal ready-made to enclose a finger. Gently, he put Grady's finger into the splint, taped it in place, wrapped it in several layers of gauze, and taped that fast.

"Ralph is gonna get a kick out of this," Grady said. "Looks like I'm shooting the bird. See? I don't even have to pull back the other fingers." The boy stood there with his hand raised, the middle finger protruding thick and stiff, a parody of the common gesture.

"Now who's grinning?" he asked Albert.

It was nearly eleven when Albert got back to the package store. He knew Vinnie Miller would be waiting. Vinnie needed his morning pint, and there was nowhere else to get it.

"I'll be down soon," Albert said, nodding at the groceries he'd retrieved when he walked Grady back to the icehouse. He let himself in by the private entrance.

Vinnie was a short man with an impressive belly, a face wrecked by alcohol. He'd been handsome once—and cocky about it—a ringleader. When they were young, he'd simper and mince for his buddies when they spotted Albert on the street. But not if he was alone when their paths crossed. The look he gave Albert then, the eyes shifting between irony and something else. Fear, Albert thought. Recognition.

Once when Vinnie's drinking could still be described as intermittent, when he'd begun to thicken but still carried himself like a bantam rooster—once years ago he'd made a pass at Albert. He came into the store at closing time and made his way to the farthest corner in the back, called to Albert, asked him a question about the brandy shelved there. Albert reached for a bottle and, turning, found himself pinned, the shelf at his back, Vinnie's face at his chest.

"You know you want it," Vinnie said, his voice raw with need. "Please." He grabbed Albert's hand and held it to his trousers at the crotch.

Albert wasn't rattled. Live very long in a small town and sooner or later you surprised most folks with their pants down around their ankles. He was inclined to think he'd seen more than his share of people at such moments. In their contempt they thought of him as harmless.

All this passed through his head in an instant while he stood there, his back against the liquor shelves, his hand at Vinnie's zipper. There wasn't a lot going on there anyway. What was that line out of Shakespeare about what drink does to a man? *Makes him stand to and not stand to.* More than once, at sixteen, Albert had jerked off with his English textbook open to those words. They wouldn't do the trick now. He removed his hand from Vinnie's equipment and put both hands on the drunken man's chest. Pushing, Albert found his fingers at the shirt front, undoing the buttons. Vinnie's eyes closed, waiting. Albert opened the shirt to expose the beginnings of a paunch.

"Look at you," he said, and Vinnie opened his eyes. "I'll put my hands on a dog's pecker before I pleasure you." It was cruel to hurt a hurting man. Unnecessary. But Albert had learned the weapon of words. To turn harm back on its source.

Something else, too, that he would barely admit to himself. When Vinnie croaked *please*, Albert had heard an answering desperation in himself. There'd been a moment when he might have done what he knew how to do with his hands, his mouth. He was thankful later that he hadn't. He'd eluded the contempt Vinnie would have felt obliged to heap on him, the furtive couplings that would have ensued, nothing between one man and the other but cock hunger.

Claude, he wrote, *it's your birthday.* He said the name to himself as Claude had said it—"Clode"—and wrote the date. *July 14, 1965. Bastille Day.* On the afternoon of this day in 1927, walking the Place St. Michel with Claude, he'd known little of the French Revolution, nothing of the Paris prison stormed at the outset.

Le quatorze juillet. Claude had made him say it over and over, smiling as Albert mangled *juillet,* its French deliciousness gone bad in his mouth.

You never said how old you were. (He'd thought thirty, his mother thirty-five, as they guessed with Claude at the table between them, offering no clue.) *How old are you today? Did you marry, Claude? You said you would. Were there children? They'd be grown and gone by now. Do they have sons and daughters of their own? Are you with them today? Where are you, Claude? Did you make it through the war?*

Most days, with Mrs. Decker downstairs at the register, Albert wrote to the page, to his journal itself, to a perfect version of himself looking over his shoulder. Now and then he wrote to Claude—always on July 14, opening a new journal to begin again. For years he'd written to the man he'd known in Paris—an older friend, but young, still—his lover of one perfect afternoon. But the decades, the package store, his mother's company, the face in the mirror. By degrees he'd realized he was years—and then decades—older than the lovely smiling man he'd known in Paris.

Albert didn't read his journals, not even the previous day's entry. It was the ritual he needed. Someone, a stranger, might find them when he was gone, might turn the pages, reading this record of his days. Or burn them—with the package store ledgers, the books of check stubs.

There were thirty-nine of them now, thirty-nine leather-bound journals—the newest on the table before him, with today's entry on its first page, and thirty-eight in a locked cabinet beside the whatnot that served as his nightstand. The first had been a gift from Claude on his own birthday. Albert had apportioned the pages to last for a year. In June of succeeding years, Mrs. Decker had driven him to a stationery shop in downtown Corpus Christi, where he'd purchased a new leather-bound journal in time for Claude's birthday, when he would start the cycle again.

During the first year, Claude had written to Albert, and Albert wrote back. He loved the thought of their letters crisscrossing the Atlantic. He took delight in mailing a letter to Claude, in the way the postmistress looked at him, uncomprehending. Albert grinned at her. The letters made him happy. He would find a way to see Claude again. In the spring, when his mother suggested they take another trip, he was elated. Paris, he said, and she said no. He pitched a fit, but she stuck with no.

Stop, Albert wrote to Claude—and put an end to his own correspondence. The letters from Paris kept coming.

Each year in the spring Mrs. Decker suggested a sojourn abroad. Each year Albert said Paris. Each year she said no. Finally he dropped all mention of Paris. When his mother broached the subject of travel, he said no. Eventually spring came and went with no talk of vacationing—not a word about Paris, except in letters from Claude, which became ever sparser as the years ticked by. Finally his letters stopped coming at all. By the spring of '45, with the war in Europe drawing to a close, Albert had come to think of Claude as a spirit from another life, like a saint to whom a believer might pray. Even the name was gone now—*Claude*—except in Albert's journals, and then only on days when he was at peace with the life he'd been given, its narrowing compass.

In 1951 several young men approached Albert on the street in Corpus Christi. Mrs. Decker beside him, he had just purchased his next journal. They didn't like the way he looked, these roving boys, so full of themselves—and impossibly young, no mark of worry on their imperious brows. Albert had been jabbed in the chest before, had learned to empty his face until the hot words cooled. Clutching his shopping bag to his chest, he waited for the leader to be done.

This time was different. One of the group didn't like what he thought he saw in Mrs. Decker's face as she looked on. Her response included the word *hoodlum*. The boy shoved her and she stumbled. Albert put his hand on the boy's arm, a plea only, and the boy hit him—hard—against the side of his mouth. The pain Albert could have taken, the taste of blood on his tongue. It was the tidings that loosed his tears, his terrible anger—the message he intuited in the boy's fist. *There is no place for you.* A howl came up out of Albert. Weeping, he raged at the boys, spittle flying in their faces with the curses he pronounced on them and their kin down through the ages. He raged until the boys were gone and the street was empty. He took his mother's hand, then, and they went home. Shortly thereafter he bought the Smith & Wesson and secreted it beneath the register. In succeeding years he purchased his journals by mail order. He never went back to Corpus Christi.

There was, still, the occasional bus ride to San Antonio, the rare anonymous encounter there, until a night several years later when things got ugly. A wiry carpenter who looked to be forty or so took the stool beside Albert at a late-night diner on Broadway. He had a story, a very long one, the kernel of which was that his wife had left him. He invited Albert to his house for coffee, laced it with honey, with bourbon. He walked Albert down a hallway on the pretext of showing him the guest room, and in the dark, against a wall, after a quick bit of business with buckles and zippers, the carpenter got rough. "I know you want it," he rasped, thrusting. "Tell me you like it."

The man was gone almost before he was done—through an open door at the end of the hall. The door closed, a lock clicked, and Albert was alone. He hurt. He was bleeding. He stumbled into the bathroom and used toilet paper to wipe blood and semen from between his buttocks and thighs. He flushed the mess, put a fresh wad of toilet paper in place at his anus, pulled his shorts and trousers into place, and stepped out of the bathroom.

The hall was empty, the door at the end still closed.

He walked toward the light at the other end of the hallway and arrived at the kitchen. Keys lay on the table where the man had dropped them. Empty coffee cups sat there—a jar of honey, a just-opened bottle of bourbon. On the stove sat a skillet of grease flecked with bits of bacon, a whitish swirl in the pan where the drippings had begun to congeal. A banana peel lay limp on the countertop nearby.

Albert carried the liquor to the sink and poured it down the drain. He struck the bottle against the sink's enameled edge and listened to quiet spilling back into the room. No sign of life from down the hallway. He studied the hand holding the bottle neck, the glistening shards that bloomed there. He lay the bottle neck on the counter and reached for a box of kitchen matches sitting nearby. Opening the box, he admired the rows of match heads lined up inside, each neatly capped in red phosphorus. He pulled a match from the box, struck it, and lit the burner beneath the bacon grease, turning the knob so that the flames leapt up, purring beneath the skillet.

The banana peel felt providential—its proximity to the skillet, Albert's knowing that if it were dropped into the pan when the bacon fat got hot enough, there would be dramatic spatters, a grease fire that could be left to do what fire can do. He didn't know later whether it was in him to do what he'd seen could be done. He knew only that for a stretch of moments his world had shrunk to a skillet, a ring of fire, a banana peel. When the grease began to smoke, he switched the burner off and the spell was broken. He turned for a last look at the carpenter's kitchen. This time his gaze lit on the ring of keys at center table. He took up the keys and let himself out. He locked the door and pocketed the keys. He did not look back.

Nothing really changed, or so it often seemed to Albert. Yesterday he'd confronted his mother, broken a figurine she loved, burned wallpaper they needed. He'd watched Grady Smith slice off the tip of his finger. Today he was back in the package store doing what he always did. True, he was summing up the hours he'd put in since they'd opened the place, but that seemed little different from the bookkeeping tasks he'd always set himself. He was busy with figures when a honking horn roused him.

Out front, behind the wheel of the family Ford, sat Grady Smith's mother Mathilda, and beside her in the front passenger seat, her younger son, his splinted hand waving at Albert.

Mathilda Smith was a stunning woman, a sunstruck blonde who would have looked at home on the cover of a movie magazine. She had the face, the hair, the curves, the come-hither look. Albert wasn't fooled. He knew the hardness, the cruelty, a woman like Mathilda could hide beneath the smile she flashed at him.

"I want to thank you," she said. She'd rolled her window down as Albert approached. "For getting my son to the doctor. He's been given the rest of the week off. We've baked gingersnaps." She nodded at the seat beside her, where presumably the cookies waited. "Grady will say his thank-you in person—you don't mind?—until business picks up?"

Before yesterday Albert's acquaintance with this woman's son had been limited to breezy exchanges when their paths crossed downtown. Now here was Grady, bearing baked goods and gratitude. But his company would make for a welcome diversion.

"I'd be delighted," Albert said, whereupon Grady got out of the car with the cookies and Mathilda drove off.

Inside, Albert took the plate of gingersnaps and set them on the counter beside the register. He handed one to Grady and took another for himself.

"Sorry about this," Grady said. "Momma's got her feathers ruffled."

"Pardon?"

Albert's question seemed all the permission the boy needed. The words came pouring out of him.

"She's miffed at Daddy. 'Scuse me, it started with Ralph—he back-talks her. Time Daddy shows up, she's got Ralph worked up and he won't apologize though she says he's got to, says Daddy's got to make him." Grady studied his cookie. "Won't nobody make Ralph do a thing when Momma's got him cornered." He took a bite, chewed, swallowed. "Momma fumes and not a word of sorry out of Ralph and Daddy bowing out—not always but yesterday he did—and there's Momma hoppin' madder than before."

The boy stopped and finished his cookie. "I guess I'm telling more than I ought."

"Perhaps," Albert said. "But your story is most engaging."

So Grady explained how things got settled at the Smith household. Sometimes he charmed his mother out of her bad mood. Others, his father got her in the bedroom and shut the door and they didn't come out until morning. Sometimes morning came, and Grady's mother worked herself up again. If she didn't feel sufficiently appreciated, this was bound to happen, as it had on the morning in question. The penance she'd exacted was to leave husband and children to their own devices for the morning. She had put on one of her nice dresses—*revealing* was the word Mrs. Decker would have used—perfumed herself and decided on a drive to the county seat. Window shopping would ease her ire.

"Momma likes to look at pretty things," Grady said. "She likes to eat a meal she hasn't cooked. Hey, what do you think of her gingersnaps?"

"Delicious," Albert said. "We must save some for Mrs. Decker. She has quite the sweet tooth."

"Why do you call her Mrs. Decker?"

"You must have noticed," Albert said, "that widowed women, especially widowed women of a certain age, are all called Mrs. here." When they'd arrived in Nopalito, his mother hadn't turned thirty-five. But she'd introduced herself as Mrs. Decker. And that was that. No point in saying more to Grady. No point in explaining that his habit of calling his mother Mrs. Decker had its roots in the bitterness that had brewed between them over Paris.

"What is her first name?" Grady asked.

Albert bit into his gingersnap and chewed. "I'm tempted," he said. "But Mrs. Decker would not be pleased."

"You don't like it when folks call you Al."

"Albert either."

"Tell me how you say it. Tell me and I'll try."

"Ahl-baíre," Albert said. "With the accent on the second syllable. It's not that hard."

"Ahl-baíre." Grady pronounced the name distinctly. "It sounds so cosmopolitan."

"Precisely."

"My daddy wouldn't like it. My daddy wants people to say everything the way they always have. I'm not my daddy's favorite. Evelyn is, so that's okay. I'm my mother's favorite. Everybody has favorites. If they say otherwise, they're lying." The boy's hairpin turns, his honesty, were breathtaking.

"Who's your favorite?" Albert asked.

"Evelyn. Momma wouldn't like it, but I'll not tell her."

The compressor turned on, and the window unit dropped into a lower register, churning cool into the shop.

"Who's yours?" Grady asked.

For a moment Albert lost the thread, but that didn't seem to bother his interlocutor. Clearly, Grady could handle both ends of the conversation.

"Bet yours is your momma. 'Scuse me. Mrs. Decker."

"No," Albert said. The word came out as a whisper.

"Who then?"

"A person I met in Paris. The only friend I ever had."

"It's hard to have friends here. I don't know that I have any. Besides Janet and Evelyn. I'm not sure they count, being kin and all."

"I see you talking to people all over town."

"I fluster folks." Grady shrugged. "They don't let on, but I can tell."

The bell on the shop door chimed, and Albert looked to see who'd come in. Robert Wahrmund nodded in his direction and turned into an aisle. Moments later he appeared with a bottle of his usual and set it on the counter.

Grady spoke to him, of course. He offered the man a cookie. Declined.

"I wonder what he'll have to say about our little party," Albert said when the door had closed behind Mr. Wahrmund.

"I'd wager nothing. Mr. Wahrmund doesn't talk much."

"He doesn't have to. He'll say something to his son, who will say something to your brother, and he—"

"I'm in a liquor store. I don't think Ralph will care."

"He might be concerned about the company you keep."

"I'm not afraid of Ralph."

From the stairwell behind them, Albert heard the hum of the chairlift beginning its descent.

"He can hurt me," Grady went on, "but I've got a nasty temper. A mean tongue. Got that from Momma—cry easy too. Ralph hates it, but I don't care. Daddy doesn't like my crying either. Doesn't say anything, just goes all stiff and distant. I don't think he knows what to make of me. Some days I try to act like the men."

While the boy talked, Albert had followed the chairlift's descent, the tapping of Mrs. Decker's cane.

"Well," she said, arriving beside him at the counter, "Mathilda Smith's gingersnaps. To what do we owe the honor?"

Grady raised his injured hand and launched into an explanation. Mrs. Decker cooed over the splinted finger.

"I don't know why," she said to Grady, "but my son hasn't said a word about your ordeal." She flicked her eyes at Albert. "Where are your manners, seating our guest here, in a place of business?" She turned again to Grady. "When does your mother plan to return?"

"Mrs. Decker," Albert said to Grady, "seems to have forgotten her manners too."

"That's all right," said Grady. "Momma needed to get away for a bit."

"I know that feeling," said Albert.

And his mother made her move—no trace of subtlety, trying to lure the boy away.

"I'd like to have a cookie too," she said. And when Grady offered her the plate, "Perhaps in a more comfortable setting. Perhaps you will accompany an old woman?" And she made to take the boy's arm.

"Stop it!" Albert said, feeling the edge in his voice, the ragged anger, as raw in the moment as something utterly new. Suddenly it was very quiet. Even Grady had come to the end of words.

Mrs. Decker looked stunned. She looked as if she didn't know where she was. She looked suddenly very old. "I meant no harm," she said, a strain in her voice as if from holding back tears.

"That's okay," said Grady. "It won't hurt to have a cookie here."

She looked at the Smith boy. She looked at the plate of cookies. "I suppose I oughtn't."

"Hey," Grady said. "I see you at the window. Up there." He gestured to the apartment above. "Sometimes in the morning when we drive by."

Mrs. Decker smiled. "I know you do." Something of the old bite was back in her voice.

"Sorry about the waving," Grady said. "I wave at everybody."

"You wave again next time. Perhaps I'll wave back." She turned to take her leave.

Albert tore a paper towel from the roll he kept beneath the register. Placing a cookie in its center, he handed it to his mother.

"Mrs. Smith will be here soon," he said. "I will be sure to thank her for the both of us."

His mother left them then, her cane tapping faintly in the background. Moments later the chairlift hummed, carrying her upstairs.

"Now *that* was awkward," said Grady. He burst out laughing.

But there was nothing of discomfiture in the laugh. Somewhere in him was a deep well of joy, his face flushed with it as the laughing quieted.

Albert put his hand to the boy's cheek. He hadn't meant to, hadn't intended to startle Grady, but that's what happened. Grady startled.

"I'm so sorry," Albert said.

"No." Grady touched him on the upper arm just below his shoulder. "That was a nice thing you did. It's just, well, no one touches me that way. My father, Ralph, they've always got their hands in their pockets. Even Evelyn. I try not to hug her, I know she doesn't like it. Sometimes my mother cups my chin, but she pretends she's being stern. Like this." Setting his jaw with a wry imitation of parental displeasure, Grady cupped Albert's chin with his undamaged hand.

He took another cookie and chatted as if there were no place else he'd rather be.

The voyage to France had surprised Albert, the one extravagance he'd been able to coax out of his mother—celebrating his graduation from high school. The first day at sea his excitement got so out of hand she had him breathing from a paper bag. He was frantic, always on the verge, until a stranger's laughter settled him.

They'd only just arrived in Paris, had found their way to a café near the hotel. The laugh startled him—rude, almost, in the uninhibited pleasure it expressed. Albert kept his eyes to the menu. He'd been trained not to gawk. But finally he couldn't resist the sensation that someone was looking from across the room, from the direction the laugh had come. He turned into those smiling eyes. His mother noticed too. She thought Claude was looking at her. At thirty-nine, the bloom was on her, and she knew it. She giggled and waved Claude over. He smiled for her and let her flirt. But Albert knew.

During the days that followed, Claude took on the role of unofficial guide. His attentions to Albert were unmistakable, and Mrs. Decker grew quiet as they admired the sights together. Predictably, when she was alone with Albert, she began to criticize Claude. He laughed too much. He looked too much the dandy. And so forth. She'd never liked it when someone else held center stage, and soon she turned her criticisms on Albert.

One afternoon, waking early from her nap, she stepped into his room as he sat waiting for a coat of clear polish to dry on his nails.

"I snitched the bottle from your dresser," Albert said. "I'm going out."

"With that stuff on?"

"You've watched me paint my nails for years."

"Only inside. Only with me."

"This is Paris. No one back home will know, and no one here cares."

"I care." Ordinarily, that would have been enough. His mother would pronounce her wishes, and he would accede. Not today.

Arching his brows at her in the mirror, Albert made his voice especially fey. "You're not invited."

His mother merely stared.

"I'm going out with Claude. We'll be back by sundown. You can have dinner with us."

"He's old enough to be your father." She said this days later as Albert prepared to duck out once again with Claude.

"Not quite," Albert said. "He's closer to my age." He didn't know, didn't care if that were so.

"It's unseemly," she said. "The two of you. Without feminine company."

In the end, with two days left in Paris, she played her trump card. "I've done everything for you," she said, and Albert turned from her, the hope knocked out of him.

He ran out of the room, took the stairs like a glissando, and headed for the Rue Saint-Jacques. The tears didn't start until Claude answered his knock.

Later, after Claude had undressed him and made love to him, Albert explained about the argument with his mother. The rest came out as Claude prompted him with questions, starting with the burn scar on his collarbone. Albert talked about life on the farm in Hempstead

County, Arkansas. He said little about his father, except for the season of the burn scar. The story, as he remembered it, was about his mother, the unflinching resolve he had discovered in her on the day of their escape, the debt he had incurred in the process—a debt she had called in earlier that afternoon.

On his outings with Claude, he had wished aloud that he could live in Paris, but he had kept the real dream a secret almost even from himself.

"I want to stay." His gaze took in the room, the window, the light pooling in the narrow interval between this building and the next. "I want to be here with you."

Claude had smiled on afternoons before when Albert spoke of staying on in Paris, had seemed to understand when Albert said he couldn't bear the life that waited back in Texas.

He smiled now, the saddest smile of Albert's life. "I am gratified," he said. "This afternoon I share your wish. But we cannot make a life together, you must know that."

Albert protested. What about the pairs of men they'd seen together in the streets, lovers clearly, for all the world to see?

The couples they'd spotted had been laughing, Claude agreed. Unafraid of holding hands. "But did you look into their eyes?"

Albert didn't answer. He was remembering that the eyes had troubled him—a glittering oddness that he could not make sense of.

Claude answered for him. "The faces smile, but not the eyes. In the eyes there is pain. Such loss, Albert. I can't bear to look at them."

"They have each other."

"They have no one but each other. And nowhere else to go." Claude walked to the window. As he stood there, the light outside waned as from a passing cloud. "Men who are lovers"—he spoke to the wall opposite, bricked in dingy gray—"they are not wanted elsewhere. Their mothers are like yours. They do not approve."

"What do I care about their mothers?" Albert was surprised by the anger burning beneath his words.

"And your mother?" Claude turned to him. "Can you defy her?"

"Yes!" Albert said, sounding to himself like a child who insists on the impossible.

"*I* have a mother," Claude said, the sound of his voice when he said *I* erecting a space between them Albert was afraid he couldn't cross. "I have brothers and a sister," Claude told him. "Nieces and nephews. I want children of my own."

"I want you."

"Think what we would lose."

"I want you."

Claude lay a hand on Albert's shoulder. "You are sweet to say so—"

Albert removed the hand and stood up. "I am not sweet!" He all but shrieked the words.

"But you are brave and I am not." Claude put a hand to Albert's cheek, and Albert let him. His anger had evaporated, in its place a weariness that would shadow many of the days to come. "Go home, Albert," Claude said, kissing him lightly, tenderly, a good-bye kiss. "I cannot do what you want."

The sound of the chairlift told him it was closing time. The sound of his mother's cane told him she wasn't heading for the side door to have her cigarette in the driveway. Momentarily, she stood beside him. He raised Mathilda Smith's plate from the counter—three cookies left— and held it out toward her.

"Thank you," she said, taking a gingersnap. "I'll have this with my cigarette. On the bench out front."

Albert took the second-to-last cookie. "You never smoke out front."

"I don't smoke half a pack at breakfast, but I did this morning. You can lock up—I'll let myself in by the side door."

His mother was slow reaching the door, slow seating herself in the bench that sat before the plate-glass window, smoke coiling where she held her cigarette like some aged gun moll, light pale as watercolor flashing from the neon sign above the window. Color. Fade. Color. Fade. A car accelerated coming out of town, and the skin at his nape prickled—something he was supposed to remember. But what?

Finishing his cookie, Albert locked up and took the plate upstairs with him, a lone gingersnap among the crumbles, a fading reminder of Grady Smith, his visit of the morning hours.

He set the plate on the table and stood at the window overlooking the driveway, blank, until his mother came around the corner and made her way down the driveway. She called, his name faint against the glass. "You left the sign on," she said when he opened the window. And so he had, the light in even flashes where the driveway met the street.

As he reached to close the window, the odor of her cigarette, a drift of warm against the skin on the back of his hand, the on-off wash of neon, a car horn, a shutting door. For the briefest moment he was at the window in their room at the Gunter, Bill behind him, waiting. He didn't close the window. Not just yet. And then he did. Nothing could be done for it.

When the chairlift began to hum, he went down, crossing his mother midway, and switched off the neon sign.

The room at the Gunter, the feeling of being there, was still with him. He wasn't ready to be upstairs with his mother. Making his way through the storeroom, he let himself out by the driveway.

It was a clear night. No moon, but stars. He walked out past the burn bin to the back of the parcel—a barbed-wire fence, a grazing pasture. He turned his face to the sky. So many stars. A dark night otherwise, the town asleep behind him.

Then, beyond the fence, coalescing out of darkness, a patch of paleness—like a white church fan levitated by an unseen hand. Albert stood looking until the apparition attached itself to a shorthorn bull, white-faced, still as a statue. The bull faced Albert as if he'd been posted here to wait, as if bearing a summons to be delivered at this juncture.

"Why, yes," Albert whispered. "I think I will." He bent from the hips and, pressing down on one of the barbed-wire strands, slipped through the space he'd made between the wires.

Years ago, on the farm outside Hope, his father had caught him playing dare with a yearling bull. He might've stayed safe with the fence between him and his father, nothing between him and the bull but a heartbeat, maybe two.

In the here and now—behind Decker's package store, at the edge of Nopalito, Texas, with July 15, 1965, nearing an end—Albert Decker raised a hand. Like a dancer long ago admired on the street in La Villita, he snapped his fingers.

The bull lowered his head and pawed the ground, his patch of white twisting like a cup towel on the wash line.

"Oh, honey!" Albert said. "You have no idea."

He raised one arm into a curve with the hand at his earlobe, fingers cupped around an imaginary castanet. He put a downward curve in the other arm, fingers at the ready along the seam of his trousers. Part matador, part flamenco, he made two quick circles and stomped the hardened ground. "¡Arriba! ¡Arriba!" he shouted—or tried to—but the words came out high-pitched, feathery.

"Sweetheart!" he said, this time to himself. "Is this the best you can do?" He laughed at the sound he had made.

And the bull startled. Turning tight circles, as if throwing off a rider, he pawed and snorted, making a show—then stilled himself, the odor of the dust he had raised fresh and peppery on the night air.

"Mother, May I?" Albert whispered. He took two steps to the side and stopped.

The bull stood there doing nothing, the white patch on his face like a map of somewhere yet to be discovered.

Albert raised his head to the sky. He took in air until his lungs were full. He wondered what came next.

CICADA SONG

GRADY SMITH, JUNE 4–JULY 4, 1967

SPRING RAINS HAD CUT little gullies into the caliche topping beyond the cattle guard—washed out the soil beneath right down to the hard-pan. Grady got off his bike and followed the curves of the lane up the rise toward the house. It was beautiful, really, though his father would have scoffed to hear him say so, the layers in swirls, the blending of colors, eggshell and gray and shadow, the trees and underbrush in so many versions of green it scarcely seemed a single word might hold them all. Still as the air was, no cool left beneath the layers of leaves, he just walked into it, thick as fog, so strong that when the smell struck, he could taste it at the back of his throat. He felt cold all over. His legs wanted to run.

An animal had died, Grady told himself, a heifer brought down by a coyote. But the rot was too close. Uncle Aaron would have tracked it, would have done something about the carcass before it wrecked a person's breathing. It wasn't a heifer he was smelling.

The handkerchief came out of his pocket as if on its own. He closed his nose with it and, walking on, got as far as the fence before the quiet stopped him, the air conditioner in Uncle Aaron's bedroom window still as stone. The silence buzzed, working its way into Grady's skull and jaw like a bad cold. He walked on, swung the gate open. Beside the back steps, perched on the footscraper, a turkey buzzard looked back at him, its head the color of lipstick no one wants to wear. Calm as judgment, the buzzard unfolded wings, tested them, let them collapse.

Grady stomped. He shouted. He waved his free hand. Nothing. He took a few steps, stomped and shouted and waved again. The buzzard lifted his wings and carried himself across the yard, where he lit on the T-top of a wash-line pole. He looked well-fed. He looked indifferent to the agitation that had moved him. *You've come too late*, his silence seemed to say. *Go home. Let my kind finish here.*

And Grady wanted that. To turn away. To forget the beating wings. Deep in him, though, he knew what he must do. Holding the handkerchief tight, he sucked in as much air as he could hold. He walked then—up the steps and across the back porch and through Uncle Aaron's kitchen. When he opened the door to the dining room, the air fell close and heavy. Summer nights, his uncle closed up the house and shut doors inside, cooling only what he needed most—his bedroom for sleep, the living room for reading before and after, the dining room for breakfast and a bank of windows to look out at the land. With the window unit stalled out, heat had thickened in the closed rooms.

The smell came at him with crushing force. It was like being held underwater and knowing he'd have to breathe and when he did the breathing would kill him. The flies were worse than the smell—a voice the smell gave itself, the flies humming and happy where the smell came from. Uncle Aaron in the living room in the light that seeped through lowered shades. Uncle Aaron in his favorite chair cranked back the way he liked it, the lamp beside him burning, a book on his little chairside table, bookmark tassel splayed on the wood grain he polished so carefully. Uncle Aaron with the flies at him, his undershirt ballooning where gas swelled in him, pajama fly wide open, exposing himself,what the bloat had done to the part of him he'd been handling at the end, the flies buzzing and feasting there, a wadded handkerchief stiff with his seed where he'd dropped it to the floor.

Grady got through the house in a run. He stumbled around the backyard, heaving spittle and bile into the flower beds while hummingbirds buzzed the flame acanthus. His uncle wouldn't have flowers that need pampering. No hibiscus—a freeze might take it out. No canna lilies—they wanted too much water. Weeds, Uncle Aaron called the flame acanthus. All they wanted was a lot of sun, a little water. Give them that, they'd burn with summer petals and reseed in wet spells, spilling their favors all over the place.

The hummingbirds hovered. The flame acanthus bloomed. Grady's stomach calmed, and he went back inside. He took a lemon from the refrigerator, cut it, squeezed the juice into his handkerchief, and tied it into place like playing cops and robbers. From a bag that hung in the pantry, he took a clothespin and clipped the handkerchief over his nostrils. Uncle Aaron kept rubber gloves in a kitchen drawer. Grady stopped when he opened it.

He'd not thought about the little canvas-clad farm journal his uncle kept, but here it was, at the front of the drawer, a day calendar of sorts, the pages filled in one by one with lists of what had been done for the place. The journal opened almost automatically between the somewhat wrinkled pages his uncle had touched with fingertips, with pencil, and the crisp, clean pages that followed. For Tuesday, May 30, 1967, notes of animals fed, of vegetables watered, of repairs on a fence line near the creek, and a final entry halfway down the page: "Watermelon with Ed and Mathilda, Evelyn and Grady. Took the new bicycle. Gave it to Grady." The intervening days were blank—nothing for Wednesday, Thursday, Friday, Saturday, nothing for today. Uncle Aaron was done with farmwork, done with making lists, crocheting, jacking off. Done. Grady closed the journal and put it back.

The rubber gloves were at the back of the drawer. He took them out and closed the drawer, put them on and went back to the living room. The smell was on his skin, in the fibers of his clothes, deeper in him every time he breathed. It was ugly business, but he got his uncle tucked back in. The flies were not happy.

The wadded handkerchief he rinsed and wrung out at the bathroom sink, then dropped it in the hamper. He fetched Uncle Aaron's throw from the end of his bed and covered him.

He meant to keep his uncle company for a while, meant to say a prayer, say good-bye. The sound of wings changed all that—a buzzard lighting on the planter box at the dining room windows. The tension in the counterweights was slightly off in the middle window. Uncle Aaron would have lowered it to the sill before he turned on the air conditioner, but it had slipped back up a couple of inches. Flies buzzed along the sill, behind them a ragged gap in the window screen—and the buzzard, peering in through his ugly red mask.

The bicycle he rode that afternoon was a Schwinn, the kind of racing bike his father'd been saying he couldn't have for as long as Grady'd been saying he wanted one. Five days he'd owned the bike, a surprise delivered during his mother's Memorial Day picnic. They had expected the watermelon his uncle had on ice in the back of his Jeep, not the ten-speed he lifted out, grinning as he handed it to Grady.

Uncle Aaron reached for the watermelon and carried it to the picnic table, Grady's mother beside him, her love of company expressing itself in the words that poured out of her. Grady's father followed behind—not a word out of him.

Evelyn stood by to admire the bike. She was in the middle, two years ahead of Grady and four behind Ralph, gone from the place since he finished high school. Grady motioned for his sister to follow and walked the bike out to the lane.

"Daddy's gonna blow," he said.

"Momma's on your side," she reminded him. "Uncle Aaron is stubborn. Go on now. Give it a spin."

He took a test run down the lane. He would have kept going, would have bicycled to the Escovedo place and let Domingo look the Schwinn over, listen to his voice while he admired it. That would have riled Daddy worse. Grady turned at the end of the lane and rode back.

Uncle Aaron had split the watermelon and cut slices. Folks said they looked alike, Aaron and Ed Smith, though Uncle Aaron was thinner.

And wiry. He'd tease his brother about going soft, said he liked home cooking too much, though he never joked about the missing hair—told Grady their own father had never let up on his younger son about his hairless pate. Granddaddy had kept a full head of hair till the day he died, Uncle Aaron too, curly, like Daddy's before he lost it, though most of the time the bachelor uncle kept his hair short as sticker burrs. He wore chambray shirts and pressed jeans over round-toed work boots. For the watermelon, he'd rolled his cuffs a turn or two. Hands, forearms, face, and neck, he was dark as a copper penny from working in the sun.

Grady's father spat a mouthful of seeds. "How much that thing set you back?"

"It's a bicycle, Ed. I can afford a bicycle."

"Fancy tires. All those gears."

"Grady's been driving tractor since he was ten," Momma said. "I think he can handle the gears."

"No need of 'em," Daddy said. "The glasses were bad enough."

He had not been happy when Grady tested nearsighted. In the world Granddaddy had shaped for him, men didn't need glasses, certainly not frames anyone might notice. Momma had let Grady choose—claimed he had good taste, though Daddy got one of his looks every time she asked what her youngest thought of a purse she had her eye on or a new pair of shoes. Evelyn said the glasses made a nice contrast with Grady's hair. People were always touching his hair, commenting on the curls and the color. Honey blond, Momma called it; he got the color from her, though hers was much lighter. Daddy didn't like that either.

Grady took another slice of watermelon and stayed out of it.

"Barry Goldwater wears black frames," Momma was saying.

"Not like those." Daddy might have left it at that, but when he turned to spit, the new bicycle stood smack in his line of vision. He did that thing he did with his mouth and Adam's apple, as if he'd been made to taste something sinful.

"Got cash to burn," he said, not quite looking at Uncle Aaron, "might want to shell out for another one. Bet the Escovedo boy would take a fancy bike off you." He swatted a fly away. "While you're at it, fix up that three-speed you never got rid of. Grady rides out with him, Mathilda might want to send you along. See if you can chaperone."

Uncle Aaron gave a soundless laugh. "I tried that once before," he said, "with my lovelorn little brother. It didn't work out so well."

The five of them stood there and studied the seeds at their feet. No one mentioned the letters Grady's father kept out of sight, from a girl he had loved and lost before he fell in love with the woman he would marry.

"Never mind the bicycle," Daddy said. "You been saving since the war—got yourself a nest egg. Wanna do somebody a favor, how about a new Chrysler for that shut-in you still carry a torch for? Let her get out some, get her out of her momma's house."

Uncle Aaron took up what was left of the watermelon, lifting it toward his brother like an offering, then let it drop. The melon broke open at Daddy's feet, the toes of his boots, the cuffs of his khakis splattered with juices.

The hackberries hushed. The stillness stretched. The birds did not call out.

Grady's father bent and brushed a chunk of watermelon off one of his boots.

Uncle Aaron walked to his Jeep, stepped up, and folded himself into the driver's seat. He started the engine and then, idling, inched forward until the bumper snugged up against his brother's shins.

"The bicycle stays," he said. "You let Grady ride it. You don't, I'll make you sorry you draw breath."

Grady had learned to shrug off his father's capacity for judgment. He had thought nothing between them would change—until he came home with news of Uncle Aaron's death.

By the time he had shooed the buzzard at the window and checked on his uncle's cows, it was getting on toward evening as he entered the house. Evelyn was stirring something on the stove, their parents sitting at the little kitchen table. Daddy had his back to Grady; Momma saw him in the doorway. She'd been worrying since Uncle Aaron left her picnic on Tuesday, and here it was Sunday. She'd called every day and let the phone ring, called Aunt Esther and wasn't happy when she said let him be, said when her big brother got over being peeved, he'd pick up the phone.

Grady stood in the kitchen door, watching Momma watching him.

"You're pale as a ghost," she said.

Daddy turned. He hadn't seen it yet.

Momma got up and crossed to Grady. "Are you sick?" She put a hand to his forehead.

"You sent the boy for news of Aaron," Daddy said. And to Grady, "What does your uncle have to say for himself?"

Grady knew the words he could use. *Jesus called him home. He's gone to meet his maker. Heaven made a place for him.* He'd been hearing old ladies talk that way as long as he could remember.

He couldn't do it.

"Uncle Aaron is dead."

Daddy stood up and faced him. His eyes were fighting what he'd heard.

Momma came at Grady with questions.

"Where?"

"He's in his chair," Grady said. "I covered him."

"You checked his breath? You're sure?"

"I'm sure."

"What if it's just something knocked him out?"

"No, Momma. He's gone." He couldn't tell her about the smell.

A sound came out of his father, knocked him where he couldn't breathe. When he straightened up, he looked wrecked.

Grady put his arms around Daddy—didn't even know he would do it—put his arms around his father and held him, felt himself being held in return. Grady felt solid, like what Jesus said about Peter.

Over his father's shoulder, he watched his mother. Her mouth was open, but she didn't say a word. A voice at his ear was saying, *Remember the day your momma was speechless.*

Evelyn was still at the stove. She had a wooden spoon in her hand. She put it on the countertop, crossed her arms and stood there. Blank. She was the most cautious person Grady knew. She held things in—or maybe kept them out.

She walked to her room and closed the door.

"Stay here with your momma," Daddy said. "Call the constable. I've got to get over there."

"No!" Grady said.

"Your uncle shouldn't be left alone."

"No, Daddy." Grady moved to stop him.

"Grady?" Momma said.

"Daddy can't see him." How could he say it? "It's been too long."

The three of them stood there—father, mother, son—stood there as if they'd forgotten who they were, where they were, what language they were speaking.

Daddy found his voice first. "How long?"

"I don't know." Grady spoke to a section of wall behind his father. He couldn't look at the man to lie, even when he needed to.

Daddy put a hand to his chin. "How long, son?"

"I'd say since the night of the picnic."

"I should be there," Daddy said. "To let the constable in. You want to ride along?"

"I'll go," Grady told him. "But you can't go in there. You have to promise."

He'd been a fixture at his favorite uncle's house from the day he was first allowed to ride his bicycle unsupervised. Uncle Aaron came to the door once, said, "What are you, a stranger, that you need to knock?" After that Grady didn't bother to announce himself.

If his uncle took a notion, he'd dial the phone and ask for Grady. "I've got some time to kill," he'd say. "Want to kill some time?"

They didn't hunt, and that was fine with Grady. It was the war, his uncle said, three years in the South Pacific. Afterward, he'd found that he was done with killing. There was plenty else for them to do. Uncle

Aaron taught Grady to identify plants by name—thorny bushes, burred grasses, all the spined and pointed desert plants that thrived in their part of the country. Together, they spied on quail, possums, turtles, toads, and left them to their own devices. The only wild thing Grady ever saw his uncle kill was a rattlesnake. Reflex, Uncle Aaron said, a jolt of adrenalin at the whir of the rattles. Nothing to do except put it to use.

Evenings over a campfire, they talked.

In the years since Uncle Aaron's mother had died—he wasn't even thirty then—he had kept up the big garden she left, said he shared her fondness, too, for plants that flowered without coddling. Esperanza and ruellia, lantana side by side with Rose of Sharon, Queen's Wreath in trellises at the west-facing windows.

"Your granddaddy give me hell about the flowers," he said, grinning. "Offered to buy me a bonnet like my momma's, ruffled apron for the kitchen. Suggested a pair of dress-up gloves for Sunday morning."

"What did you do?"

"Taught myself to crochet," Uncle Aaron said. He dug into the chest where his mother had stored her things, found patterns and a how-to book, yarn, a crochet hook. "Two birds with one stone," he said. Pissed off his daddy, huffing behind the newspaper, and gave Uncle Aaron something to do of an evening. Calmed his nerves, especially after his father died—this was 1960, Grady was nine—and Uncle Aaron had the place to himself. The throw Grady covered him with—Uncle Aaron had hooked every stitch with his own hands. He kept at it—crocheted afghans for the nieces and nephews, booties for newborns, tablecloths for the women in the family.

The garden and the flowering plants, farming the home place, trekking the woods with a nephew he clearly favored—Uncle Aaron seemed reasonably content with the life he had. When the sun went down, he had a book waiting beside his favorite chair, his crochet hook and yarn. But then came an afternoon when Grady walked into the smell death brings, when he saw what his uncle had been doing as he breathed his last. Perhaps all of us have hungers that can't be quenched in quiet.

Grady had heard the noises his mother and father made sometimes in the dead of night. He made a joke of it with Ralph, though he was certain their parents wouldn't laugh. They reached for something no one had the words for, something that would not be held back.

On a Saturday morning in April, Grady had risen early, pitch dark weighting the dream that woke him. He'd been sleeping but aware—the way a dream allows. A voice whispered—no words but lips and breath against his ear. The night was cool, and the sheets were lovely. He woke into the dream, a spill of sticky wetness in his boxer shorts, the air heavy with the smell of it. The voice was gone, but all over he felt its murmuring touch. It was Domingo's voice.

He got up then and dressed, left a note on the kitchen table and biked to Uncle Aaron's, slipped in quietly—the sun was just up—thinking he'd tap at the bedroom door, and while the light inside was still soft, he'd sit in the bedside rocking chair and maybe find the words.

Uncle Aaron wasn't in bed. He was standing in a pool of light by the dining room windows, face upturned as if to the cool that hovers at an open window when morning comes. As Grady stood there, he raised a hand, touched fingertips to the window screen, let them linger.

He turned suddenly, his face a map of sleeplessness, and made no mention of the private moment Grady'd walked in on.

"Hadn't figured you for an early riser," Uncle Aaron said. "Let's rustle up some breakfast."

He took care of the bacon; Grady fried eggs. When they sat down, Uncle Aaron asked why the sunrise visit. Reaching for the coffee pot at center table, he poured himself a cup, sugared it liberally, added cream. Grady watched the coffee swirling while he stirred. "Well?" Uncle Aaron said, blowing into his coffee.

"There's someone."

"Of course there is. Happens at your age."

Grady tried again. "There's more."

"You haven't done anything?" Uncle Aaron set his cup down. "You and the girl? You know what I mean?"

"We haven't done anything."

"You don't want a baby out of this."

Grady laughed. That's what he did at such a moment.

Uncle Aaron said it again. "You don't want a baby out of this."

"That's not going to happen."

"You think that now. Get alone with her somewhere, you might find otherwise."

Grady reached for his knife and fork. He had no appetite, but eating would give him something to do while he tried to think what he could say to make his uncle understand him.

"You know about rubbers?"

"Yes sir, I do."

Using the tip of his knife, Uncle Aaron broke the yolk of an egg on his plate. Grady watched the yellow run and pool, watched his uncle dab at it with a corner of toast.

"You get to that point? Can't hold yourself back? Armor up. You want me to, I'll get you some."

Grady shook his head no.

"Don't ever use an old rubber," Uncle Aaron said. "Ralph left any hidden, throw 'em out. Boys got no business fathering babies."

They finished breakfast in silence, and Uncle Aaron poured himself another cup.

"Want to tell me who?" he asked.

While he sugared and creamed his coffee, Grady studied the smears on his plate.

Old-timers in the community, Germans, they had a word. *Verboten.* For hungers in the body that must not be satisfied—forbidden yearnings no one puts into words.

By the time Grady woke on the morning after he found Uncle Aaron, the kitchen had been cleaned and the countertops cleared. His mother and Aunt Esther were sitting over a cup of coffee. Cousin Janet, Aunt Esther's only daughter, had been put in charge of labeling dishes as they arrived. She had cut slips of paper into a little stack; she had scotch tape at the ready and a notebook to record who'd given what so thank-you notes could be sent. Ralph had been called; he was driving in from Odessa with his best friend, Jimmy Don Wahrmund. Evelyn had gone with their father to make the funeral arrangements.

Aunt Esther had a reserve their mother liked to poke at, as on Easter Sunday back in March. The meal was barely over when Momma leaned back—her necklines were much too low for Aunt Esther's taste—leaned back, stretching like it was nap time, then leaned forward and reached where no one could see. Little snapping sounds came from under the table, Momma tugging and wiggling, and then—pop!—waving her girdle over the table like a flag.

While Aunt Esther's face curdled.

Uncle Aaron got a kick out of these moments. "Mathilda," he said after Momma had stashed the girdle in her purse, "if you weren't already spoken for, I think I'd get down on my knees right here at Esther's table and ask for your hand in marriage."

Daddy said, "Don't encourage her."

"Mathilda needs no encouragement," Uncle Berndt put in. Grady could see he was trying not to smile.

And here, three months later, differences put aside, Momma and Aunt Esther sat sipping coffee together.

Neighbors arrived, bringing with them a casserole, a ham, barbecue brisket, sliced and ready to eat. Mouth-watering kolaches, too, warm from the oven. Grady was standing on the back steps with his mother, his aunt, his cousin, a welcoming committee of sorts, when a 1950 DeSoto pulled into the outer yard, its grill grinning like giant chrome teeth. A rear door opened, and Bunny Jamieson got out. Grady'd never heard Bunny so much as mentioned at the supper table, never seen his mother exchange a word with her, though he couldn't see how chance would have offered. The polite word for Bunny Jamieson was recluse—about as likely to be seen outside the house where she grew up as that crazy woman locked in the attic in *Jane Eyre*. Bunny had been married. Actually, she still was, though the husband had been out of the picture for as long as Grady could remember. His name was Adler; hers was too—by law.

Momma and Aunt Esther exchanged a look. "I'll go," said Aunt Esther. She went down the steps and across the yard.

"Who'd have thought?" Momma said. "Hope Bunny's gone before your daddy gets back."

"Why?" Grady and Janet came down on the word together.

"Never mind," said Momma. And to Grady, "Go help your aunt. I can't have you and your cousin conspiring." She put a hand to his chin. "Look at me." He did. "Not a fresh word out of you. Offer to carry whatever she's brought."

Bunny was wearing a gray print sleeveless housedress and plain black flats. All over—face, arms, ankles—she was pale as the flesh on the inside of an old lady's arm in the dead of winter. A lovely voice, though, like wind chimes through a window on a cool fall morning.

Her voice, the look on her face, the way she carried herself—*fragile* was the word that came to mind. And this morning there was something more, a care in the way she held herself, as if she knew a crushing weight had dropped and some mix-up in physics had delayed the impact.

"I hope you don't mind," she was saying to Aunt Esther. "I just had to come. You know how highly I—" She stopped. "We—" She glanced toward her sister, still sitting behind the wheel. Connie Jamieson nodded, as if in encouragement, and Bunny finished her thought. "The family," she said, "we were all so fond of Aaron. Momma says to send her sympathy. Connie too."

Aunt Esther led Bunny across the yard; they stopped at the back steps. Grady and Janet went inside with the bowl of potato salad he'd taken from Bunny. He put the Jamieson sisters on a label and taped it to the bowl while Janet added the dish to the list in her notebook. When he and Janet got back outside, their mothers were letting Bunny go. Aunt Esther walked her to the DeSoto.

As Bunny got in, an old flatbed truck rounded the corner into the yard, and Grady felt an uptick in his pulse. Behind the wheel sat Domingo Escovedo.

"What's *he* doing here?" Janet sounded both mystified and displeased, as if she'd just got a whiff of the pens.

"Mind your manners, miss," said Momma. "Domino's our neighbor. He's your cousin's new friend."

Janet's look said, *You will never learn.*

"Go on," Momma said. "Ask Domino in. He won't do it, but ask him." She'd called him nothing but Domino for the months they'd known him. It made him smile. Grady's father didn't like it, but that could be a bonus with Momma.

Domingo offered a Dutch oven full of stew, chunks of pork cooked up with hominy and chili peppers and spices the Smith household didn't stock.

Momma was right; he declined the invitation to come in. Grady accepted the Dutch oven and set it on the truck bed so he could visit with Domingo. Between what one had picked up of English and the meager Spanish the other had managed to wrap his tongue around, their words were limited. Grady didn't care. They would say what they could. They would let their eyes do the rest.

Sleep kept Grady restless that night, a recurring dream of Bunny Jamieson threading the dark—her face at the passenger window, the DeSoto slowing to a stop, and the window rolling down, her voice like notes on a glockenspiel—*We were all so fond of Aaron*—her gloved hand waving as the car drove on.

He'd seen that once before—Bunny Jamieson waving from the family DeSoto. He'd been in town with Uncle Aaron. Three years ago, thereabout. They were coming out of the package store, bells chiming as the door closed behind them, when Connie Jamieson drove by, Bunny in the back seat. Her voice came trailing out the open window. "Stop the car!"

Connie slowed and pulled to the shoulder. And then nothing. The DeSoto just sat there. Grady was about to run up the street and see what was the matter, but Uncle Aaron put a hand on his shoulder. A car door opened, and Bunny stepped out. She stood there looking their way while her sister spoke from inside the car. Grady couldn't distinguish the words, but Connie seemed to be encouraging movement—whether to get back in the car or walk down to meet them, he couldn't tell.

Bunny gave a tentative wave. She was wearing wrist-length white dress gloves. On a Wednesday morning. In June.

Uncle Aaron gave Grady a nudge, and together they walked to meet Bunny.

She was pale, of course—a life spent indoors would do that to a person—but her eyes were bright, and there was color in her cheeks. What Grady saw in her face was joy. The adults he knew, when they laughed or smiled, it was like a chord. He heard other notes; not all of them were happy. Bunny's voice had just the one note, like the pleasure a child shows taking the bow off a gift.

There wasn't much said between Bunny and Uncle Aaron—five minutes, no more—before she said, "I must be going."

Uncle Aaron offered to walk her back to the car, still sitting at the curb half a block away. "I haven't seen Connie in ages," he said.

"No!" Bunny put a hand on his arm. "No, thank you, Aaron. I want to remember it this way. Just the two of us." She paused. "And Grady, of course." Such tenderness in her when she said *Aaron*.

She took his hand in both of hers—Grady remembered the contrast of her white, white gloves against Uncle Aaron's sun-darkened hands—and Bunny walked back to the car.

Grady made himself wait until she was safely inside and her car door shut before he turned his curiosity loose.

"What was that all about?"

"We were young once," Uncle Aaron said. "We meant something to each other."

"But Bunny had a husband."

"What happened between us—it was before she married."

Tires squealed and they looked toward the sound. Connie had pulled into the street, likely without looking, and only quick reflexes had saved a pickup truck from hitting the DeSoto. While they watched, Connie maneuvered the clumsy old sedan into the beginnings of a U-turn. Whoever had braked to avoid her just sat there waiting. The DeSoto backed up and stopped, then turned again and came back down the street, toothy as a jack-o'-lantern. Bunny raised a gloved hand and waved.

"Why didn't *you* marry her?"

"Some things are private."

"But what happened to her husband?"

"I imagine you'd have to ask Bunny. Or Lucas Adler." Uncle Aaron cleared his throat and spat. "If he could be found."

"She's still sweet on you."

"Whoa, son. There's danger here."

"Bunny's free. You're free."

"I'm not sure that we are."

"She could get a divorce. I bet Lucas Adler wouldn't care."

"What you saw just now," Uncle Aaron said. "Bunny used up every ounce of courage she's got making Connie stop the car. She'll be in bed for a week, won't come out of that house for who knows how long."

"You should have someone. Bunny too."

Uncle Aaron shook his head. "We're damaged goods, son."

"But I want you to be happy."

Was it something in Grady's voice, the way he said *happy*, as if wishing it would make it so? He didn't know, but Uncle Aaron turned and walked to his Jeep. He crouched there—Grady watched him from behind—shoulders stooped, arms bent, hands on his knees. He straightened, finally, and stepped into the Jeep.

Grady walked around and took the passenger seat. Uncle Aaron's eyes glittered like a calf just gone under the knife.

He put a hand on Grady's shoulder. "You've got some surprises in store," he said. And they drove on.

What is said and done when a person dies—Grady knew the words by heart. Uncle Aaron's visitation service differed only because of the closed casket and the little clucking pity sounds the women made, as if the sad thing were lying dead and alone for five days.

There was a brief homily. There were prayers and hymns. Afterward, the family made a receiving line—Aunt Esther and Uncle Berndt with Janet and her brothers, Grady alongside his parents, his brother and sister. Ralph had driven in that morning with Jimmy Don, who'd gone outside for a smoke while Uncle Aaron's kin attended to the shaking of hands, saying, *Thank you*, saying, *Yes, we'll miss him*, saying, *Yes, he was taken too soon.*

None of it reached Grady. He was outside himself, hearing a voice that sounded like Grady Smith say what needed to be said. He was safe. And then the oddest thing, like dozing—one moment there but removed, and the next somewhere else entirely—he dropped into a memory, blurry as the pieces of a dream barely remembered on waking.

He stands in a space like the funeral chapel, hushed and smelling of wool fresh from storage. He's a child. All he can see are shapes and shades of black—black wingtips, black trousers, black skirts, black pumps. Through the maze of grown-ups, a small casket, a veil of gauzy black tenting over it. Beside him is Ralph, Grady holding his hand. By the casket, a woman is weeping. Daddy taps her on the shoulder. She turns, pale and lovely. Grady knows this woman. He saw her yesterday, holding a bowl of potato salad beside a car with a garish chrome grill. Older. Paler still.

Bunny Jamieson is taking his hand, saying, "I can see why you were Aaron's favorite."

"You remember that?" Ralph asked afterward on the drive home.

"And what do you care?" Jimmy Don added. He'd taken the front passenger seat. Ralph was driving; it was his car, a sporty Pontiac he'd bought off a used car lot in Odessa.

"But what do I remember?"

"Cleave Adler's funeral," Ralph said.

"Who?"

"Bunny Jamieson had a son."

"What?" The questions spilled out of Grady. "Who was he? What happened to him? How come I don't know about him?"

"You gonna tell him the rest?" Jimmy Don asked.

"Drop it," Ralph said. He eyed Grady in the rearview. "I don't see how you remember. What were you—two, three—when Cleave died?"

"How old was he?"

"Eleven—twelve, maybe."

"What happened?"

"Swing set collapsed on him."

"Know what else?" Jimmy Don said. "Your uncle was swinging him."

"An eleven-year-old?"

"He wasn't actually swinging him," Ralph put in.

"But Jimmy Don said?"

"Look." Ralph had a limited supply of patience. "I wasn't there. Only one there was Uncle Aaron. Cleave was swinging high. Something broke."

"Where was this? What broke?"

"Granddaddy's place," Ralph said. An old swing set, not solid soldered iron piping like the one their father had built for them about the time Grady was born. The swing supports were made of wood—not even anchored at the ground, Ralph seemed to remember. "Something give out. Broke the boy's neck."

Granddaddy called Momma right away. She grabbed Ralph by the hand, and they ran for the car. "Our momma don't scare," Ralph said. "Should've seen her that afternoon. Drove like Judgment Day was upon us, wouldn't say a word about why. Wonder we didn't wind up dead in a bar ditch."

Uncle Aaron was at the swing set with a crowbar when they drove up. He wrecked it, piled the pieces, threw dried brush on top, and lit it.

"Stood there," Ralph said, "until weren't nothing left but ashes. No one trying to stop him, not a word spoken. I didn't even know Cleave was dead. Undertaker got there 'bout the time the fire burned out, carried him out of the house, Momma saying hush every time I tried to get a question out."

It was quiet for a minute—just the rush of air at the windows. When Jimmy Don spoke, he didn't bother turning to face Grady.

"Asked enough questions, cream puff?"

Grady tried another tack with him. "You said there was more."

Ralph cocked a brow in the rearview.

"Earlier," Grady said. "Remember?"

"You've heard enough." Ralph's look said he was finished.

"Way this story's been told," said Jimmy Don, "the best part's missing."

"Slander," Ralph answered him. "Kind of thing a man spreads when he's had too much to drink."

"We heard it from my daddy. You ever seen him drunk?"

Ralph turned off the highway, crushed rock of the county road growling beneath the floorboard. "You tell him then."

Jimmy Don swiveled, dropping an arm over the seat, and whispered lewdly, "Cleave Adler was your uncle's *love child*."

That was all they knew, a fragment of gossip passed along to Ralph and his best friend by Jimmy Don's father—a little moral lesson about the folly of sniffing after skirts.

"Here's your story." Jimmy Don made an O with thumb and forefinger. Pointing the other forefinger, he poked it in and out of the O.

Three members of the Escovedo family came to Uncle Aaron's funeral. Rafael was the family patriarch. He walked up the aisle—hat in one hand, cane in the other—and paused at the casket. Beside him was his son Serafin, and behind them, Domingo, wearing black trousers with a white shirt and tie, his hair combed back dark and shiny as ink.

Rafael looked to be in his seventies, though like many men who worked the land he'd been aged by more than time. Didn't miss a thing, could look right through a person. He'd taken a mortgage on the farm across the creek from the Smith place when Grady was barely out of diapers. Before the ink was dry on the papers, Momma said, Uncle Aaron drove over there to welcome him. Grady grew up hearing them talk, Uncle Aaron peppering his sentences with Spanish, the old man teasing him about his way with the language and sometimes correcting him—an ease between them Grady never felt when his father had business with Rafael.

At the cemetery after the funeral, when the burial service was over, folks hovered, their number thinning as last words were left with Daddy and Aunt Esther. A line of cars moved along the lane and turned onto the road away. Among the gravestones, a whirlwind humming dust. Evelyn nudged Grady and pointed. In a spot of shade beyond Uncle Aaron's open grave stood Domingo, hands in his pockets, clearly waiting.

Before Grady could think to ask, before his mother noticed, his father spoke. "Go on, son, your friend's waiting."

He didn't know how that had happened—friendship with Domingo—from opposite sides of a line he'd hardly even noticed until Domingo beckoned from the other side. For reasons of her own, his mother wasn't vigilant about the divide. Domingo had arrived on the Escovedo place last fall. Shortly after, Grady mentioned him when he found his mother alone. "Sure," she said, "invite him over." When he came, she sat him down at the kitchen table and set a plate of gingersnaps in front of him.

One evening, washing up on the porch, Grady heard the tail end of a conversation between his parents as they entered the kitchen from elsewhere in the house.

"You want him to be out among men," Momma was saying.

"But that Mexican boy."

"Domino knows how to work," she answered. "He can handle a bat. He likes being outdoors." She was borrowing from her husband and firstborn, the litany of things they admired in others.

"Have you listened to him?" Daddy asked.

"He makes himself understood. Would you pass a grammar test?"

"Folks don't like that kind of mixing."

"What you mean is you don't like it. That Grady's friend is not a white boy. Doesn't drink, doesn't hell around like Ralph."

"Nothing wrong with a little fun."

Momma might have raised her voice. She might eventually have lost her temper. Not this time. When she spoke, it was a single blunt sentence.

"I want my son to have a friend."

Grady heard the ache in her words—something she'd not have been able to name. His father either, though he must've heard it too.

Come spring, March 10, when Grady turned sixteen, when they could not have known how soon Uncle Aaron would be taken from them, Daddy had stayed out of Momma's way. When it was time for the bus that morning, she came along—a special occasion, she said, proceeding from the weather to the planting season to the work Domingo had done in Uncle Aaron's fields and the few afternoons Grady'd been made available to help.

"You've had no time to spend with Domino," she said, adding that after school Grady should stay on the bus until his friend's stop.

"I'd like nothing better," Grady said. But he hadn't been invited. He said as much.

"I phoned Serafin," Momma announced. "He says you're welcome to drop by."

And that's what happened. Grady rode past his stop that afternoon and got off with Domingo.

At the Escovedos, he dropped his books in the dining room and followed along out to the barn. One side of it was stacked with baled hay, the dusky air smelling of sunshine on cut fields and—just beneath that—not quite an itch, a tremble in the air at his nostrils. Domingo stepped ahead and dissolved for a moment in the shadowy light. A hinge creaked, a sliver of shadow opening in the opposite wall, the dry scent of corn spilling from the feed room—and voices from inside shouting, "Surprise!"

In the space of an instant, Grady was surrounded by Escovedo cousins, eight of them, ages six to seventeen. The younger ones came at him like bumper cars, the word *piñata* peppering their shouts.

"*¿Donde esta piñata?*" Grady asked. He followed their pointing fingers to a shaft of light cutting down through the barn's upper reaches. The light came in thorough a high opening that had once served as access for augered grain. Suspended there was a little papier-mâché horse.

Behind the noise of the younger children stood Evelyn and Janet. Momma, he learned later, had crossed by the old bridge, driving like the wind to get them there. She'd been recruited by Uncle Aaron, who'd hatched the party with Domingo. It was clear, from Janet's studied calm, that the event had been a surprise for her too. No other sign. The others, Domingo and his cousins, who didn't know her, would've just assumed that she was quiet like Evelyn.

Domingo loosened the piñata rope where it was tied to one of the barn's support posts. He lowered it to eye level and let it hang while the voices swirled. Motionless, fringed with bands of color—orange and hot pink and blue—it might have been a little donkey balking at what was to come. Esmeralda, a year younger than Grady, took hold of the piñata and started it swinging in a wide circle. Domingo raised and lowered, raised and lowered the little horse, working the children into a frenzy. When the swinging slowed, he raised it one last time and secured his end of the rope at the post.

He led Grady to the space beneath the piñata and, taking a large bandana from his hip pocket, folded it into a blindfold. He turned Grady around and knotted the bandana into place. Grady was handed a bat and turned in circles until voices were his only clue which way he was facing.

"I tell you when," Domingo said. Then his hands were gone.

The barn was quiet while Grady stood there, and when Domingo shouted, he began to swing the bat. A voice cried out—*¡Mas arriba!*—and before he could swing higher, another cried the opposite. *¡Mas abajo!* Grady had no aptitude for this kind of thing. Any sport that involved a ball and something you hit it with, he was hopeless. He picked up phrases, like bits from a cheering squad. One voice calling—*¡Dale frijoles y tortillas!* Another finishing up—*¡Para aserlo fuerte!* Others taking up the chant.

Domingo came to his rescue—a hand on Grady's shoulder, a voice saying, "I help you," the warmth of breath at his ear, a whiff of comino, the cushion of arms cradling his, the warmth of hands on the bat by his hands. "*Mira*," Domingo said. "*Como este.*" Grady un-tensed and let the bat move where Domingo willed it, a solid thwack as they connected. "*Otra vez*," Domingo said. "You can do it." Then he was gone.

Grady let strength, certainty, flow up his arms and into his grip on the bat. The piñata would not move, not yet. Domingo would allow him this chance. He swung and connected, swung again and broke open the piñata, little candies pattering on the hardened earth of the barn floor. The children's voices eddied around him as they scrambled for the goodies.

The next morning, stepping into the feed room back home, entering the powdery scent of milled grain, he felt himself smiling. He walked past a haystack on his way to the pens, a hint there of the air beneath the piñata. "*Mira*," he said to himself. "*Mira.*"

A couple of days after Uncle Aaron's burial, Grady got his mother alone and asked her about the snippet of scandal Jimmy Don had passed along.

"Not a word of this in front of your father," she said.

It was like a love story in one of her soap operas, which is to say a tale of happiness tripped up on bad timing and interference by third parties. Uncle Aaron had shipped out to the South Pacific before Bunny knew she was pregnant. He would have married her, but the child was due long before his return. Old man Jamieson wouldn't have it, wouldn't brook the shame.

"Next thing we know," Momma said, "Bunny's walking the aisle with Lucas Adler."

"Was he sweet on her?"

"I don't think the man much cared for anybody."

Lucas was older than Bunny, Momma explained, ten years or more. Looked to be a confirmed bachelor. Bad knee had kept him out of the army.

"Then why?"

"Mr. Jamieson played Skat with the bridegroom to be," Momma said. "Your uncle Berndt suspects they came to terms while they studied their cards."

"What happened to Lucas Adler?"

"No one knows," Momma said. "Spring before Japan surrendered, he up and left. Gossip was she run him off."

"What does that mean? Did Bunny tell him to go?" Grady couldn't imagine how she'd have summoned the nerve. "Did she take to drink? Was she too sad missing Uncle Aaron?"

"Bunny is delicate," Momma said. "She's high-strung. I imagine Lucas Adler's patience wore thin."

Curiosity got the better of Grady. Uncle Aaron and Bunny had loved each other. They'd had Cleave. They could've been a family.

Momma wouldn't have it. She cut him off.

What survives then? Grady wondered. Of anyone? A gravestone, names and dates, who married whom? Was that it? His father loved his mother. But he had loved someone else before, and she broke his heart. Momma wanted that part of him erased.

"Cleave Adler is dead," she said. "His momma had her wings broken. Your uncle was a private man. We got no business digging here."

Going through Uncle Aaron's things, Daddy came across the old Raleigh bicycle he'd kept to ride with nieces and nephews when they were coming up. One by one, Ralph, Evelyn, and their cousins found other pursuits until it was just Uncle Aaron riding the back roads with Grady. He had to stop when he tore a cartilage in his knee. Promised he'd ride with Grady again, but when the knee healed, there was a catch in it that never went away.

Daddy stowed the Raleigh in the bed of his pickup truck. When he got home, he took it to the tractor shed and leaned it against a wall.

"What are you keeping that for?" Grady asked.

"Your friend"—he nodded toward the creek, the farm beyond—"is good with his hands. He puts it in working order, he can have it."

The very next morning, Grady loaded up the Raleigh and drove to the Escovedo place. He had time on his hands, so he hung around watching while his friend worked on it. Domingo was short for his age, a wiry little guy. Slender fingers—long, graceful, deft—knobby at the knuckles. Grady could see strength working there like little pulleys, a movement in the tendons from fingers to wrists and upward beneath the shirt cuffs Domingo had rolled a turn or two. A patch of sweat on his shirt just below the top button. Grady wasn't sure he had words for what he felt watching. What he wanted. For a start, on the tip of his tongue, a taste of the salt-sweat that glistened in the hollow beneath Domingo's Adam's apple. Grady could feel it in what his hands wanted to do when he was with Domingo and no one else around. But it was other things too. The way words fell away and Grady didn't feel the need for them. The way Domingo looked at him. The way breath felt when Domingo smiled.

There was something else, something more, something about Uncle Aaron that Grady didn't want to ponder—a secret only Grady knew. What had happened after the rupture at his mother's picnic on Memorial Day, what had kept him away from his uncle's house in the days after.

The dust from the Jeep had barely settled when Daddy made an excuse to be elsewhere. He said the cattle needed checking.

"Fine mess you've made," Momma said to his retreating back. "I'll deal with you later."

Evelyn helped her clean off the picnic table while Grady gathered up pieces of broken watermelon and tossed them over the fence into the hen yard. He hung back till they were safely inside, then mounted the new bike and rode to Uncle Aaron's place.

They sat on the front porch steps and talked. Side by side. What if they'd sat down at the kitchen table, somewhere face to face? Would Grady have looked into unblinking eyes and lost his way?

Uncle Aaron lay a hand on his shoulder and spoke. "I don't like what your daddy said. I don't like that you had to hear it."

"He was mad at you. I bet he's sorry already."

"Not that. What he said about you."

"That's just Daddy."

"It's not right. What he said about you and Domingo. Insulting your friendship."

The next words came out as if Grady were meant to say them.

"He's right, though."

The shade palled, the breeze gusted. Grady smelled summer coming—sunlight and dried grass and caliche dust all mixed together.

"What do you mean, he's right?" Uncle Aaron asked.

Grady knew by the voice that his uncle was just this side of knowing.

"About me," he said. "I don't know if he's right about Domingo, but Daddy's right about me."

"Don't say anymore."

Anger flickered awake, and the words came. Grady had no will to stop them.

"I like Domingo," he said. "I want us to be more than friends. Like how you feel about Bunny." He spoke to the widening shadow cast by the house, to the brightness beyond, with Uncle Aaron as witness, blurred by side vision.

"You cannot say that." The hand on Grady's shoulder gripped hard. He turned into eyes that burned. With what? Anger? Pain?

"It's the truth."

Uncle Aaron got up and down off the steps and strode across the yard. He stopped half in, half out of the sun, from the waist up blazing with light. The breeze came again—heat and cured hay and dust.

He turned and walked back into the shade, a silhouette now, Grady's uncle, clothed in dusk. When he got to the steps, he leaned forward, crouching, and grabbed a fistful of Grady's shirt at the top button.

"Understand me," he said, his grip tightening. "I can't hear that. Ever."

"Let. Me. Go."

In a single motion, Uncle Aaron pulled Grady off the steps, feet dangling, their noses all but touching. He let go then. Grady lost his balance and fell into the lantanas beside the steps.

Uncle Aaron was sorry already, his eyes said so. But Grady was past caring.

Scrambling out of the lantanas, he sucked in all the air he could hold and shouted. "I'm telling the truth!"

He yanked away from hands that reached for him, got out of the gate and onto his bicycle, riding blindly then, eyes spilling over, Uncle

Aaron's voice behind, a name in the sky—*Grady! Grady!*—as if calling, *Come back.* Five days before that happened—and too late by then.

On the afternoon of July 4, Domingo installed dynamo lights on their bicycles. This was Grady's idea, a way of getting around the dog days' heat: they could ride at dusk and after. Domingo tested the lights, and they rode to the cemetery. Uncle Aaron had often spent the holiday with the Smith family, and though he couldn't abide the explosions that go with fireworks, he'd loved watching children wave sparklers. At nightfall Domingo and Grady would light a box of them for him.

Sunset was perhaps half an hour off as they approached the graveyard, heat softening in shadows that stretched to cover everything. Along the lane that led into the cemetery, beneath an ancient mesquite, sat the Jamiesons' DeSoto. The driver's door gaped open, and Connie Jamieson sat there fanning herself.

"Little sister had to come today," she said, and waved at Bunny's figure among the gravestones beyond. "Her son's daddy loved Independence Day." A pause. "Suppose you know who that was."

"Yes, ma'am."

"You don't look the worse for knowing." Connie turned away and flipped open the glove compartment. A match rasped, and when she turned back, a lit cigarette unfurled smoke at her fingertips.

"I took my daddy's side," Connie said. She put the cigarette to her lips, the sides of her mouth caving in as she drew smoke into her lungs. She held the smoke then, her lips pursed, the skin around them hashmarked with short, deep lines where the muscles pulled taut.

"Poor Bunny," she said, the words coming with a burst of smoke. "No match for us."

She put the cigarette to her lips again. All around, as if the air itself were pulsing, cicadas chorused, their song rising and falling.

Connie's voice cut through. "I'm going to offer you a piece of advice. No charge. Fourth of July special."

The cicadas crescendoed; the air swirled with Connie's smoke.

"Steer clear of folks who claim to know what's best for you. We stick a wrench in the works. Can't help ourselves, that's what we do."

They turned from Connie and walked up the rise, passing between rows of stones, passing the Smith family plot, the fresh scar of Uncle Aaron's grave. Cenizo, agarita, and yaupon holly, the occasional clump of yucca, dotted the land where the dead were buried. Clusters of huisache cast long splatters of late shadow over the patchwork grass at their feet.

Bunny turned as they approached. "I'm so glad you're here," she said, and when introduced to Domingo, "Pleased to meet a friend of Grady's." She was standing at her son's grave, a small headstone claiming it among a cluster of Jamieson family graves. Grady'd been coming to this cemetery since before he could walk, had traipsed the rows and studied the headstones, yet this marker had escaped his notice. The inscription held another surprise.

Cleave Aaron Adler, September 23, 1942–October 19, 1953

"Cleave was my husband's favorite brother," Bunny said. "He died in childhood."

Grady studied the gravestone and held his tongue.

"My husband objected to the middle name," she said. "No one need know is how I looked at it. I can keep a secret." She reached through the crook of his elbow and lay a hand on his forearm. "While he was still with us," she said, "Cleave, I mean—sometimes I got out his birth certificate and just looked at it."

"I'm glad you put it on his gravestone," Grady said. "All of it."

"My daddy raised a stink." Reaching, she ran fingertips over the inscription. "It's your grandson's name, I told him, the name his momma and daddy gave him. It's how God will call him—loud as *this*." Bunny raised herself erect and stirred the air as if she were directing the cicadas.

"*Chicharras*," Domingo said, the r trilling like a song of its own.

"*Chicharras*?" Bunny said, the syllables rolling off her tongue as if she'd spoken Spanish every day of her life.

"*Sí*," said Domingo. Then to Grady, "Now you."

"*Chicharras.*" He took all the music out of the word.

"*Mi amigo es un gringo que no tiene remedio,*" Domingo said to Bunny, putting his hand on Grady's shoulder as if to present the evidence.

Bunny lay a hand against his cheek. "You have a lovely smile," she said. "Do you see it, Grady, this lovely boy's smile?"

She did the oddest thing then. She took Domingo's hand and turned it palm up, took Grady's hand and turned it into Domingo's, then placed her own hand over theirs.

"Be good to each other," she said.

She left them then, receding down the rise, a darker shadow against the graying day, the DeSoto beyond her a faint glimmer against the big mesquite's darkening silhouette, the sky pink and graying behind it.

As the DeSoto edged away from the mesquite and out to the county road, Grady and Domingo crossed to the new grave, the earth piled loose and crumbling, dusk thickening with insect voices. They stood together, saying nothing as the last of the light drained out of the sky, and then from somewhere down by the creek bottom, some farmer's yard, likely, came the kind of muted report that goes with darkness on Independence Day. They turned to see streamers of color and light erupting against a blue-black sky.

"*Mira,*" Domingo said.

Again and again, as they stood watching, fountains of light exploded in the sky over the creek.

Domingo's left hand, hanging loose at Grady's side, rises, brushing in an arc across the back of a well-worn cotton shirt, comes to rest on a shoulder that registers the hand as if new. Soft pressure—lovely—against the upper arm where a head leans. They will linger here, Grady and Domingo. Later, one by one, they will light their box of sparklers, watch the tiny embers fizz against the night and fade. They want not to go beyond this moment. Grady knows without words that Domingo is with him in this—knowing how soon the fireworks will be over, how soon they must return to separate houses, separate days. Knowing their days will pass too quickly, not knowing how many will be given them. Knowing troubles will greet their mornings. Still, standing here with Domingo as the sky goes light and dark and light and dark again, Grady feels certain. He is young, if not quite ready. While the fireworks last, they rest against each other, the warm night cooling as it deepens, the song of the *chicharras* cresting around them in wave upon wave.

WAKING GRADY

ED SMITH, SEPTEMBER 1967–AUGUST 1970

ED CHECKED HIS POCKET watch. It was half past four, the creek bottom of the Agua Dulce humming with warmth that filtered down through live oaks and glowed as if from the leaves themselves. As he raised his eyes, a shard of light glinted from beneath an agarita rooted in a cleft at the base of the creek bank, its spiny branches swept cock-eyed by the rush of water after thunderstorms. He wondered later why God arranged the trick of timing and light, the angle of reflection, the alignment of gaps in the canopy that allowed a pinpoint of sun to rebound from the fraction of one lens washed clean of silt.

In the instant he knew he was seeing Grady's glasses, the breath went out of him, and Ed dropped to his knees in the dry creek bed. The swirl of soil around the glasses was cool, clean, silky. With the briefest motion of his fingers, Ed further exposed the visible hinge, grasped the glasses, and pulled them free.

No one else in Nopalito had worn such glasses. The general opinion seemed to have been that they were as odd as Grady, humming Buddy Holly songs his every waking hour. Who besides Ed's youngest would've cared to look like that near-sighted goof, several years dead by the time

Grady needed glasses? Leave it to Grady to find a pair of frames like this, wide across the brow and narrow-rimmed so that the odd rectangular shape of the lenses called attention to him as he walked around town, jabbering at everybody. "Plain black frames," Ed had insisted. Be careful what you wish for.

The black of the frames had dulled with eight months' exposure to sun and water. Ed held them to the light coming through the trees. The lenses were unmarked, the light beyond them thick and murky from the thickness and the grinding of the glass. It was like looking through water. A sound came out of Ed, and he stumbled to his feet. Something tore loose from his ribcage. The sound came again. Ed took off up the creek, hugging himself against spasms that yanked at his insides. He had to get home.

The house was empty and still. He opened the closet he shared with Mathilda, a kaleidoscope of Sunday dresses in rayon and flowers, her tailored Sunday suits for the short Texas winters, and dancing dresses—their low-cut necklines and flouncing skirts. The shelf above was stacked tight with hatboxes, the floor below boxed in like a shoe store. But his wife had stopped wearing nice things. For the café, she had several plain white dresses and a pair of nurse's shoes. At home, she wore faded dresses or old jeans with one of Ed's cast-off dress shirts.

To the left of Mathilda's dresses hung Ed's two Sunday suits and several pairs of trousers. Beneath them sat black wingtips for church and a pair of fancy dancing boots, their shine powdered with dust. Ed pulled the shoes and boots out onto the bedroom floor and, reaching into the back corner, pulled out a hatbox that had once belonged to his mother. Inside were the few things he'd kept from his school days—report cards, faded pictures of friends with toothy adolescent grins, a photograph of himself trying to look somber in a football uniform. He touched a bundle of yellowed letters Laurie Lindeman had sent to him in the South Pacific, including one that broke his heart. Mathilda had never accepted that these letters had a place in Ed's life. Rattlesnakes might have nested in the hatbox. Grady's glasses would be safe there.

In bed that night, Ed ached from the tearing he'd felt in the creek bottom. He thought about his little Jersey cow and her breech calf two years back, the sound she had made when he tugged at the rope and the block and tackle pulled the calf's protruding leg taut. You could say she bellowed, but it sounded like suffering distilled into sound. *Unbearable.* That's what Mathilda had said afterward, and she didn't mean how the cow felt. She meant unbearable to witness. That was before Grady went out to look at the flooded creek and didn't come back. In the months since, she had begun to learn what a body can bear.

"Momma's just practicing."

It was Grady's voice, more often than not, that came to Ed at times like this—Grady still trying, from wherever he'd gone, to explain his mother's rages. Grady, with his head of unruly hair, wild even beneath the comb—more curl than Mathilda's, less curl than Ed's when he'd still had hair. Grady's had been darker than Mathilda's, though if he'd grown it halfway to his ass, like the fools out roaming city streets, sunlight might have lightened his hair as it did his mother's in the summer. Ed's imagination regularly defied the common sense he lived by. His son had surely drowned. Still, he was visited by pictures that insisted otherwise, like this one, of Grady in long hair and fringed leather, stepping onto the cable car at Hyde and Lombard, as had Ed a lifetime ago, fresh out of the morning fog, Russian Hill sloping beneath him toward the Bay—and the Navy waiting, the war distant, unimaginable.

Grady had liked it when breezes stirred his hair. He wanted nothing to do with the burr cuts Ed had tried on both his sons. After each turn under the clippers, Ralph gave him a look that burned straight through. He would not beg. But Grady was heartbroken. There was no light left in his half inch of bristle. He went to his mother, and Mathilda took his side.

"Momma's boy."

That was Ralph with his pecker in a knot because Grady could brave whatever Mathilda flung in his direction and minutes later loll on her bedside while his mother sat at her dresser primping, the two of them fluttering like a hen yard. Grady had understood something about his mother that slipped past Ralph and Evelyn. He had learned by watching Ed, who went still when Mathilda got going, who set his face in an attitude of listening but didn't take her words to heart.

As things stood now, Ed would've welcomed one of Mathilda's rages, harmless as a whirlwind blustering that rain was on the way. She'd started to quiet when Ralph finished high school. He'd left the next day—that would've been five years ago—threw over a track scholarship he said was too close to home and went roughnecking out by Odessa. Last August, Evelyn had left for college. She'd spent most of her time holed up in her room, studying. Wasn't until she was gone that Ed came to realize how much comfort he'd taken from knowing she was there. His only daughter had been a cushion against their rough edges. In the weeks after she left, he and Mathilda and Grady had bounced around the place—talking in fits and starts, lapsing, looking past each other. Until the twenty-second of September, after Hurricane Beulah, after the floodwaters had crested and begun to ebb.

Something terrible had got loose in Mathilda that day. It started with a flash of fear in her eyes when she asked where Grady was and Ed said, "I don't know." There'd been several days of storm, what with boarding up and winds gusting to a hundred and downpour following hard upon the wind. Mathilda stayed safe at Norma Pfeiler's house in town, afraid of rising wind after she'd helped Norma batten down at the café. Having waited out the 1919 hurricane on the safe side of a haystack, Norma had built herself a brick house with the only cellar in the county.

Four days Mathilda was gone. A low water crossing still pounding in her blood, she walked straight from the backdoor to Grady's room and then to Ed, pacing in the dining room as dusk sucked the light out of the house.

"What do you mean, you don't know?"

"He went out to look at the water."

"You let my son out of the house to look at *this*?" She flung a hand at the window Ed had left unboarded so that he could monitor the storm—with the Agua Dulce beyond, its silvery sheen in the darkness gathering over the fields, so far out of its banks, so close to the house you could hear the flood humming, the pull of the current like a sea-shell to the ear, the voices of frogs calling from every watery direction.

"Have you lost your goddamn mind?"

Grady was a born swimmer, Ed reminded her. He knew to keep away from the current. Mathilda shrilled at him that he was crazy to have let their youngest go out there alone. Against the force of his own unease, Ed tried again, reminding his wife that Grady regularly stayed outside until twilight. Mathilda flung herself at Ed and swept him from the house to search. Pitch dark came quickly, and with it, dread.

At midnight Ed called Evelyn. "Lynnie," he said, spilling everything in a rush. "Grady went out to the creek, he ain't come back. Your momma's beside herself. I don't know what to do."

"Oh, Daddy. No." He could hear it in his daughter's voice too, a crossing over, and when she walked into the kitchen in the early morning, her face was a map of worry and loss. Evelyn exchanged a look with her mother, haggard in the dress she'd worn since the day before. They looked nothing like one another, his wife and daughter. Mathilda, with her curves and the shock of her hair like sunlight through honey. Evelyn, all bones and angles. A dishwater blonde, her mother called her, with the emphasis on *dishwater*. Everything about Evelyn, from the simple flats at her feet to the blunt cut of her hair, said, *I am not my mother's daughter.*

"Don't look at me like that." Mathilda's words rippled at the morning quiet.

Ed had noticed something too. It was the first time in the last dozen years he'd seen his daughter look at her mother as if she could see something of herself looking back.

"What happened?" Evelyn asked, her grave eyes turning to Ed.

Behind him, through the window, the chorus of frogs rose up. Their calling emptied his mind of all but what he heard, like conjurers repeating his son's name. *Grady, Grady, Grady.*

"Daddy?"

"The rain quit yesterday morning," he said. "Drizzle and clouds was all. Till five or so. The sun came out." He stopped. He didn't have the words.

Mathilda did.

"The sun came out." Her eyes burned. "It rained like Noah's goddamn flood, but the sun came out."

Ed swallowed and went on. "Grady wanted to look at the water. I said fine, just be careful." He opened the refrigerator. On the top shelf, in a metal pie tin, sat a single slice of coconut cream pie, his favorite. Norma Pfeiler had sent a whole pie home for him. Five days ago. The meringue had shrunk to a puny dollop atop the coconut custard, a puddle of goo congealing beside it.

"Look at you," Mathilda said. "Take *one* bite." Her threat caught him there, aware that his mouth was watering, that he hadn't eaten since yesterday. It was a reflex, he told himself. A lifetime he'd turned from the kitchen sink and rummaged for a bite to eat.

He closed the refrigerator and turned to his wife and daughter. He didn't know what to do with his face.

"Something happened," Mathilda said. "Between you and Grady."

"No." The lie festered at the back of his tongue.

Mathilda turned to their daughter. "Starting at the sight of each other. Days before that storm come into the Gulf."

"Daddy and Grady are always at nines and elevens." Evelyn stopped. Ed wondered if it was because she heard herself say *are*.

"Your father wouldn't look at him. He won't look at me." Mathilda thumped the table with her fist. "Right now. Look at him. He won't look at me."

Ed had turned away without thinking. He found himself at the sink with his back to the room. In the gray light at the window, he felt Grady's eyes on him. *I'm your son.*

"And what about Domino?" Mathilda's words spun him back into the room.

"His name is Domingo." He felt sick at the feel of his tongue giving shape to the name.

"What's Domingo got to do with any of this?" Evelyn asked.

Mathilda kept her eyes on Ed. "Go ahead," she said, "pronounce his name for us—*Domingo Escovedo.*" Her voice mocked his contemptuous precision with the boy's name. "You make him sound like he swam the river just last week."

"I know what *I'd* call him."

Evelyn spoke. "You shouldn't say words like that."

"Domino ain't no improvement."

"He answers to it," Mathilda said.

Ed felt cornered. He let his ire slip out in Evelyn's direction. "Your momma had no business baking cookies for that boy, calling him Domino, making him welcome around here."

"I'll bake cookies any time I goddamn please."

"She. She encouraged it." Ed couldn't let himself say more.

He turned back to the kitchen window and looked out at his fields, the floodwaters receding to a band of brackish gray along the trees that marked the creek. The frogs were still at it. Behind him, Mathilda took up the thread.

"Something happened with Domino."

"Your son"—Ed turned and took a step toward his wife—"had his hands on that boy."

"Grady never laid a hand on anybody," she said.

"That's not what I mean."

"Momma's right," Evelyn said.

"They—"

"Daddy, don't."

The frogs called out. The pie beckoned. Evelyn looked at him. Her eyes said *please.*

She knows.

"There's something you're not telling," Mathilda said. "Whatever you say you mean, you're hiding something."

Ed stepped across and put his hand on the table. The room—the house—could not hold this. He leaned down, locked eyes with his wife. "You got no idea," he said.

Mathilda reached up—he let her. She took a fistful of his collar and pulled at it until their noses all but touched. Her breath was stale and acrid.

"Momma. Daddy." They didn't move. "Grady's gone."

"Where's my son?" Mathilda's voice rose to something like a howl, the word *son* hot on Ed's face. "What have you done to my son?"

It happened a couple of weeks before the hurricane. Finished early with the fieldwork, his tractor parked in the shed, Ed wandered among the mesquites of the feeding area, looking over the yearlings, then decided to rest for a few minutes before going to wash up. Out past the feed lot, he sat down at the base of an old hackberry ringed by cedar fence posts propped against the trunk. For a few minutes no one would know where he was. There was pleasure in stealing away.

He had just begun to relax when he heard Grady and Domingo—wrestling and tickling each other, by the sound of their voices. He smiled, thinking of his brother, the roughhousing they'd done coming up together. Then he caught himself and frowned. He'd wanted Grady to fit in with younger brothers of Ralph's friends. He hadn't wanted *this*. He'd gone along with Mathilda, resentfully, when she made the Mexican boy feel at home with them. His wife seemed to have absorbed some of their daughter's ideas about where and whether lines should be drawn.

Ed stood and peered around the cedar posts. The boys were beneath the live oak tree, its outer branches about twenty yards from where he stood. The tree was old and huge, its canopy draping a splash-work of green almost to the ground, the shadows beneath the branches shot through with afternoon light. Evelyn had discovered the space beneath the tree soon after she learned to walk, and she insisted Grady be carried here the day they brought him home from the hospital. They'd grown up together in the lighted space beneath the leaves. Small wonder that Grady had brought his friend here.

The Mexican boy was short, thin, wiry—clearly stronger than Grady and more experienced at wrestling. But they were playing, and neither was handling the other like an opponent to be pinned. It unnerved Ed, the absence of aggression, and he felt odd spying. Mathilda would have his hide if she knew. But just as he started to turn away, Grady rolled on top of Domingo. Straddling the Mexican boy's hips, Grady straightened up and raised his hands in a gesture of triumph. Domingo didn't move; he let Grady have the moment. And then, so natural Ed didn't see it happen, like dancers attuned to each other's signals, liquid in their movements, Grady and Domingo were holding hands. Ed could not see Grady's eyes, but he could tell by the angle of his face, a kind of fierce repose in the way he held himself, that his son was looking into the Mexican boy's eyes.

What Ed saw, for a fixed moment, was Laurie Lindeman looking up at him when he'd lounged beside her on a picnic blanket in the spring of 1941. He saw hunger in her eyes, answering hunger in him. He could hear her heart beating. When he came back to himself, spying, he saw Grady and Domingo disengage their hands, and then as Grady leaned to undo the top button on Domingo's shirt, his friend unfastened the buckle at Grady's waist. Ed watched, transfixed, and then Grady turned and looked right at him. Father and son, their eyes locked. Grady's look said *please*, and he took Domingo's hands in his, stopping what the Mexican boy had been about to do. Otherwise, Grady didn't so much as flinch. He looked at his father, his eyes saying *please*. Something snapped in Ed, and he found himself rushing away. He had to get to the house.

Nausea caught up with him as he approached the back porch, where he stepped behind Mathilda's pampered hibiscus and gagged. He kicked dirt over the bile and went inside to wash up, then lay on the bed pretending to nap until Mathilda called him to the table.

He said grace and reached for a platter of salmon croquettes.

"Coming down with a bug," Mathilda said, "you might not ought to eat something fried."

"I'm not sick."

"I heard you," and she turned to Grady. "Your daddy gagged in my flower bed."

Against his will, Ed looked at his son. Grady did not look away.

Ed turned back to Mathilda. "Let go of that platter. I'm hungry."

"You throw up later on, don't blame it on my croquettes."

After supper, Ed claimed he was tired and turned in early. He dozed eventually, half aware that at some point Mathilda had slipped into bed beside him. He held still when she cozied up to him. She ran a hand through the hair above his navel, slipped deft fingers beneath the waistband of his pajama pants. Nothing.

He got hold of her hand and removed it.

"You are plucking at my last nerve," Mathilda said, scooting to the far edge of the bed.

She slept while he lay there waking, weak with the shame, like an infection transmitted through his eyes in the moment that Domingo reached for Grady's buckle. He'd felt his father's presence beneath the hackberry, the old man standing behind him, snickering, his breath hot against Ed's neck. "What do you say now, pretty boy? Your chickens done come home to roost." The voice was as throaty and lewd as if his father had risen from the grave to goad him, as he had about Laurie, touching every pleasure Ed had discovered alone with her.

She had been lovely and slim. *The closer the bone, the sweeter the meat.* The first time his father put these words to him, Ed burned with anger and loathing. Afterward, at the supper table, when the old man felt the need to test the son he accused of being sensitive, he'd pass a platter of fried chicken to Ed and suggest he take the piece his mother cut from the back—a length of spine with precious little meat clinging to the thin splintings that made chicken bones a sometimes fatal pleasure for cats and dogs. "Take this back piece, son. You know what they say? The closer the bone, the sweeter the meat." Then he'd loose that nasty chuckle of his while Ed's mother squirmed—she knew what he was up to—and said, "Adolph, please."

Somewhere in the wee hours, Ed slept. In his dream he was in the latrine at boot camp, standing at the urinal, admiring himself in a mirror that was there and then not there, his beautiful curly hair, the pride of his youth, winking back at him like neon—never mind the camp barber. Rough hands grabbed him from behind, shoved him against the mirror. He felt the whisper of lips against his ear—wet, obscene—something about pretty curls, a sweet mouth. And the punch line: "I got something for you to suck on."

Ed woke. He needed to pee. In the bathroom, finished with his business, he turned and sat on the edge of the tub, propping elbows on knees and chin on fists, ragged with wakefulness in the room's harsh light. The door opened and Grady stood there, pale and lean in boxer shorts, tousled hair framing a sleepless face, his eyes intent, unfaltering.

"Don't tell Momma."

Ed couldn't face his son. He opened his hands and cupped his face in them, looking into his own lap. The fly on his pajama pants had gapped open when he sat down. He stood up, running a hand quickly along the bunched cloth to flatten the gap.

"I don't have words," he said. Elsewhere, unbidden, the refrigerator motor clicked on, the floorboards beneath his bare feet humming with it.

He leaned over the sink, scooped water from the faucet, rinsed his mouth, and spat. When he straightened, Grady was watching him as before.

"Get on back to bed."

"Daddy."

"Don't call me that. After what I saw. No son of mine—"

Grady moved as if to console him. The boy didn't get through a day without putting his arms around someone.

Ed put a hand up, and Grady stepped back.

"You can't fix this by hugging," Ed said. "Now get."

Back in bed, he lay awake until first light. Beside him, Mathilda slept soundly.

In the weeks after the hurricane, Ed wanted Mathilda. He wanted her badly, his body accustomed to the hungering, the easy pleasures of their lovemaking. They'd been like two animals behind their bedroom door, with bodies that fit when they came together, so that afterward Ed ached while Mathilda trembled beside him.

It was deep in December, with Grady three months gone and a blustery north wind rattling the bedroom windows, when Mathilda reached for him one night, her touch like the jolt of an electric fence, the hard throb of need it loosed in him. They grabbed at one another, no pleasure in their coupling. And then it was over, Mathilda sobbing at the side of the bed while he rode out the wild beating of his heart. Afterward, at intervals, they reached for one another under cover of dark. Each morning after, he woke remembering, each time Mathilda lost to him again, and Grady's absence like a wound they'd opened.

One morning in February they woke to the smell of their coupling on the bedclothes, and before they could shrug into robes for breakfast, Domingo Escovedo knocked at the back door. Ed recognized the imprint of shock in the set of the boy's jaw, the odd brightness of his dark eyes. Clearly he had left the Escovedo farm before the hurricane, following work or crossing the border for a season with relatives in Mexico, and had only learned about Grady on returning. Domingo extended a dark, work-calloused hand, and Ed watched himself shake hands. Short at seventeen, the boy carried himself with wiry grace. His hair was heavy and black and straight. He wore a starched white shirt frayed at collar and cuffs, wool dress slacks of a cut Ed had worn when Ralph was in diapers, and a plain dark tie.

This was to be their only formal sympathy visit. In the frantic days after Grady had disappeared, the men of Nopalito had helped search the muddy creek bottom, sodden thickets along its banks, while the women brought casseroles and company. After they'd searched the watershed all the way to the Gulf, without finding so much as a shoe, their friends and neighbors slipped away. There was no body, no funeral, no grave. The neighbors didn't come to pay their regards. They wouldn't have known what to say. Ed didn't know. Domingo did.

"*Condolencias*," he said, and then, heavily accented, "I am sorry for your loss."

Mathilda stepped past Ed and took the boy's right hand in both of hers. "Your kindness is a comfort," she said.

Ed watched their exchange. He understood Domingo's terseness, recognized the way Mathilda rescued the boy from himself, let him step back, slip his hands into his pockets as if the casual posture of men were the only possible behavior in the face of grief.

His wife came to the rescue again. "Won't you please come in and set for a minute?"

Domingo almost bolted. "No, ma'am, thank you. I come to ask for work." The boy turned to Ed. "I help you before. This year, I plant with you, no?"

I plant with you. In lieu of an answer, Ed had a flashing vision of the live oak tree, dripping with September rain, and beneath the tree, on a trestle improvised of scrap lumber, a weathered wooden casket, open to the raindrops, and Grady asleep in the casket in work shirt and jeans—Ed could see breath in the rise of his chest—and Domingo beside the casket, dressed as he was today, Domingo bending from the waist, waking Grady with a kiss.

No. It was the one word Ed needed to say. *No, thank you, I can do my own planting.*

Mathilda answered for him. "My husband appreciates your offer. Rest assured he will pay you a decent wage."

And that was that.

On Monday of the last week in February, Ed climbed onto his tractor, Domingo behind him on the old drag planter, and for weeks they planted the crops. The boy brought a sack of burritos the first day, but Mathilda sent them back with him. At midday she put him through the washup she'd trained the Smith men to follow. She sat him at Ralph's old place at the dining table, opposite Grady and Evelyn's empty chairs. She made conversation. She called him Domino.

He was Grady's age. He'd been Grady's friend—if friendship could spring up through the Mexican boy's paltry, stilted English and Grady's few dozen Spanish phrases, so tortured that Domingo's face split ear to ear with grinning when Grady bit into a proffered *pan dulce* and said,

"*Me gusto mucho.*" Even Ed, who'd learned his meager Spanish in the fields, could hear Grady's mouth take on each vowel like a playground slide.

The Mexican boy knew how to work, Ed had to give him that. As for himself, he'd learned to shut his mouth and work with men who hit their wives or cheated. He found that the habit of not talking, which had served him in so many ways, could get him through long days with Domingo Escovedo, who seemed, for reasons of his own, to welcome silence.

After planting season, the boy moved on to other jobs. Ed hired him now and then. Domingo was good with a hoe. He knew how to attack Johnson grass. He worked tirelessly at whatever Ed charged him with doing. But weeks went by between tasks that needed help, and Mathilda turned bad as ever each time the boy said *adios* and headed for another farmer's offer of work.

In June, several days after Ed found Grady's glasses and hid them, he drove to the Escovedo farm and arranged for Domingo to help him grub mesquite and huisache from the grazing land along the slough. Two weeks, he offered. He could have done the grubbing himself. He could use the cash he'd fork over. But he knew that Mathilda would welcome the boy.

She fed Domingo and watched him eat, hardly touching her own food. Claimed she didn't have an appetite. Ed suspected she wouldn't allow herself the pleasure. More than once, when Mathilda had eaten a plateful, he'd heard her in the bathroom afterward, throwing up. She said it was a nervous stomach. Maybe so, but once, through a sliver of light along the partially closed door, he saw Mathilda lean over the commode and stick a finger down her throat. It seemed a pity, really, that she would punish herself like this. As long as he'd known her, his wife had loved rich food—gravy that gleamed with drippings, her homemade ice cream, so rich in butter fat it made your teeth feel greasy. She'd always doled treats out to herself and never left the house without what his mother had called foundation garments. She didn't need them anymore. The curves they shaped had dried up.

These days, Ed ate enough for both of them—pancakes and bacon, fried pork chops, bread pudding. One day he ate a plateful of Norma Pfeiler's cobbler at the café on Main Street, stopping only when Mathilda's gaze finally got to him. He'd been a real catch once, had admired himself in storefront windows—proud of his trim build, aware of the magic he worked on women. At twenty-five his hair had begun to thin, leaving him at thirty with his build, his smile, and a shiny pate. His father had said Ed looked like a jackass fighting the bit when he grinned, nothing but air to keep his ears apart. The old man plumbed new depths in ridicule over the hair loss. Ed shrugged off what his father said and learned to face himself in the mirror.

At forty-six he'd let himself go thick and soft, a bulge at the waist that gapped his shirt between the buttons. The grin was mostly gone, except as a reflex when he met people on the street. One morning shaving, he caught a glimpse of himself—the pinpoints of his pupils, the dark of the irises, glinting. He looked like someone who'd done murder.

After they hospitalized Mathilda, Evelyn phoned Norma Pfeiler at the café where her mother worked. "I'm afraid I have bad news," Ed heard his daughter say. "It's Momma. She's had a breakdown." Norma was tight-lipped. Only the few who needed to know would hear from her that Mathilda was in the hospital. They would tell the rest of Nopalito, and Ed's friends would have trouble looking him in the eye until his wife was back again.

He would've had a hard time saying exactly when things got out of hand, but he supposed it was the early afternoon of March 10, 1969. It would have been Grady's eighteenth birthday. His seventeenth had passed unremarked during the period of sleeplessness and waning hope that followed their fruitless searching. Ed had wanted this one to pass unnoticed too.

After the hurricane, Ralph had come home to help search for Grady, but one night in the house with Mathilda had driven him to the Wahrmund place, where he slept in the bed his best friend had vacated when the two of them took up roughnecking. He'd not been back to Nopalito since the searching ended. Evelyn had tried both years at Christmas. Both times, Ralph had put her off. With Grady's eighteenth looming, Ed had called his daughter and begged her not to come. She wouldn't have it. "I don't want us to forget Grady" is what she said. She'd called Ralph. She'd insisted. And here they were—Ralph in running shoes on the couch beside Ed, Mathilda in her reading chair, and Evelyn in a corner rocker.

Not a dozen words had been spoken before Mathilda got up and walked out of the living room. Seconds later, a crash erupted from the direction of Grady and Ralph's bedroom. Evelyn went to investigate and came back.

"She's digging in Grady's junk drawer. I'll stay with her for a while."

Minutes passed—and then a sound of wood scraping on wood followed by hurried footsteps. Ed caught a glimpse of Mathilda headed through the kitchen to the back porch, Grady's flimsy old bureau drawer perched on her shoulder and Evelyn behind her, saying, "Momma? Momma?" Ralph was up and out the front door by the time Evelyn disappeared out the back door with her mother. He'd run his old cross-country training route. He'd be back by sundown. Ed went to see what he could do about Mathilda.

She had carried Grady's drawer through the backyard gate and tossed it on the scrap lumber Ed kept neatly stacked out past the tractor shed. She rushed back to the house, whisked past him on the porch, and came out again, this time with a drawer holding Grady's shirts. Ed put a hand on her shoulder, and she whirled, knocking against the doorjamb. He stepped back, and she whirled again—it felt oddly like dancing—and was gone. She added a third drawer to the pile, this one with boxer shorts and socks—and then two armloads of clothes from Grady's closet. Evelyn appealed to her each time she arrived at the lumber pile and each time she left. He followed her from porch to bedroom, saying, "Mathilda, honey, stop this," and from bedroom to porch, saying much the same.

When she stepped away from the lumber pile and headed for the tractor shed, Ed left the porch and joined his daughter at the woodpile. He knew by the sounds coming from the shed that Mathilda was pumping gas out of the drum he used to fuel his tractor.

"We've got to stop her," Evelyn said.

He put a hand on his daughter's shoulder. "Best we can do is keep an eye on her."

"We can't let her burn Grady's things."

"Your brother's clothes are no use here. If burning them will get your momma through to sundown, let her burn them."

"But Grady's *things*," Evelyn said.

"Junk, Lynnie." Postcards, ribbons from the county fair, a miniature Alamo his son had carved out of a bar of soap—there was nothing in that drawer that needed saving. "If you want something to remember your brother by, there's plenty left in the house."

Mathilda appeared with a gasoline can and doused the shamble of their son's clothing and souvenirs. She tossed a kitchen match, and as the gasoline lit, the heat whooshed against them, sucking the breath right out of their lungs. Mathilda stood there briefly, her face and dress shimmering. Then she turned and went back to the house.

Moments later she came down the porch steps with a box of family snapshots. Ed knocked them out of her hands, and as his daughter scrambled for the scattered images of their lives together, he got a bear hug on Mathilda and started talking to her, the same husky, soothing phrases he mouthed into the ears of a young calf trembling after the knife or a puppy swollen with snakebite. Mathilda let loose a hoarse and desperate cry. Then she let him take her inside to bed, broken. She was all but eager, the next morning, when Evelyn suggested a stay in the hospital. A rest cure, he'd heard it called.

Ralph stayed on for a few days while Mathilda was in the hospital. Together one night, they finished off the bourbon left in the house. The next afternoon, before returning from a drive to Nopalito, they stopped at the package store on the edge of town.

Albert Decker was behind the counter. Increasingly in recent years, he'd taken over the daily operations of the business from his elderly mother, known so long as Mrs. Decker that Ed wasn't sure he could dredge her first name out of memory. Albert would've been pushing sixty by now. He'd always been too thin, but the flesh had begun to turn loose from his jawline and throat—at odds with his whispery girlish voice, the pompadour he'd slicked his hair into for as long as Ed could remember, black as shoe polish from the dye jobs his mother had been giving him for twenty years.

"I don't believe I've had the pleasure," Albert said, looking at Ralph.

"This is my firstborn," Ed said. "You remember Ralph? He's been gone for a while."

Albert turned back to Ralph, smiling. "Perhaps I do remember. I'm Ahl-baíre, Ahl-baíre Decker."

Ralph took the limp hand Albert offered—fingers plumped and smoothed by lotions and emollients, nails carefully manicured and coated with a colorless polish that shone like water through fog.

"Good to see you again, Al." The sparkle that lit up Ralph's voice was all ridicule.

Albert Decker had learned to smile through worse. He turned his attention back to Ed. "We haven't seen you in a while."

"I don't drink so much these days," Ed said. He had pretty much quit liquor after Grady disappeared, hadn't stopped at the Decker's package store since the summer before the hurricane blew in.

The smile left Albert's face. "Please accept my heartfelt sympathy," he said.

The words took Ed by surprise—the hurt they loosed in his ribcage. He made himself remove his hands from his pockets. He let his right hand be squeezed by both of Albert's.

"Mrs. Decker and I were so sorry to hear about Grady." Albert turned from Ed to Ralph. "I miss your little brother."

Ralph scuffed at the floor with the soles of his boots.

"A sweet boy," Albert went on, his voice dreamy and wistful. "He always got my name right."

"We miss him too," Ed said.

"I know you do. I can see it in your eyes." Again, Albert turned to Ralph. "Your father was always laughing with his eyes."

Ed asked for a bottle of their usual and made his way to the truck with his son. No sooner had Ralph closed the passenger door than he shook himself like a dog fresh out of the creek.

"Ahl-baíre," Ralph said. He rolled down the window and spat. "Someone ought to cornhole that old nancy boy."

Ed gave his son a look.

"What? You don't think he wants it up the ass?"

Before them, through the windshield, sat the ramshackle package store shelved floor to ceiling with the honey burn of distilled grain. Under a gray sky, the neon sign cast its watery light—Decker's, Decker's, Decker's—against peeling clapboard walls with slatted windows to the second-floor living quarters Albert Decker shared with his mother. Except for a month in Paris forty years ago, *this* had been his life.

"I'm not sure it's my place anymore"—Ed paused—"to judge what a body might want."

"He pisses me off—talking about Grady was a sweet boy, Grady said his name right."

"Your brother was nice to Albert."

"I don't like it that he was. I don't like what it made people think."

Ed turned the key in the ignition, shifted the truck into reverse, and turned to Ralph.

"What you think people think—it might be better left unsaid."

"You don't want to hear it," Ralph said. "That Grady was a faggot. And he wasn't. My brother was *not* a faggot."

Ralph had been in Odessa, a safe remove from the Gulf Coast—his mother biding the time in Norma Pfeiler's cellar—when Hurricane Beulah blew in. At home the wind and rain kept Ed and Grady occupied. They'd left two windows unshuttered, one on either side of the house. Ed couldn't breathe otherwise, couldn't see what the storm was doing. As the wind tore at the place, he and Grady hovered at the uncovered windows. They rolled bath towels into place along the sills, wringing them into mop buckets. Hours they worked at it, their fore-arms sore with wringing. The immediate risk lay in the wind and what it could blow through a window, a more lasting risk in what Mathilda would do to them if they let the water warp her floors.

When the wind died and the rains came down, there was nothing to do. By noon of the second day—their fourth day in the house together—they had trouble facing each other. It was like goofed-up swordplay, each man sighting for an instant, then pointing just past his opponent. When Ed left the room, he felt worse. As soon as he returned, Grady came up with a lame excuse to be elsewhere.

On the afternoon of the twenty-second, Ed sat in his chair by the radio, drifting, when he felt a hand on his shoulder. He jumped at the unexpected touch.

"Where've you been?"

"Out back. The creek is bad out of its banks."

Ed adjusted the radio dial. Against a backdrop of static, faint voices, wavering lines of song, rose up and ebbed.

"Wish I could get across," Grady said. "Wish I knew everything was okay at the Escovedos."

"I *wish* " Ed stopped. What he might've said hung in the air between them.

"I started it," Grady said. "What we did. I started it."

"You will not say—"

"You didn't see the worst of it. After you left. The worst thing I've done." There was pain in Grady's face, a plea written there. "I slapped him, Daddy. I made us stop. For you."

Outside the floodwaters hummed. "I've done a hurtful thing," Grady said. "I can't get across the creek to make it right."

Ed took his son by the shoulders. "You will not go to that Mexican."

"You don't want me." Grady looked around. "Here." His voice was calm.

Father and son, they looked at each other. Outside, the frogs called, and closer by, on the radio, a woman's voice, singing—*We didn't find it there, so we moved on*—her voice far away and fading.

"I'll be outside for a while," Grady said. "I want to watch the water."

Ed didn't know when he'd started shaking. He had to clench his jaw to keep his teeth from chattering. It felt like chills, like fever. He needed to say the right thing.

"Clean up before you come back in this house" is what he said. "Bring any mud in here, your momma will skin us both."

Grady hugged him. It was as simple as the doing of it. Ed stood there and let him, his own arms limp and useless.

"I'm your son," Grady said. And he was gone.

On August 3, 1970, Hurricane Celia made landfall at Corpus Christi. Norma Pfeiler called beforehand to offer her cellar, but Mathilda would not be moved. Skittish and silent, she kept to the house while Ed got the place ready. The hurricane tightened as it moved into the brush country west of the bay, rain beating against the walls and roof until Ed feared he might howl with the noises tearing at the place. When it was over, he couldn't keep his wife inside the shuttered house. Nothing would do but she must see the water. The sight unraveled Mathilda. She had a second breakdown.

Early one evening after a visit to the hospital, as Ed turned into the wide main hall on the ground floor, a custodian turned from his work there. A short, wiry Mexican who looked to be sixty, with cheeks that showed the skull beneath, the man put out a hand to say *stop*, then raised a bony forefinger to his lips. He breathed one word into the fading light between them. *Mojado.* Ahead, the floor was covered with freshly slicked-on wax gleaming like the surface of a tiled swimming pool. In the stillness of the waning day, with the old custodian beckoning beside him, their secret glimmering to the far end of the voiceless corridor, late sunlight pouring in like butter—Ed looked down and down beneath the wavy surface of the waxed floor to a place in the deep where light and shadow fluttered, like a swimmer going the length of a pool underwater.

The next morning he took Grady's glasses from the hatbox in his bedroom closet and drove to the Escovedo place. Domingo, still short but clearly a man at almost twenty, came out to meet him, and they stood together in the yard, exchanging pleasantries about the weather and the farming life.

"You want me for a job?"

"Not now," Ed said. "Maybe when the fields dry out. I come to show you—to give you—something." He pulled the glasses from his pocket and handed them to Domingo. The young man looked blank for a moment, and then his jaw tightened. He looked at Ed and swallowed, his dark eyes shining.

"Where?" was all he said.

"I found 'em in the creek. Couple years back, spring after we lost him."

"You think he drowned?"

"There was a lot of water when he went out there."

"You think he's dead." It was both statement and question.

"Son—" he had not used that word with Domingo—"he's got to be somewhere."

"Here." Domingo touched his fingertips to Ed's chest. He put the glasses in his shirt pocket.

"I will keep these for Grady."

He walked Ed to his truck and stood there on the caliche drive, a lone figure in Ed's rearview mirror, smaller and smaller beneath the August sky.

THIS BUSINESS OF NOT FORGIVING

RALPH SMITH, JIMMY DON WAHRMUND, AND CANDACE MEYER,
SPRING 1976

A STRANGER WANDERED INTO the Wellhead one night. Tassels on his shoes. He tried to make conversation with the woman tending bar—asked what might be seen in this part of the world before moving on.

"Odessa?" the bartender said. "Only thing worth looking at is the city limit sign driving out. In the rearview. All the letters backwards."

"Nail. On. The. Head," Ralph said, emphasizing each word with his fist on the bar. "Let's get the fuck out of here." He'd only ever known two places—Coastal Bend brush country and this godforsaken piece of West Texas—a toss-up when it came to words like *empty, desolate, flat*.

But with Jimmy Don beside him, and Jimmy Don was always beside him, seem like the road out of one only led to the other.

Next morning, when they pulled away from the shabby house they'd rented for how many years now?—a baker's dozen—Jimmy Don wasn't even driving.

"Where to?" Ralph asked. He should've known better, should've said Ruidoso, Taos, Durango, routes marked on the map he kept in the glove compartment.

"I need a Lone Star at the Triple Six," Jimmy Don said, and Ralph drove him there, 475 miles to Jimmy Don's favorite watering hole on the stretch of coastal plain inland of Corpus Christi. A stop for lunch and gas, pit stops before and after, a stretch of hill country to make Ralph think *anywhere but home* and then drive there anyway to spite himself.

A week, maybe ten days later—Ralph lost track quickly—Candace Meyer walked into the Triple Six, took the stool beside them and didn't even say hello, just set her clutch on the counter and asked for a double shot, neat.

She clicked Ralph's glass—he drank his bourbon on the rocks—and raised a silent toast to Ralph and Jimmy Don in the mirror behind the bar. She took a sip and held the glass in front of her as if studying the liquid glowing there. Ralph waited, he always did, stretching the interval before raising a glass to his lips, letting the liquor ease into his bloodstream and feeling the calm as it settled in him. Anticipation was one of the pleasures of drinking, though succeeding sips never delivered the release of the night's first taste. Jimmy Don teased him, called him an alchy in slow motion. Ralph shrugged him off, watching his friend put away half a dozen longnecks while the ice melted in his bourbon as he made his way through a double shot.

"A bit of a drive," Candace said, and when Ralph turned in her direction, "from Odessa. What are you two doing here?"

"Quit our jobs. Taking some time off."

"Why bother with the middle of nowhere?"

"Might ask you the same," Jimmy Don put in.

"Two shotgun weddings." Candace took another sip. "Got myself stuck in Nopalito. You boys got out. Why not keep going? I imagine Odessa has roads headed someplace worth driving."

"You sound like Ralph," Jimmy Don said. "Up to me, we'd bunk at my folks or his for a while."

Ralph hadn't even been over to see his family since the drive down. "Can't breathe in that house," he told Candace. "Makes me itch." Instead, he'd made a couple of phone calls, secured an empty trailer on ranchland near the Triple Six.

"His momma used to would say things," Jimmy Don offered, "could turn a person to stone."

On the afternoon of Ralph's high school graduation, he'd packed and hidden an old suitcase beneath the bed he shared with his little brother. The plan was to escape Nopalito, he and Jimmy Don together. Destination West Texas, the oil fields. That evening, diploma in hand, he rode home with his family and made himself endure the celebration there. An hour in, Jimmy Don arrived, his presence arousing no suspicion. Ralph waited for the noise to enfold his friend, then stepped into his bedroom, took up the suitcase, and tried to slip out of the house unnoticed. In the kitchen, he came face to face with his mother. Jimmy Don could have distracted her until Ralph was safely out of the house, but confrontation was Jimmy Don's style. All these years later, though Ralph had never accused his friend, he was certain that somehow Jimmy Don had maneuvered his mother into that kitchen.

She erupted. Grabbed at Ralph, followed him out of the house. Where did he think he was going? That suitcase wasn't his, goddammit. He would kindly turn around and get back inside. "*Now.* Do you hear me? I will make you regret this."

Jimmy Don soft-shoed ahead of them and put himself behind the wheel. Ralph took the shotgun seat, disengaged his mother's grip, and closed the door.

"Spitting mad," he told Candace. "Shouting about eighteen years of disrespect, eighteen years of my guff. Told me I'd made her appreciate folks who drown cats at birth."

"You got the last laugh," Jimmy Don said, tapping the neck of his beer bottle against Ralph's glass of bourbon.

"How's that?"

"You're not the one who drowned."

The summer Grady was seven—Ralph would have been twelve—they went boating with friends on Lake Corpus Christi. The boat had just tied up at the pier, so Grady jumped out and started splashing. Ralph had been behind the boat on skis; he joined his brother. His mother and the friend who'd invited them out were sitting on lawn chairs near the water's edge, sipping daiquiris. Ralph had long forgotten the hostess woman's name, but he had not forgotten that, like his mother, she loved dressing up, no occasion needed. That afternoon, both women were wearing bright sundresses, bright lipstick. Both had somehow traversed the weedy expanse between the lake house and the shore in some kind of open-toed ankle-strap shoes. Ordinarily Ralph paid little heed to women's shoes. What he noticed today was how out of place his mother and her friend looked—as if they'd parachuted into place for a glossy, full-page cigarette ad. On the shores of a muddy lake.

Water along the pier was chest high for Ralph and deep enough that Grady needed his life jacket. The ski rope trailed from the back of the boat, buoyed by a Styrofoam lozenge near the end that fastened to the boat. Without thinking, Ralph took hold of the Styrofoam and slapped the short end of the rope in the water. Not once did it occur to him that the rope had somehow come loose from the boat, that the section he slapped into the water ended in the hook that should've secured it. With the bad luck of bad timing, Grady chose this moment to holler and splash in Ralph's direction. Ralph splashed back with the rope.

The hook raked across Grady's scalp, and then Grady was shrieking and blood was pouring from the gash in his scalp and all hell broke loose. Their mother made it to Grady in the speed of a time lapse. She was holding her youngest, alternately cooing at him and shouting at Ralph, like a cartoon of mixed signals, fear for the one son at war with rage spilling out of her at the other, the front of her sundress drenched with blood while Grady added to the uproar by cursing a blue streak. Where had he learned such words, such fluency?

Given shots along the gash for the pain and then stitched up, Grady was quick to forgive. Not so their mother. She railed at Ralph for days. Periodically, until the day nine years later when Grady went out to look at hurricane floodwaters and didn't came back, she branded Ralph careless, spiteful, a descendant of Cain.

"You." Candace nodded at Jimmy Don. "Are still an asshole." She slipped off her stool and disappeared into the restroom.

"All washed up," Jimmy Don said.

"I've had a glance or two." Ralph indicated the mirror behind the bar. "I kind of like what I see."

"Not again." Ralph's friend put a hand to his brow, a gesture of mock despair. "Charlie Chump. Always ready to grab hold when the woman is smoked out, fucked out, can't stop telling her sad story."

Jimmy Don tipped a splash of beer into an ashtray sitting there, made a couple of stirring circles with his forefinger, then raised the smudged fingertip. "Put your mouth on this. Give it plenty of tongue. That's what it's gonna be like."

"I know what you're up to," Ralph said. "You messed up once and for good. Girl like Candace, as I recall. Bit of sass in her, bit of spine. Stop trying to rescue me."

"Well, hello," Jimmy Don said. Ralph followed his gaze into the mirror and swiveled with him to take in the young woman who'd paused just inside the door. His friend's type, this girl—stunning breasts, face unlined by age or worry, young enough to be carded. Her makeup put Ralph in mind of the woman who'd raised him—lipstick, eyeliner, mascara, eye shadow—expertly but heavily applied. His mother had cured him of tarted-up women in pushup bras.

Jimmy Don patted the stool beside him.

The girl hesitated, but just then Candace stepped out of the restroom.

"They're harmless," she said, as if that were the truth about anyone. "Come. Join us."

"Hi," the girl said, taking the seat Jimmy Don had patted. "I'm Lucinda. Please don't call me Lucy."

"Lucinda," Jimmy Don said. "I like the sound of Lucinda. Might I ask the bartender to prepare a libation for you?"

"Why yes, thank you. I'll have a Harvey Wallbanger."

No one so much as cracked a smile, but Ralph knew what they were thinking. A Harvey Wallbanger. But Jimmy Don wouldn't care. He'd order half a dozen frou-frou drinks for the girl. Vodka was his ally, however disguised.

As Ralph had expected, the bartender asked for ID. Lucinda produced a driver's license, then slipped it back into her pocketbook.

"Could've passed it around," said Jimmy Don. "Fess up now. How old are you?"

"I'll tell if you all will."

"Thirty," said Ralph.

"Thirty-one," said Jimmy Don.

And Candace, "Thirty-two."

"I'm twenty-two," said the girl. "But I'll try to keep up."

"You'll do fine, darlin'." Jimmy Don tapped his longneck against the rim of her glass. "I'll give you some pointers."

"Before thirty, after thirty." Candace took a sip of bourbon and seemed to contemplate the numbers. "Doesn't much matter. One age or another, life goes off the rails."

"Disappointment," Jimmy Don said. He paused as if to let the word sink in. "Disappointment has hardened your heart."

"I've lost the knack for smiling when a handsome man suggests I ought to."

"Heartless." Jimmy Don made clicking sounds with his tongue. "Just plain heartless."

Without pausing, he launched into a story about a hard-hearted woman back home in Nopalito, a woman he swore he'd known, a woman of indeterminate age who would remain nameless in his telling.

"A light sleeper," Jimmy Don said. "I think it was a guilty conscience kept her awake. Or meanness. Ask me, I think she liked sharpening her grudges while other folks slept. This one night, though." He took a sip from his longneck. "This one night it was the family dog, name of Duke as I recall. She claim he howled all night, and this part might be true. Eyewitness testimony? Duke was one stupid, exasperating, tail-wagging dog. Howl if the breeze was blowing, howl 'cause the sky was blue, howl 'cause the moon was bright."

"You're making him sound like a cartoon dog," Lucinda said. "I think this is a made-up story."

"Swear on the Good Book," Jimmy Don said, one hand in the air, the other on an imaginary Bible. "One night, soon as our heroine's head hit the pillow, one night Duke started up. Didn't stop. Ought to have barked himself hoarse, barked himself into hound-dog laryngitis. But not Duke. That dog howled Mrs. Cantankerous into a headache so bad *she* wanted to let loose and howl. Except by then the sun was coming up, and she was planning her revenge."

On the word *revenge*, Candace signaled the bartender, who poured her another double shot. "To bullshit." She reached across and tapped the neck of Jimmy Don's beer bottle. He put both hands over his heart and made a face of mock dismay.

"Go on," said Lucinda. "I expect a trick. Like from Wile E. Coyote."

"This is the best part." Jimmy Don winked at Ralph in the mirror. "Mrs. Insomnia got up and got herself to the family gun closet. Tiptoe. Didn't wanna wake anyone who might try and stop her. Took the loaded twenty-two and got herself outside. Whisper-called, 'Here, Duke.' Dog come right away, of course. He was that stupid. One shot was all it took. One shot. Middle of the forehead. Half an inch above the eyeline." Jimmy Don made an imaginary pistol of his hand, pointed at himself, and said, "Bang!"

"*Stop*," Lucinda said. "Stop it. This is an awful story."

"Know what I call it?" Jimmy Don chuckled. "I call this story 'The Dog Who Died of a Headache.'"

"Why would you make up such an *awful* story?"

"He likes to think the worst of people," Candace said. "Stick around long enough, he'll put you in one of his unflattering fictions."

Jimmy Don had looks on his side. Charisma. The girl he'd dazzled in high school—smart enough to know she was being conned—Ralph heard her say once that his friend could charm a diamondback out of its rattle.

Already, Lucinda was falling; her objection to the dog story seemed forgotten. Jimmy Don had lowered his voice to a husky, conspiratorial near-whisper, creating a space for two, Ralph and Candace excluded. He signaled the bartender for another Harvey Wallbanger. Another. A fourth. When he and Lucinda got up to leave, he leaned in and whispered to Ralph, "You can have the trailer. I've made other arrangements." He winked and walked out with the girl.

"I'm way ahead of you," Candace said when the bartender poured for her again. Ralph had just started on his second double shot.

"I like a quiet place," she added. "Couple of regulars at the bar. I appreciate a bartender"—she raised her glass to him—"who knows how to keep his mouth shut."

Behind them cues sticks clicked, stripes and solids tumbling into pockets.

"Your friend," Candace said, "does not have the knack." When Ralph looked a question at her, she added, "For keeping a rein on his tongue. Good thing the young ones fall under his spell. I never cared for the famous good looks. Jimmy Don is entirely too pretty."

"I can't explain him," Ralph said. "We're best friends, no question. I can't count the times I've tested Jimmy Don's patience. Doesn't matter. He'd do anything for me."

"I've never had that kind of friend. My husband, I guess, but if I drop my guard for long, I say too much. Makes him afraid I'll up and leave."

A round of whoops erupted from the pool table.

"Women, though," she said, when the noise had calmed, "the ones I know, they're more like that *creature* in Jimmy Don's story, the one who shot the dog. They might pretend otherwise, but I'm not fooled."

Behind them the sound of balls being racked for another game.

"Even on my worst day," Candace went on, "when I want a dynamite plunger to blow the town apart, I'd point a gun at myself. Maybe one of the men I've known, but they all got old and sad."

"You're not that kind of woman."

"I'm not sure anyone is that bad."

"Jimmy Don exaggerates," Ralph said, "but that story is true. He heard it from a reliable source."

"Who?"

"His best friend. You'd believe him, wouldn't you, sitting here beside you? My mother shot the family dog."

Ralph rattled the ice in his bourbon. Was it the liquor? Jimmy Don's way of inserting unblunted memories into his ribcage? This woman on the barstool beside him, her refreshing candor?

"She changed," he said. "My mother. Into someone else. After Grady. Like body snatchers came in the night and traded. I used to believe if there was any justice in the world, my mother would get what was coming to her. And then worse happened."

"Worse always does," Candace said. "One minute I had my escape planned, the next minute I was pregnant. One minute I was a dreamy pregnant girl wanting a milkshake, and then my husband was dead. They used to call me Candy, some still do. I don't know who that girl was."

"I only know one of me," Ralph said. "Some guy in the Sunday funnies. Jimmy Don's roughneck buddy Ralph. How'm I gonna get away from *him*? Get away from *this*?" He made a waving motion that took in bar, pool tables, brush country.

"Oh, honey," Candace said. "You've got a car."

"I could leave right now. Or maybe head out tomorrow."

"Do it," Candace said. "Do it for the both of us." She slipped from her stool and settled up with the bartender.

"I can drive you," Ralph said, and she accepted.

"My husband would thank you—saving him from taxi duty. We'll come back for my car tomorrow." Before Ralph could ask, she added, "We have an understanding. Stan allows me an evening like this. I behave myself. I don't drive when I've had this much to drink."

When they pulled out of the parking lot, against his better judgment Ralph mentioned the trailer. Candace was kind but firm. "I have a husband at home. He loves me. I don't know why, but he does."

The night beckoned, dim glow of dashboard lights against the surrounding dark. Slowing for a curve, Ralph ached for another hour with

Candace. He wished for a long drive with her going home to her husband. Simultaneously, he wanted Candace—wanted someone like her—to be going home with him. Staying longer than the time it would take them to bed each other.

"What's it like?" he asked. "Being married? You've done that twice."

"You might want to ask someone else. I am not a reliable witness."

Up ahead, lightning marked the horizon, a spring thunderstorm out there in the night.

"I'm asking you."

"Some days I'm content. Some days I live in a cage."

Crushed rock crunching beneath them, they reached the end of the county road, and then blacktop hummed by in the dark.

Three or four miles short of Nopalito, they drove into the storm. Rain hammered at the car so heavily that Ralph slowed almost to a stop, his car buffeted by powerful gusts. Windshield wipers at top speed, headlights on bright, he steered the car into the center of the road and followed a ghostly blur, the center line. When lightning struck, the countryside lit up for an instant, the black cloud so low it brought one word to mind.

Tornado.

He knew it wasn't a funnel cloud. Still, it made his pulse jump.

Time stood still inside this kind of punishment. It might only have been a minute they'd driven into the storm, but in the moment of anticipation between a flash of lightning and the thunder that would pound them, beside him, Candace said simply, "I'm scared."

Ralph stopped the car. Right there in the middle of the road, headlights shining into the rain.

"I'm scared," his mother had said. "We've got to pray."

When? Where? He didn't know. But the storm had come on them like this. Sudden. Fierce. The two of them only. His father, his sister, Grady—elsewhere. And his mother, who had loomed over his childhood, monstrous in the power she wielded, his mother—suddenly vulnerable, suddenly afraid—asking him to pray. She'd been driving, and like him tonight, she'd stopped the car. Ralph had been merely frightened before his mother said, "I'm scared," before she said, "Please pray," her words releasing a terror in him he thought would blow them off the road that had held them so securely until the storm unleashed itself inside his mother.

Ralph had thought he was immune from prayer, all that mumbo jumbo during Mass—swinging censer, clouds of incense, endless, indecipherable intoning in Latin. But the words were in him. And that night, for a few endless minutes alone with his mother on a road in the storm, he prayed with desperate conviction.

Hail Mary full of grace the Lord is with thee.

Blessed art Thou among women and blessed is the fruit of thy womb Jesus.

Over and over, Ralph prayed, the words a frantic hammering in his throat.

At some point he was aware that his mother had curled up on the seat between them, arms cradling her head and ears. Praying, Ralph shrugged out of his jacket and covered her with it. She took his hands and held them until they hurt. One minute he was praying Hail Marys, a frenzy, a madness of prayers, and the next the storm was gone, the night so quiet for a moment he thought they were dead.

It was near two when Ralph arrived back at the trailer, the night pitch black when he shut off the headlights. He felt his way up the steps and inside, closed the door behind him, sat down on the floor, leaned against the door, and wept. He'd cried before, quick tears and quickly over—behind the barn the morning his mother shot the goofy dog he'd grown to love, beside the phone the night his father called him in Odessa to say that his Uncle Aaron had died. He'd cried when his grandparents died, cried over a snake-bit cat, cried when Elizabeth Taylor succumbed to pneumonia in *The Last Time I Saw Paris*. Jimmy Don had teased him for years. "You cry often as a girl," he'd said, though Ralph had never cried for Grady.

At the door of his trailer, at two in the morning, after drinks at the Triple Six and driving into a storm with Candace Meyer, he cried for all of them. For Grady and the life he wouldn't have. For his father, who'd let Grady out of the house to look at the floodwaters and could never undo the moment, never say, "No, son, stay here. With me." For his mother and himself in the storm he'd locked away until this evening, when a woman he hadn't seen in years said to him, "I'm scared."

At six the next morning, Ralph turned into the short drive leading to the farmhouse where he'd grown up. He'd tried sleep but without success. At four, he gave up, got up, put on the pair of jeans he'd dropped beside the bed, and sat in a folding chair on the trailer's ramshackle stoop. The night had cleared, almost no moon but a sky stippled with starlight. Now and then a hint of breeze stirred in the mesquite, and cool Gulf moisture breathed against his chest, his arms, his face. After a while he fetched a shirt from inside, got in his car, and headed for home.

As he pulled into the outer yard, his mother stepped out the back door and walked toward him. "Let's sit," she said, indicating two old Adirondack chairs, a long-ago gift from Uncle Aaron, who'd been able to work magic with his hands.

"Your father will be up shortly," she said. "He's making up for a bad night. I wake like clockwork whether I sleep or not. Every single godforsaken morning at five."

They sat immersed in sparrow chatter, no talking between them, no awkwardness in the lack of words, Ralph realized with surprise. He could not remember when he'd felt at home with his mother, just the two of them, no buffering little brother, no sister, no father, no one to soften their edges.

"I have learned something," his mother said, no hint of what was coming. "You can love somebody and not be able to forgive him for a hurt you can't get over. That shouldn't be possible, but it is."

Ralph let silence settle between them again. He could feel that his mother would say more, that she had no need of words from him.

"It's a bitter knot," she said, "this business of not forgiving. For a long time I was afraid it would be the end of me."

His mother was fifty, fifty-one. She looked sixty and more. Her hair, once bright and blonde, once a mark of pride, had lost all its light, uncombed this morning and streaked with gray. She hadn't worn makeup in years. She was thin to the point of gauntness, her face, her eyes stamped by grief.

Grief was the word carved in her.

Again Ralph felt tears coming, but this morning he held them back. His mother had howled her grief. His sister, in her quiet way, had let grief in. His father had carried a double load—grief weighed down by shame for letting Grady out of the house to his death. But Ralph? Ralph, Grady's brother, had gone back to Odessa and put his brother's death aside. The loss was in him now, but he would feel it later. Now there was something he wanted to say.

"I stayed away, Momma. I'm sorry. I shouldn't have stayed away."

"Your sister has stepped in. Sometimes more than is helpful. She has been here when I cannot bear company." She reached across the space between them and brushed his wrist with her hand. "This is between us. Not a word to your sister—she has been a godsend. I would not want her to think otherwise."

The sparrows were still at it, a brighter sound in the light of day, the morning clear and sun-washed. Somewhere behind them, in the trees down along the slough, several cows erupted in a bout of call and response.

Ralph had no idea he would say what he said when the cows quieted. "I need to get away for a while. Jimmy Don won't like it, but I have to get out."

"Where?" was all his mother said.

"New Mexico. Colorado. I want to be in the mountains."

Ralph felt no resistance in her silence.

"I have some money saved," he said, as if to reassure himself.

"And when it's spent?"

"There's work waiting. In Odessa. Jimmy Don will be there. You've never cared for him."

"You know what your father said to me once? He said, 'Mathilda, everbody knows you're the prettiest woman around. Everybody knows Jimmy Don is more'n nice to look at. Let the boy strut when he's in the room with you.'"

"And how did that go over?"

"About as well as could be expected."

From nowhere a tabby cat materialized on the arm of her chair, light gray stippled with dark markings that showed him a descendant of leopards. The cat hissed once in Ralph's direction and then flopped into the boneless posture that always made him think of a bear rug. Without remarking on the cat's arrival, his mother scratched him behind an ear.

"All this talk," she said, "has made me hungry." The cat was purring loudly now. She took her hand away and stood. "Let's have some breakfast. If I know your father, he's already spied on us from the bedroom window. He'll want to see you before you go."

Moving toward the house, they fell into step beside each other, and then momentarily, as they reached the back steps, in the space between Ralph's shoulder blades, the lightest touch, his mother's hand.

THE LIGHTING, THE SINGING, THE UNSPOKEN WISH

FOUR FRIENDS AND A HUSBAND, OCTOBER 11, 1985–JANUARY 1, 1986

I
—

Albert was frosting the cake for Candace, crisp October air drifting in through the open windows, when Mathilda called out from below. Footsteps clicked up the stairs, and then voices livened up his kitchen, Mathilda at her usual volume, Dorene calm and balanced beside her, and Albert doing the feathery lilt he'd always thought sounded most like him, with forays into the emphatic, the flamboyant Ahl-baíre he'd almost forgotten was in him until Mathilda coaxed him out again— seventy-five now, but who was counting?

"I stopped a while back," said Mathilda. "Counting. Wish I could see myself through silk when I look in the mirror—you know?—like Gloria Swanson way back when." She struck a pose right out of *Sunset Boulevard*. "Suppose I could fool Eduardo? Sweet, gorgeous Eduardo!" Putting thumb and forefinger to her mouth, she released a wolf whistle that made Albert wish he were hard of hearing.

Eduardo Maldonado had been managing the package store since

the year Albert's mother died. Actually, Eduardo owned the business. Albert had signed it over several years back, with the proviso that the upstairs apartment remain his for life.

"I'd pay rent," he said. "But he won't have it." And then, wishing aloud, "I hope he finds a man who deserves him. And soon. Do you suppose the neighbors"—he glanced toward the window and the town beyond—"will behave decently?"

"Michael is the right age," Dorene said, a pensive hush to her voice as she named her youngest son.

"The homosexual in absentia," Mathilda put in. "Do you suppose he'll ever fess up? Use that word in front of you? Bring home a sweetheart?"

"Jimmy Don is the one I miss," Dorene said. Recognizing the wistful timbre in her tone, Albert exchanged a look with Mathilda.

"It shouldn't even be legal," he said, "for a man to be *that* good looking."

"Seven years," Dorene went on as if lost to the interruption. "Every day for seven years."

"Doesn't matter how long," Mathilda told her. "Missing one of your own. It won't ever let up."

"He wouldn't pity me," Dorene said. "On my worst day, Jimmy Don would not pity me."

"We have that in common," said Mathilda. "You brought the candles, right?"

"I don't know." Caution was Dorene's fallback. "Maybe we shouldn't do candles. Or just a few?"

"I *adore* birthday candles." Albert brandished a fistful of them from the bag Dorene had produced. "Do you suppose next year I can have a cake big enough for all of mine?"

"Candace Meyer is not even fifty, not even close." The words drummed out of Mathilda, a mockery of her trademark impatience. "I'm old enough to be her mother. She has been through childbirth. These candles"—she grabbed them from Albert—"will not be her undoing."

She poked one into the cake—another, another—a random arrangement, counting under her breath until the last one.

"Forty-two," she said. "Voila! Done!"

"Oh, it's lovely. Thank you." They turned to find Candace standing at the stairwell landing.

Albert had been watching her since she was ten, wondering about this dazzling fairy child given to aged parents, wondering what would become of her in dusty, blinkered Nopalito. Would beauty be her ticket out? Or disappointment hem her in? When she didn't get out—Albert had feared she wouldn't—his interest became personal, as if in Candace he might find the key he'd needed when he was seventeen, twenty, thirty-two, fifty. Since the way out was blocked, a way in.

Mathilda Smith—he would never have imagined even a few words with her—Mathilda Smith had been his own ticket to a life outside the package store. Some weeks after his mother's death—coming up on nine years ago already—Albert had looked up from his roses one afternoon as Mathilda pulled over, got out of her car, and approached him.

"I am not a grateful person," she said. "I'm not sure I can learn this late in life. What I want to say is—" She paused. "I have been remiss. I have never thanked you."

"Thanked me?"

"You were kind to my son."

"I rather think it was the reverse," Albert said. "Grady was kind to me."

"I went to the creek," she said. "Yesterday morning. Restless after breakfast. Told myself I shouldn't and walked out there anyway. My feet just took me."

Albert snipped a bloomed-out rose and deposited it in the basket he carried for deadheading.

"Hasn't rained in ages," she said. "But you know that. The creek was dry as cornstalks in August. I just stood there and looked."

Albert snipped another stem and waited.

"The breeze picked up," she said. "Sounded like water, you know, how it rushes by on its way to the Gulf. Like this." She paused as a gust blew among Albert's roses. It didn't sound like water, but he knew that didn't matter. His roses fluttered, calmed, and then words tumbled out of Mathilda.

"I had one of my panic attacks. Haven't had one in ages. Couldn't breathe. No water in the creek—didn't matter—I was in the water swimming after Grady, and the current was pulling us under." Mathilda touched a hand to Albert's elbow. "When I came back to myself, the tears were flooding out of me. I knew I had to come here. Had to say thank you. For Grady."

"My roses have a magical effect," Albert said. "They make me happy when I'm not. Spend a few minutes here. You might leave feeling calmer."

Mathilda lingered. Minutes later, Albert bent to sample the bouquet from his favorite climber, a Don Juan at the peak of its crimson bloom. As he straightened, she remarked on the band of gray along the part in his hair. "You have looked better," she said.

"My mother always did my color. I could have it done, I suppose. At my age, though, it would seem like vanity."

"I know that feeling," she said. "Have to remind myself to wash my own. Coloring is out of the question." She seemed to consider—and then this: "You've got to buck up. Look after yourself."

"You might want to consider your own advice."

Mathilda merely stared. For a moment she looked as if she might get her dander up. He'd witnessed that side of her before.

"I was never any good," she said, "at talking around what's on my mind. How old was your mother?"

"Mrs. Decker was eighty-eight. It was time for her to be gone. She wanted that."

"Grady was sixteen. I cannot let myself *think*—about him being twenty-five. If I picture him alive and breathing—standing right here in your rose garden—I might start howling. Like I did before."

"He was the only person in this town," Albert said, "who looked at me and didn't change expression."

"Tell me something about Grady, something he said. What he was like around you. If I'm not trapped in my house, if I'm here with you, maybe I can stand it."

A week later, having stopped at a drugstore, Mathilda arrived at his door with two packages of hair color—shiny black for Albert and a dusky, smoky blonde for herself. Albert had forgotten the sensation of someone else's fingertips on his scalp. And Mathilda talked nonstop, her voice like notes on a scale running up and down his spine. Several times that afternoon he giggled.

A curious friendship emerged. She'd lost a son; he'd spent a lifetime cut off. They held each other up. On a Saturday afternoon two years later, Albert's phone rang while he and Mathilda were doing each other's hair. Mathilda had set the timer for his dye.

"I'll get it," she said. In the few seconds that she held the receiver to her ear, all the color drained from her face.

Jimmy Don Wahrmund was dead, killed in a car crash the night before—lifelong best friend of her son Ralph, who was unhurt, who wouldn't let the ambulance attendants even touch him.

"Oh!" Mathilda cried out. "I feel so relieved. That's terrible—isn't it?—to be glad someone else's son is dead. And not mine."

"Oh dear God! Dorene!" Mathilda spoke as if her mind would not hold still. "Grady was my favorite. I'm certain Jimmy Don was hers." And Mathilda was out the door. She regularly ascribed credit to Albert—that knowing him had taught her to reach out.

"Albert Decker," she would say, "you rescued me." She tried the French pronunciation he preferred—*Ahl-baíre*—grinning when he joked about her wayward vowels, saying that in her mouth, his name sounded like an aspirin ad. *All Bayer*.

"That man is my savior," Mathilda announced to her husband, her daughter, her neighbors.

Candace opened a small bottle of lavender water from Mathilda, who looked at Dorene and smiled. Dorene had been using lavender water since a day on her honeymoon when she tried a sample at a gift shop in San Antonio and her husband bought a bottle for her. She well remembered the heavy, cloying perfumes Mathilda had once favored. She knew about the little crystal atomizer Grady had given his mother for Christmas when he was ten. Tears had brightened Mathilda's eyes when she spoke of it—and the moment some months after losing Grady, when she sat down at her dresser and could not bear to look at the things she'd used to make herself pretty. She had raked lipsticks and compacts into the little trash can beside her dresser chair, opened her makeup drawer and dumped the contents, then walked through the house with Grady's perfume decanter and smashed it against the concrete slab at the base of the back steps. Mathilda's first bottle of lavender water had been a gift from Dorene, a gesture of appreciation in the weeks after Jimmy Don's fatal car wreck. It was the first perfume Mathilda Smith had worn in years, the only fragrance she'd splashed on since.

Next was a decorative tin from Dorene (Albert wanted his gift saved for last). Candace opened the tin, full to the rim with Mexican wedding cookies. Dorene spent hours of her time baking. Luckily, Robert had a sweet tooth, and what they didn't eat, she packaged up and took to her mother's bakery and café on Main Street.

"I don't see how you do it," Candace said. "Such pretty edibles. I've tried but I have no patience. I make a mess and then give up."

"Cookies are my therapy," said Dorene. "I just disappear into them."

Candace opened Albert's gift then, an elegant leather-bound journal nestled in tissue paper. "This is lovely," she said, opening the journal and running her fingers over a page. "I'm afraid I'll ruin it. What will I write?"

"Anything," Albert said. "Whatever pops into your head. What the sunrise looks like, what it's like being a Libra, quirky things your husband says."

"I'm not sure that Stan has quirks."

"Ahl-baíre"—Mathilda put special emphasis on her pronunciation—"writes to a lover he had when he was young, when he got as far away as Paris. Claude"—she said *Clode*—as Albert had taught her. "But you all know about him."

"I've only ever had two lovers," Candace said. "The one died. The other has lived with me since I was eighteen."

"That's it!" Mathilda said. "You can write to Buddy. Write about Buddy."

"I didn't really know my first husband," Candace answered her. "It's not something I like to admit, but I didn't love Buddy Grant. I chose him. Some girl named Candy chose him. Maybe I should write to her."

Something about her voice, an almost tremor in the words—something was amiss, though Dorene kept quiet about it. Albert and Mathilda didn't seem to notice the tension in their young friend's face, her smile, her hands as they stirred the air when she spoke.

One morning several years back, Dorene had stopped in at the package store to pick up a bottle of sipping whisky for Robert. Eduardo had gone to lunch. After paying Albert, she settled onto the barstool he kept at the counter for just such occasions. As chance would have it, Eduardo came in from the back entrance, ready to take over, just as the bicycle bell on the front door sounded and Candace stepped inside. She looked up, and for a moment her gaze met Dorene's. A flash of recognition arced between them.

Dorene's own bad time had come upon her unannounced when she was thirty years old. It had left in her a cold, hard space she'd carried gingerly ever since. She had studied other women, how they managed the disturbances of motherhood, the unbearable silences that sometimes marked their days—husbands at work, children at school, children eventually grown and gone. A moment looking into the younger woman's eyes—a glance—was all it took. Candace Meyer had heard the silence, had felt it in her bones. Of this Dorene was certain.

Candace approached the counter. "I know where to find my bourbon," she said, "but what about Bailey's? I think I might want to try some in my coffee."

"You'll be glad you did," said Dorene. "I'll show you."

"Ages since I've been in Decker's," Candace said. They were standing midway down the aisle that shelved liqueurs. "Pardon my lack of manners, but I'm surprised to see you here. Sitting at the counter. Making yourself at home."

"We're having a nice chat."

"I suppose you are. Odd place for it."

"That's part of the charm."

"Wonder what you talk about."

"I don't think that matters anymore. It's the company I enjoy. Hearing voices mix with mine."

When they returned to the counter, Eduardo turned on his gift for gab. His patter had been keeping customers at the counter, keeping them coming back, for years.

At a pause, Dorene made her move.

"This is lovely company," she said. "I have an empty house waiting for me. The quiet can be unnerving."

"I know that feeling." Candace looked as if she'd said too much.

"Spend a few minutes with us," Eduardo said. "Takes the edge off a quiet house."

"I have homemade cookies," Albert said. "Gingersnaps. Mathilda Smith's famous recipe."

"Fresh coffee?" Dorene said. "I'll make us some fresh coffee."

Albert took Candace by the hand. "You must join us," he said, raising her hand, cupping it in both of his, a gesture Dorene had experienced as invitation, as pleading, as thanks. With receptive women customers, he'd been doing this for years—the laying on of hands, Mathilda called it.

After the gifts, Dorene did the honors at Albert's dinette table, putting out a plate of tuna sandwiches, a relish tray, a dish of assorted nuts. They served themselves on Albert's dainty party plates and sat around the coffee table, talking and taking the occasional bite. Whatever the weight Candace had carried when she entered, the younger woman seemed to have settled in with them. For her own part, Dorene wished for nothing more than afternoons like this one, immersed in the leisurely voices of friends, with cake and candles and no rush toward the ritual of the lighting, the singing, the unspoken wish, the breath that would extinguish candles and close out the loveliest of days.

The moment came. Albert lit a match and held it out for Mathilda and Dorene, who lit theirs from his, and the candle tips flamed up one by one as Mathilda joked that the first of them would melt entirely into the frosting before the last was lit. Then they were singing, and as the phrases repeated, Candace looked at the flame-tipped cake before her as if it signaled the end of the world. She closed her eyes when they were done, inhaled deeply, and blew out all her candles.

"What am I going to do?" she said. "They want to chop my breast off."

Between Mathilda and Albert, the questions rained at her.

She'd found a lump, Candace said. Without alerting Stan, she'd driven to Corpus Christi. There'd been a biopsy. She'd known the results since yesterday. She hadn't slept the night before.

"I must look awful," she said. "I could scarcely face the mirror getting ready to come over."

"When?" Dorene asked, and when Candace looked a question at her, "The surgery. When have your doctors scheduled it?"

"I told them no." Candace looked from Dorene to Mathilda to Albert. "Surely I can't let them."

"You've *got* to," said Mathilda.

"Look at me," Candace said. "Look at my necklines. Who am I gonna be if I can't show these off anymore?"

"Our dear friend Candace," said Dorene. "That's who you'll be."

"Oh! I know you all don't care if I switch to high-necked collars. But what about me? What'll I do when I look in the mirror? My breasts have always been my ticket out."

"Oh, honey." Albert dabbed at the corner of a glistening eye. "*This* is your place. Right here. You don't need a ticket anywhere."

No one spoke for a minute. The condenser in Albert's window unit switched off, heavy silence eddying among the birthday celebrants.

"What about Stan?" Candace clearly wasn't ready to concede. "He loves my breasts."

"I had breasts once," Mathilda said. "They shriveled, but I'm still here. God help Ed Smith if he dares to comment."

"But my husband."

"Your husband," Dorene said. She hadn't realized such anger had awakened in her. "Your husband be damned."

II

Stan had felt inhabited since Candace told him, as if just beneath his skin he'd developed some kind of exoskeleton, like a humanoid roach taking the villain's role in one of the comics that sometimes still said *buy me* from the magazine stand. Every movement awkward, every word the wrong word. He simply could not make her understand. It was her he was afraid for, the suffering he could not save her from that made him awkward. Even the words for what she was going through. *Mastectomy, radiation, chemotherapy.*

Of course, it bothered him that she had lost a breast. Because she had heard the news alone, because the malignancy lived in her. *Malignancy.* Another of those words that put him on a distant planet. Because no one could endure this in her place. No one but Candace—the one and only madness that had got inside him and rooted itself, feeding off his blood, his pulse, his heartache.

Nothing to be done for it. They marked the calendar for the day of her surgery. She made herself lie down on a gurney, succumb to anesthesia, go under the knife, let her breast be cut off, wake up and face the rest. Face him, the fear he felt written in him.

He drove her to radiation, drove her to chemotherapy. He stayed home with her when she could stand him, drove to the office when she could not. Chemotherapy knocked the wind out of her anger. Small favors, he thought—he should have been grateful. Nothing in the years he'd known Candace had been able to tame her when she let her temper loose. Only time had worked. Let her burn at him, get out, come back, let her flare at him some more. Her anger had always burned itself out. But the chemo. The chemo turned her a shade of ash that made him think what she might look like if she didn't make it. The chemo drained her. Three weeks in, he found himself wishing for the fire, the light in her ignited by anger.

And then a gift. On Friday of the first week in December, three weeks into her treatments, he went into the office for the afternoon, took care of some paperwork, phoned clients who had questions about their policies, talked his secretary through a week of what she could do to keep the office going. Afterward, when he arrived home, Candace was sitting in his recliner, her resting place of choice. He stopped in the doorway, leaned into the jamb—he'd been doing this for as long as they'd lived in this house—and asked her the question he couldn't help and she likely didn't want.

"How was your afternoon?"

She raised a shot glass and said, "Fine."

Beside her on the end table was a bottle of black label, the bourbon she'd been sipping since the early days of their marriage.

"This one is almost empty," she said.

"Jack Daniels. With chemotherapy."

"I called," she said. "The oncologist. Says yes. To small amounts." *Oncologist*, another word he loathed.

Stan was a cautious man. The idea of liquor with chemotherapy bothered him, but as he pondered what he might say, Candace gave him a look. "I'll be fine," she said. "The oncologist. Said so."

He let it go. With the chemo, most foods tasted like poison. Chicken-fried steak, which had been a lifelong guilty pleasure, sent Candace to the bathroom gagging.

"This afternoon was bad." She paused. "I would have considered"—she paused again—"suicide."

It was agony for him, but since the chemo had taken effect, his wife conveyed her thoughts in fragments, slowly, breathing between, hoarding her depleted energy.

"Don't get. That look. On your face," she said, her pacing at odds with the words themselves. "I'm kidding. About suicide. You know. I'm kidding."

There was no point trying to reassure her. She wouldn't believe him anyway.

"In my condition," she continued, "I couldn't lift. A gun. Pills? I'd only barf."

In the hallway, his mother's grandfather clock chimed the quarter hour.

"Then I thought," Candace said, "about my Jack. And—joy!—it doesn't taste. Like mosquito repellant." She raised the shot glass, held it to the light of the lamp on the end table, and took a sip. "It tastes." She sighed luxuriously. "Like bourbon. Only better."

Monday morning, Stan stopped in at the package store. He'd no more than said hello to Eduardo when Albert materialized behind the counter.

"I saw you drive up," he said, and to Eduardo, "I hate to come between you and this handsome man, but I must."

Eduardo shrugged, grinned, winked at Stan.

"I've got a fresh pot on," Albert told Eduardo, nodding toward the apartment upstairs. "Relax for half an hour. Have a cup. There's a plate of apple fritters on the table." He blew a kiss at Eduardo, who laughed and did a little soft-shoe toward the stairs.

On any other morning in any other year, instead of putting his confusion into words, Stan would have made small talk and headed for the aisle where bourbon was shelved. But his wife's crisis had robbed him of guises.

When Eduardo's steps sounded on the stairwell and Albert turned back to him, Stan voiced his conjecture.

"Eduardo is . . . ?"

"You can say the word, dear man. I promise not to blush. And yes, Eduardo is gay."

"I wouldn't have thought."

"I am not the representative type."

"I didn't mean." Stan felt that he was fumbling. But clearly his host was in a mood to be frank.

"If I'd been born fifty years later." Albert paused as if imagining his life thus altered. "Or perhaps somewhere else—New Orleans comes to mind—I might have been a career drag queen. A rather successful one, I like to think."

Stan didn't say anything. It's not that he was shocked, exactly, or that he disapproved. He'd just never pictured a man in this town—well, any man anywhere—prancing onstage in fancy women's clothing, makeup, wig. When he came back to himself, Albert was looking at him intently.

"I've let my guard down," Albert said. "My hunch tells me our words are safe between us."

"Strictly confidential," Stan said.

He'd always thought of Albert Decker as someone who absolutely did not fit. He'd heard the liquor store proprietor identified as a freak and worse. As a younger man, Stan had thought Albert made his situation worse than it might have been, what with eyeliner, rouge, and shiny pearl nail polish. As Stan got older, though, and settled into his own version of loneliness among the locals, a kind of begrudging sympathy rose up in place of judgment.

This morning, sensing an opening between them, he just asked.

"How have you stood it? This." His gesture indicated the register, the store, the town beyond. "All these years?"

"Getting older takes the edge off," Albert said. "If you will pardon a reference to matters anatomical, prostate surgery helped."

Stan was used to the company of older men, their ribald comments about frequent nighttime urination and other prostate discomforts. He supposed he could handle what Albert had to say.

"Perhaps the surgeon used a magic wand." Albert waved as if he, too, were inciting magic. "A week or so after the procedure, I woke to a revelation. What my body had wanted before, even as I got older—that kind of want was gone. I still enjoy *looking* at a handsome man." His eyes seemed to indicate that Stan was included in this category. "But nothing more. I can't tell you how peaceful my life has become."

"I might could envy you," Stan said.

"Are you ready to be done with it? For good and all? Today?"

Stan laughed out loud. "I'm forty-eight," he said. "Ask me in another twenty years."

"I've been mostly lucky," he added. "I have Candace. I have only ever wanted Candace."

"Your lovely wife," said Albert, "is the reason I shooed Eduardo away."

Stan felt as if in that moment he'd stepped through a portal in one of his comics, a door that wasn't there but was, a door opened by this kindly gentleman, the risk he'd taken speaking of things not spoken. The words poured out of Stan.

"I don't care about her missing breast. *She* cares. She says she thinks I should. She turns against me. Says bitter, hateful things. Says it's my fault she says them."

He paused, then came home to the truth.

"But always she is Candace."

"Get her out of here," Albert said. "She needs to be gone from herself for a while."

"She won't go."

"Get her out of here."

"Where?"

"Anywhere but here. Anywhere the sun is shining. Anywhere it's warm."

III

During the weeks of chemo, Candace had a recurring dream. It should have been a nice dream: there was a beach in it, with sky and palms, a dramatic cliff set back from where she walked. In the dream, she knows she's never been to this place by the sea because it is so beautiful. She almost knows she's in a dream, though that has never helped. On and on she walks, an endless shoreline, the sand luscious and cool between her toes, an exquisite chill flickering at her ankles as the surf breaks and the silvery scrim of wave beneath it rushes in, its edges liquid lace, and then, without transition, she is waist deep, the ocean dragging at her skirt. A wave looms, crests, immerses her, pulls her in deep. She cannot struggle, cannot breathe, and the ocean drags against the incision where they removed her breast, the salt sea a searing pain.

Awake, she was too tired for anger, too tired to think about what lay ahead, too tired to tend the space that separated her from others.

When she was done with chemo, Stan suggested getting away. Some place nice, he said, with a picture window and a view, a chair where she could sit and look and get her strength back.

"I'm wiped out," she said. "I can barely move. From room to room." When he persisted, "Go yourself. Leave me. In peace."

"You need a break," he said. "From all this."

"What I need. Is this rocker. My Jack."

Stan was a comfort, though she wanted him quieter even than his usual. She wanted Christmas not to happen, let alone with company. But Stan would not say no to her daughter, their son—the children they had raised together. She had thought herself worn out before they came. Two hours with them in the house proved her cynicisms true. *Things can always get worse.* She'd been saying that one for years. *If you think it's bad now, just wait.* And the variant she used on Stan. *If you think you're hurting now, I'll practice up.*

It took more energy than she felt she'd saved up to convince her daughter and son that she was hopeful, that she was glad to have them for the holiday. She seemed always to have a glass of bourbon at hand. She knew she was sipping more than she should. When they gathered for gifts, the tree lit up like Vegas, her son remarked as she poured for herself. She raised a silent toast and said, "It's Christmas. I'm celebrating."

Christmas Eve and Christmas Day. For hours at a stretch, they gathered at the laden dining table—turkey and dressing, baked yams and scalloped potatoes, Waldorf salad, bread pudding, pecan pie—the mix of odors tilting her into nausea. When it was time for presents, the living room turned into a chaos of ripped giftwrap and yanked bows, gifts no one needed cluttering every surface. And the chorus of their voices—talking, talking, talking.

Three days and they were gone.

With the house quiet again, she sank into bed and slept for twenty-four hours, rose and sat at the kitchen table for a while, then slept again. On the morning of the twenty-eighth, she found herself in the recliner, looking out at gray and gray and grayer.

By the time Stan came home for lunch, she really was inclined to do herself harm.

"Let's get out of here," she said. "Now."

By sunset of the twenty-ninth, they had checked into a little hotel in La Jolla a few steps from the Pacific—bedroom, kitchenette, sitting room, terrace. Stan must have spent a fortune, but it was only money. Candace spent the next day mostly in bed, marshalling her resources. The morning of the thirty-first found her in a lovely overstuffed chair looking out at the glorious light. In the afternoon she ventured onto the terrace. La Jolla sat above the Pacific, with a steep drop to the beach, so she could not see the shoreline. Instead, out there beyond, an expanse of blue she felt that she could watch as long as she breathed.

New Year's Day began with coffee at her bedside, dark, dark coffee as she had learned to prefer it during chemo—no cream, though perhaps now she could chance it. Afterward they sat on the terrace, Candace waking and dozing while Stan read and dozed. Noon surrendered to one of those mild afternoons that give the lie to winter in Southern California. Eager to be out, they made their way to the shoreline, Stan beside her, and she was grateful. He stopped when she needed to and stood while she leaned on him, reveling in sunshine, in delicious warmth.

As they turned to walk along the water's edge, Stan remarked on the waves, thin shallow leftovers sneaking up the sand. He suggested she take her shoes off—he was barefoot already—and walk closer to the water, let the shallowest edges of the waves run up over her feet.

"You used to call it footsie," he said. "At Padre, remember? Why did we stop going?"

"Have you *looked* at Padre Island?"

"It has beaches. The Gulf. Waves." Dear Stan, so easily satisfied.

"If I want to look at flat," Candace said, "I can just look out the picture window at home."

"But this," she added. They walked a thin strand of beach, with ocean to the right and cliffs to the left, ahead of them stone shelves the waves splashed up against, lit up in every shade of copper, bronze, gold, sandstone.

"Come on, then," he said. "Let's get your shoes off."

She wanted only to look, she insisted, and told him about her wading dream that turned into a drowning dream.

"Afraid of a dream," he said. "My wife, who isn't afraid of a single person on the planet."

"Buddy Grant's mother," she reminded him.

"Saint Peter himself is probably afraid of her."

"She pulled me off a bus once. I was coming here. Well, the bus station in downtown L.A." Candace stopped, memory surging in her. "I had a panic attack. Right there beside the gas pumps, some grease monkey staring at me while he wiped a windshield. My drowning dream is like that. I can't breathe. I can't get away."

"You got away. We're here."

If only it were that simple. If somehow she could quiet the girl she'd been when first she tried her escape, the voice still in her, insisting, as if tomorrow she could board the bus that drove away, like a time traveler in one of Stan's comics, having what couldn't be had.

"Which one?" she said to her husband. "Which Candace got away?"

"We've been over this," he said. And they had, more times than she could count.

"But which one do you see? Right now. Choose."

"I've only ever known *one*. This woman right here beside me. You."

"What if I never figure it out? What if I'm sixty—and still this back and forth?"

"Let's get you to forty-three. Sixty will take care of itself." A couple of steps more and Stan put the flat of his hand at the center of her back and pressed lightly. "I didn't mean." He stopped. "That you wouldn't." He stopped again.

His words, their implication, made her missing breast ache. For a stretch of minutes, here along the beach, she'd all but forgotten. She hugged herself, glad for the sweater she'd draped on her shoulders before they left the hotel. They'd stepped from sunlight into shadow, a slip of cloud moving overhead. Stan put his arm around her.

"You're all talked out," he said. "Let's get you back."

The cloud moved on as they retraced their steps, but the light had turned wintry, the ocean gone from a vibrant, sparkling blue to a cold, glinting gray.

Beside Candace, Stan dropped into an easy silence, a blessing of their marriage, of the man himself, that made her feel, if not exactly happy, then what? Once, her answer would have been *resigned*. Over the years, though, she knew she'd changed. They had changed together.

A scattering of seagulls, their calls a pleasing patchwork, swooped from the palms along the brink, arcing out over the waves and back around over a farther stand of palms. Then gone.

More wisps of cloud blew over. The light grayed and brightened, grayed and brightened. As they approached the stone stairway up the cliff, more gulls came over, tilting in the currents. Climbing, Candace could feel a buoyancy in Stan she didn't share. Hope, she would have called what lifted him. She didn't have the strength, but she was grateful for the foothold he offered, here beside her on these quarried steps, with the Pacific behind them now, the waves a receding whisper.

BENEATH A NOVEMBER SKY

EVELYN SMITH, NOVEMBER 1998

EVELYN SMITH WAS IN her fiftieth year when her father lay down for a nap and didn't wake up. Her mother was certain he knew what was coming. He'd been napping in a cranked-back recliner every day of his life for the past forty years. He was on the couch when she found him, flat on his back with his hands folded at the chest. Ready for the casket, Momma said. She fetched a straight-backed chair from the kitchen, set it beside him, reached for his hand and sat with him, said her good-bye, then picked up the phone and made the necessary calls. The constable was first, Evelyn second. "Call your brother," she said. "I'm afraid he'll cry. I can't have tears right now." Evelyn closed her office door and called Ralph. He did cry, quick choking sounds coming out of him, then a ragged voice saying he'd get on the first flight out of Midland. She hung up and called George at his office. Go, he said, and she did. George would pack a suitcase for her and head for the farm.

Her mother wanted a simple burial. No visitation service, no funeral mass. If folks wanted to shake hands and blather nonsense, they could come to the graveyard.

A scattering of neighbors converged on the appointed morning. Outside of the rare encounter when she stopped for food or gas in Nopalito, Evelyn had seen none of these people in years. Her parents had been here, her life elsewhere. Aggie Doyle hugged her. Long ago they'd been friends. She was aware of Ralph having a difficult moment when Max Wahrmund approached him. Max's brother Jimmy Don, killed in a car wreck somewhere outside Odessa twenty years ago, had been Ralph's best friend. Ralph had stepped out of that car without a mark on him. Evelyn had never had that kind of friend. She'd envied her brother—until Jimmy Don died and she saw again what that kind of loss could do to a person. It closed the gap between Momma and Ralph, an unspoken understanding between them that each knew the other's grief.

After a brief service at her father's grave, Evelyn stood with her mother and Ralph. One after another she shook hands with old neighbors, accepting murmured words of sympathy. And then Domingo Escovedo took her hand. She had run into him several times over the years since the flooded Agua Dulce took Grady from them, each time wanting to say something. But what? That Grady had told her what he felt? That she wanted Domingo to have heard these words, to have spoken like words in return—at least that. And maybe they had. Maybe that explained why Domingo's face lit up every time she'd seen him since, why he took her hand today and held it as if he didn't want to let go, why an unbearable ache rose up in her as they spoke.

Afterward, on the way to the car, George asked about him.

"Domingo was a neighbor," she said.

"Did he know your father well? Were they friends?"

"Why do you ask?"

"The man is in pain. It's written all over him."

"No," Evelyn said. "Domingo and my father were not close."

"What then?"

"Domingo was in love with Grady. At least I think he was. I know that's how Grady felt."

"You are a sealed court record, Evelyn Smith. A classified government document."

"I'm talking now. What else do you want to know?"

"How they felt about each other. Did they act on it?"

"I don't know. They were so young. It was a different time. This place—" She looked around her, flatland of the coastal plain stippled with brush, gray beneath a sunless November sky. "It was like living in a strait jacket. Though Grady acted otherwise."

They arrived at the car. George got behind the wheel, and they drove away. Evelyn waited until the cemetery was well behind them. She put her wish into words then—a private hope it had been, spoken now for the first time.

"I want to believe Grady had that." George didn't take his eyes off the road ahead, but he was the best listener she knew. "Silly, isn't it?" she added. "Like making a trade."

"Heaven can have your brother," George said, "if he and that striking black-haired man got to have a tussle first."

They giggled like schoolchildren. George would have known that this was what she needed. He stayed on for a day and then returned to Corpus.

Several days later, acceding to their mother's request for some time to herself, Evelyn took her brother for a drive. They crossed the creek below their childhood home and followed the county road up the slow rise beyond, the air at the windows chill with fall, a cold front moving into the damp Gulf air and the windshield stippled by drops of rain. Ralph rode along quietly beside her, wiry as the day he'd left home—a gray, sad-eyed version of himself, the top of his head hairless like his father's, shiny as a plate since the day he turned thirty.

"So. George Sanders," he said, apropos of nothing. "Ever gonna make an honest man of him?"

Evelyn arched her brows at Ralph and gave him a sketch of her life with George—their weekends together, the evening meals they shared at her downtown condo or his little house in Flour Bluff. Aimless as chickens in a barnyard, the two of them, nowhere to go and plenty of time to get there. "We're old maids. Marriage, moving in together?"

Irony edged her words. "We wouldn't last a week." She suspected George would outlast her.

They passed the gate to an old house, long empty, occupied briefly years ago by the Matthews family, a father and sons who worked cattle for the Doyles, a daughter who kept house for them. Ralph chuckled and pointed through the scrim of rainy gray.

"Do you remember that wacky day we spent with Opal Matthews?"

"What are you talking about?"

"That magazine we found on the coffee table, you know, the robber's trick she played on us." Ralph made a derringer of his hand, took aim at Evelyn, and pulled the trigger, miming the click of it from the back of his throat.

She turned into a little-used gate to one of the Doyle pastures and stopped the car.

Years ago, in a hurry to get somewhere, Evelyn had lost control of her father's pickup truck when a cottontail hopped into her path. The truck had slued wildly and done a complete roll, coming to rest at a right angle to the road, tires beneath her once again, bumper snubbed against a barbed-wire fence. Caliche dust everywhere, its pall on the sun-shot air. It was as if she'd crashed through a barrier between the world she knew and one that only looked the same.

The sensations of that long-gone afternoon blossomed in her as she stared through a padlocked gate into the rain-spattered landscape beyond, a grazing pasture clustered with Spanish daggers and huisache. Several cows trotted up to the gate and stood there staring their cow-eyed stare as if they knew a secret she'd only just discovered.

Evelyn killed the engine and turned to Ralph. She made a conscious effort to sound matter-of-fact. "Grady told you about that day?"

"What do you mean, Grady told me? I was there."

"You were not. It was Grady came with me."

"Grady was home with Momma. Remember? They were playing jacks. He sweet-talked her into letting him stay."

"No."

Ralph's eyes said yes.

"You were gone off with Daddy, Grady and I, we—" Evelyn felt cold all over.

"I don't know where Daddy was." Ralph sounded as if he'd been handed someone else's cue cards.

"Grady went everywhere with me."

"Except when he got a chance to monopolize Momma."

"You and Daddy were gone."

Ralph shook his head, but Evelyn went on.

"Grady and I went with Opal."

"Did not." Forty years dissolved in the tone of Ralph's voice.

"Momma was there by herself." The words were like sand in Evelyn's throat. "I thought she must've planned it that way. I thought—"

"What?"

"Not then. Later." The cows on the other side of the gate waited for her to say the one ridiculous thing, a murky, half-formed suspicion she had never put into words. "She was all full of perfume. I couldn't make sense of it. What did I know? I was six years old. But later—oh, years later—I half suspected maybe Momma was having an affair. And she was trying to get us out of the way—Grady and me."

"You thought she was cheating on Daddy?" Ralph turned away.

Evelyn followed the line of his gaze to a clump of huisache, shivering and wet, the gray band of rain moving beyond the pasture with the edge of the front.

"Do you remember the sounds they made at night?" Ralph asked.

In the space that opened up then, Evelyn was back in her childhood bed, listening to her parents through the wall between her bedroom and theirs—going at it (Grady's phrase)—while she held herself rigid and wished for a momentary lapse in her hearing.

"What about her clothes?" She could see the rickrack swirling on her mother's skirt. "She'd put on one of her dancing dresses."

"Momma loved dressing like a floozy, you know that."

Her objections bounced evenly as a little handheld rubber ball, and just as evenly, Ralph scooped up every one.

"But the perfume?"

"Grady was always spritzing her."

"But she was such a flirt."

"Do I have to draw you a picture? Grady was home with her." Ralph pointed in the direction of the creek and the house where they'd grown up. "*I* was with you at Opal Matthews. And, yes, Momma was a cocktease. But that's all she was. With any man but Daddy. *Him* she never denied."

Something like envy had crept into Ralph's voice. Evelyn stared at him. She had only ever wanted her parents to stop.

"How many of us find what they had?" Ralph asked. "One in a hundred, maybe? I never did." He shrugged. "Nothing ever cocked my trigger like that woman on the magazine with a snake wrapped around her."

A sudden gust slapped rain against the windshield.

"Just give me that picture in one hand." Ralph spoke with boyish pleasure. "And a room to myself and the other hand free." With his right hand, he started the old, well-practiced gesture, but then he looked at Evelyn and stopped.

"I found your magazines," she said. "The ones you hid."

"You were such a wet blanket."

"It's not that. I don't care about that."

"What then?"

"I was hearing Grady laugh. Remember? You would make that jack-off motion. To tease us."

"You got so mad."

"But Grady laughed. He made me forget to be mad."

"You got the lion's share." Ralph's voice had turned husky, wistful. "He wouldn't even go hunting with me."

"Grady couldn't shoot straight."

"Grady was a girly boy."

It was the truth, spoken with no insult. But there was more to it.

"He was fearless," she said.

"I'll give you that." Ralph paused, and then, as if musing, from far away, "He might oughta been afraid of water."

Evelyn started the car and turned back. What little rain there was had stopped. The country would go crisp now with cold.

"I've always wondered what you saw." Ralph's voice came from the other side of a barrier.

Evelyn trained her eyes on the road. She remembered a kitchen table, windows dripping with rain, Opal with her skirt up, a man with his pants down, his butt going back and forth against her pale thighs. Opal afterward with a black eye. Until minutes ago, Grady had been with Evelyn that day, upstairs behind a loveseat playing his part in a game of pretend robbery while she took the role of spy.

Ralph broke into the silence. "You sneaked downstairs. I dared you."

Was that how it happened?

"Come back not five minutes later. Eyes big as pie pans. White as a sheet."

The planks on the old bridge clattered as they crossed the creek.

"You're not gonna tell me, are you?"

"I promised Opal."

"You were six." Ralph spoke with quiet emphasis. "You made that promise more than forty years ago. And where's the other party to the contract? Opal Matthews could be dead."

"I promised."

"She scared a promise out of me too. Had me repeat some nonsense about a horse kick give her that black eye. Made me promise not to pester you. Threatened to get Momma riled."

"You kept your promise."

"I didn't have a thing worth telling. I don't know how she come by a black eye. And you went mute. I was afraid to look at you, let alone say anything."

They rounded the curve and there was the farm. Evelyn thought of the promise she'd kept, the choices she'd made during the years she carried Opal's secret. It was her secret too, the surge of excitement and fear kept safe by her promise not to tell, by the promises she'd made herself, the safe life she'd chosen, the safe man.

"I'm used to my secrets," she said, turning into the lane that led to her mother's house.

Ahead of them, in the side yard, stood the rusty cast-iron swing set their father had put up when Evelyn was barely out of diapers. It was still there, thanks to their mother, waiting for grandchildren that had never arrived. As they rounded the corner in front of the house, the norther gusted, setting the one remaining swing into motion.

When Evelyn woke the next morning—much earlier than usual—she got up and went to the kitchen for coffee. Ralph and her mother, early risers both, were at the little table there, halfway through the first pot, the friction between them long ago abraded smooth. There were two chairs. Ralph rose to grab a third from the dining room, but Evelyn stopped him.

Excusing herself, she put on a heavy robe and walked out to the front porch. She hugged herself against the cold. She took deep breaths of the crisp, lovely air and blew them back at the morning. Halfway through her coffee, she heard the low throb of an engine revving up the county road from the highway. This road was little used anymore, almost never by trucks. Evelyn turned to investigate, and for a stretch of moments she could not breathe. It was an old yellow school bus coming down the road as if for her and Grady and Ralph, though today the bus didn't slow as it approached the lane to the farm. She was not a sentimental woman, but the old bus touched something in her as she watched it recede toward the creek and disappear into the line of trees there.

"Eye-dot," she said to herself, and chuckled. She would have been—what?—seven, eight, maybe, when the word first showed up in one of her books. *I-d-i-o-t.* Sounding it out, she'd pronounced the first letter as a syllable of its own with a long *i*, but she couldn't wrap her tongue around a second syllable with the same vowel. She puzzled over the second *i* and finally decided to leave it silent. *Eye-dot* was the best she could make of the word. Until one day on the bus with Grady beside her, a whiz-kid second grader reading aloud—showing off, really—while she looked on. "Idiot," he said when he came to the word in his book—three syllables instead of two, a perfectly recognizable English word.

"No," she said, pointing. "That's not right."

Grady rolled his eyes. "How would *you* say it?" he asked, his emphasis on the second-person pronoun reminiscent of their mother's gift for insult.

"It's too rude for one of your books" was all Evelyn could think of to say. Already, she knew she'd been wrong.

"Idiot," Grady said. "That's how you say it."

What struck Evelyn decades later, sitting on her porch after the school bus had passed, was a long-lost association. For years when she was young, even after Grady pronounced the word correctly, *eye-dot* had been her private word for Opal Matthews, who in the aftermath of her family's moving away, had shrunk to a single image in Evelyn's mind. A face with a black eye.

"Eye-dot," Evelyn said again. And then, in perfect mimicry of her lost brother, "Idiot." She giggled, another reminder of Grady. More times than she could count, he had found the tickle that made her laugh. Once, she'd thought such lightness in her gone for good, the silence of his disappearance carving itself inside her, impossibly empty, impossibly still. Until Grady started sneaking back—a gesture, a facial expression, a snippet of talk—impish at first, goading, insisting she let him in. Grady, reminding her to breathe. To smile. For him.

But her coffee had gone cold. Evelyn rose and stepped into the house, voices but not words reaching her from the kitchen. She would refill her cup and let Ralph fetch the chair he'd offered. She would sit down with her mother and brother, listen. She might tell them about the school bus, the mispronounced word, and Grady beside her, saying it right.